EBU

SA

Saksham Garg is an editor at Penguin Random House India. For seven years, he studied at Woodstock School, Mussoorie, from where he could see the snow-capped Seven Hills of this story. He currently spends his time between New Delhi and Jaipur, and, outside of work, is often found on the football field or practising the violin.

He loves to interact with his readers; connect with him on Instagram, Facebook or LinkedIn @sakshamgarg94. To get updates on upcoming book events and workshops on writing and editing, log on to www.sakshamvgarg.com.

ADVANCE PRAISE FOR THE BOOK

'This book will define the Indian fantasy genre for years to come'
—Akshat Gupta, author

'*Samsara* is a fresh and fantastic read with epic-level world-building and unforgettable characters. Finally, India's answer to *Harry Potter*'
—Krishna Udayasankar, author

'*Samsara* takes you on an amazing voyage. This is magic, mythology and mysticism, all rolled into one delicious Hinduism-inspired story. Narrated beautifully, the plot and pace are gripping. What a fantastic debut novel by a young writer whose talent shines out on every page'—Harish Bhat, author, marketer and columnist, and brand custodian, Tata Sons

'Absolutely fascinating creation of a new world and imagination at its best'—Anand Neelakantan, author

'*Samsara* is a unique and intriguing story that takes us to the hidden heart of the Himalayas, where mountains and mythology meet. Saksham Garg has a compelling story to tell, and he conjures up an exciting, thought-provoking tale'—Stephen Alter, author

'*Samsara* is the newest addition to India's growing fantasy fiction genre. It's an unputdownable read where you encounter demons and gods'—Stuti Changle, author

'*Samsara* introduces its readers to a never-seen-before world of mythology. Every part of it is so visually powerful'—Kevin Missal, author

'Saksham's pen whispers incredible, fantastical tales to you in your grandmother's voice. Finally, a *Harry Potter* in India'—Ayush Gupta, author

'*Samsara* is the kind of mytho-fantasy that is so jaw-droppingly brilliant that it leaves you wide-eyed with wonder and begging for more! A phenomenal new talent has arrived!'—Anuja Chandramouli, author

'Saksham Garg's *Samsara* brings to life a world of Indian mythology and fantastical adventure. A creative and entertaining read'—Shashi Tharoor

SAMSARA
ENTER THE VALLEY OF THE GODS

SAKSHAM GARG

EBURY
PRESS

An imprint of Penguin Random House

EBURY PRESS

USA | Canada | UK | Ireland | Australia
New Zealand | India | South Africa | China

Ebury Press is part of the Penguin Random House group of companies
whose addresses can be found at global.penguinrandomhouse.com

Published by Penguin Random House India Pvt. Ltd
4th Floor, Capital Tower 1, MG Road,
Gurugram 122 002, Haryana, India

| Penguin
Random House
India

First published in Ebury Press by Penguin Random House India 2022

Copyright © Saksham Garg 2022

All rights reserved

10 9 8 7 6 5 4 3

This is a work of fiction. Names, characters, places and incidents are either the
product of the author's imagination or are used fictitiously, and any resemblance
to any actual person, living or dead, events or locales is entirely coincidental.

This book is a reimagination of mythological stories, some of which have origins
in religious texts. The views and opinions expressed in the book are those of
the author only and do not reflect or represent the views and opinions held by
any other person. This book is based on various sources, including published
materials, stories from religious texts, and stories that have been passed on from
generation to generation orally. This book reflects the author's own understanding
and conception of such stories, and the stories are presented in a simplified form
in a manner accessible to readers. The objective of this book is not to hurt any
sentiments or be biased in favour of or against any particular person, region, caste,
society, gender, creed, nation or religion.

ISBN 9780143458289

Typeset in Adobe Garamond Pro by Manipal Technologies Limited, Manipal
Printed at Replika Press Pvt. Ltd, India

This book is sold subject to the condition that it shall not, by way of trade
or otherwise, be lent, resold, hired out, or otherwise circulated without the
publisher's prior consent in any form of binding or cover other than that in
which it is published and without a similar condition including this condition
being imposed on the subsequent purchaser.

www.penguin.co.in

FSC
www.fsc.org

MIX
Paper from
responsible sources
FSC® C016779

To Grandad, who recently returned from Vanyasa

The hut grew silent and people turned towards the man who had entered, carrying a musical instrument. He sat right beside the sleeping boy, tuned his *veena*, cleared his throat, and swept into the Song of the Valley. Everyone knew better than to sing along—at least not before the last Adwaita of the valley.

> *'Tucked within brambles that may,*
> *Shielding boughs and keeping at bay;*
> *Every* dashak *centres a blue rose,*
> *Scent of which dale invariably knows;*
> *Watered, it riots by the nights,*
> *Sheeny, eliciting awe from sights;*
> *But in the valley fortified by the one that slithers,*
> *For the sake of home, that flower must wither.'*

The Souls

Aman
Idhika
Fayza
Prithvi
Ujal
Aarti
Payal
Dhara
Jagrav
Savitri
Yuvan

Prologue

More than anything, what you hold is a map—a guide that will allow you to find the mythical valley of Vanyasa. But know that this book will only help you as far as Nandana, the tree that keeps the valley a secret. Once you get there, you're on your own.

You may have heard of Vanyasa, or you may be wondering what it is. If you have ever chanced upon some mention of it, you probably think it is fictional. But I assure you that Vanyasa exists. In fact, even today, there are many who spend years—sometimes entire lives—meditating, hoping to be led to this valley that exists only for the enlightened.

Vanyasa is known in different cultures by a multitude of names: Gyanganj, Shambhala, Swakipur, even Shangri-la. Nestled within the hidden folds of the Himalayas—on the roof of the world—the valley is completely inaccessible. However, every ten years, for its own survival, Vanyasa opens its doors to let in ten new Souls from the plains of the Indian subcontinent. They must take to the valley, its ancient ways, its sacred lessons, and know that they have no more than one year to prepare for the Mahayatra, the ultimate journey. They must survive the Mahayatra in order to join the ranks of the immortals that live in the valley.

Aman is one such Soul. Although his life is one in which few choices happen to be his own, he goes on to determine the fate of a nation. This is his story.

PART I

1

Aman

'How about you,' the teacher asked, 'you in the back?'

The boy to whom these words were sternly directed did not react. Seated in the last row, he continued to look in his textbook, rhythmically shaking his leg and tugging at a red thread around his wrist.

The teacher cocked her head in a dramatic gesture. 'Excuse me? I'm talking to *you*!'

'Ma'am, he can't hear you,' a girl said, trying not to laugh. The entire class sniggered and began muttering under their breaths. The commotion finally stirred Aman, who looked around, not realizing he was the target.

The substitute teacher quickly checked the register to figure out the boy's name and asked again, louder this time, 'Aman Chandra?! Can you hear me? Did you get a chance to read the first three chapters as Kulkarni Sir had instructed?'

What are the odds that I'm picked? Aman thought, feeling cornered. Time was running out. Everyone was probably staring at him.

Aman cleared his throat. 'Umm—'

'No, it's not that he can't hear you, Ma'am,' another boy interrupted him. 'He just can't spe-spea-speak, but he can . . .' He looked around for approval. 'He can *surely* cry.'

Aman stiffened. *Are you kidding me? Cry? That was more than ten years ago!*

He had always been a quiet kid, but it wasn't like Aman wanted to be tongue-tied at such a moment. His reticence had festered over the years as he'd backed himself further and further into a corner. The silence in his world had enveloped him completely after the loss of his father back in 2009, thirteen years ago. His father, the infamous Avi Chandra, had been an army officer. When Aman was five years old, an official letter had arrived at their home in Delhi, informing him and his mother, Upasna, of Avi's death. But it wasn't accompanied by any of the outpourings of poignant glory reserved for the deaths of soldiers. No gun salutes. No badge of honour. No eulogies in the press. In fact, there was no state funeral for him—the army had said disobedience and abandonment of duty lay behind Avi's death.

With little time offered to grieve, Upasna and her son were thrown out of the army staff quarters. She had tried looking for work, but even when the hope of a job glimmered, any inquiry about her family and husband put an end to it. She had no alternative but to take the low-paying job of a dishwasher at a local canteen.

It wasn't long before the consequences of this unfortunate situation spilled over into Aman's life. In the second grade, he was called 'son of a traitor' by a classmate for the first time, and he ended up sobbing in front of his class. That event bred new bullies who continued to torment him the entire year. The taint of his father's disrepute seemed to be the only thing people spoke about when it came to him. But changing schools was out of the question—this was the closest public school to where he lived, and they couldn't afford anything else.

Aman's survival mechanism had become all about avoiding attention. First, he started watching his actions and weighing his words. He called in sick as often as possible. In the third grade, he completely stopped engaging in any discussions, and from the fourth grade onwards he only spoke when called upon by a teacher.

By the sixth grade, Aman Chandra had sidelined himself to the extent that the older students appeared to have forgotten about him. He was also careful to never engage with the new students, and even went to extraordinary lengths to hide his last name.

By the seventh grade, he had succeeded in his mission to be invisible. His classmates avoided him and the teachers— the regular ones, not the substitutes—clearly knew better than to ask him questions, whether out of pity or sheer weariness. Aman kept a poker face and would admit to no one that he wished he had a friend. Just one person to talk to honestly. But one day rolled into the next, and time went on.

So imagine Aman's surprise when the substitute teacher addressed him directly. Of course, he wasn't going to answer. Other than the occasional 'yes, ma'am' or 'yes, sir', Aman's voice was scarcely heard by others. So if he was going to speak—if there was no other way out of it—then it had to be done early.

Here goes nothing, loser. He readied himself to speak. But time had already run out. It no longer mattered that he had indeed read the chapters last night and knew the answer to the teacher's question. He knew that even if he tried to speak, he wouldn't get past the dryness in his throat. So instead, like always, he offered his classmates a callous smirk, hoping they would mistake it for indifference.

The boy sitting right in front of Aman turned around and snapped his fingers in Aman's face. Then, deftly manoeuvring his hands so that the teacher couldn't see, he pulled out a device from his pocket and clicked on its screen. Sneers formed on all the faces looking at Aman as he recognized the tune of 'Lonely' by Akon.

That moment shook him out of the belief that he had recovered from the trauma of elementary school. He had been a fool to think that the strategic planning and distancing of so many years had washed away all the stains of the past and insulated him in his cocoon. Aman felt undone. Broken. That old feeling came rushing back into his veins, and he felt like he was back at his desk in classroom 2B—instead of 12B—when it had all started.

He felt heat travel up from his belly and his eyes well up with tears. But he would not, could not, give them the satisfaction of seeing him cry. He tilted his head back and blinked the tears away.

'Is that *a phone*?!' the teacher barked.

Aman bit his lip, gathered whatever belongings he could from his desk and stood up. Everything seemed to be happening at lightning speed, and yet it felt as if time stood still. The atmosphere in the room was heavy with expectation—everyone was waiting to see what he would do next. He felt all eyes on him. When he finally stepped into the corridor, he heard the entire class burst into laughter.

Where's Prakash when you need him? Clutching his bag, Aman walked hurriedly to the administrator's office, where he was told that Prakash hadn't come to school in the last two days.

I don't care; I will go to him.

Since he had no idea where Prakash lived, Aman pretended he had an urgent assignment to hand-deliver to him. The office staff disclosed his address.

Prakash was the only person in school with whom Aman exchanged words that didn't involve insults. But it wasn't as if he was a friend. It was just fate, or more likely the fact that no one could stand Prakash's company either—the ill-mannered individual that he was—which meant they were often grouped together for projects.

When Aman reached Prakash's doorstep, Prakash happened to open the door.

'What the hell, man! What are you doing here?' Prakash said.

'It's nice to see you too, Prakash,' Aman said, rolling his eyes. 'What's keeping you from school these days? Are you up to the usual—'

'How'd you find my place?' Prakash nervously looked past Aman and then put his arms on Aman's shoulders to steer him towards the lane beside his house.

'Quit it.' Aman shrugged off Prakash's hold. 'Why are you trying to get rid of me?'

'Am not!' Prakash looked cross. He paused and then, after a moment, smiled anxiously. 'Okay, fine! It's just that . . . How do I put this . . .? Umm . . . My parents are old-fashioned.'

'So . . .?' Aman asked. *Of course! How could I have been so stupid? Even scum-of-the-earth Prakash is embarrassed to be associated with a traitor's son.*

Aman felt like turning his back on Prakash and running home. Or maybe yelling at Prakash, maybe even smacking him. But he couldn't. He'd been conditioned to weigh his words, watch his actions and be as passive as possible. There was no way he could make an enemy of the one person who provided him company. He swallowed his pride and said, 'Nothing really, Prakash. Rohan and gang were extra desperate for attention, and today I became their muse.'

Prakash nodded. 'Yeah man, listen . . . that all stinks . . . Like I said . . . I'm going to have to go back inside. But I wanna leave you with a gift . . . And I *know* you said last week that you weren't interested, but THIS-IS-IT, Aman. I repeat, *this* is the solution to all your problems . . . Wait right here. No closer though. I'll get it. Be right back,' he said. Before Aman could respond, Prakash was already walking away.

He returned shortly and handed Aman a book. 'Just give it five minutes. That's all I'm asking.'

Aman looked at the rare hardback edition of *The Alchemist* by Paulo Coelho and put it in his backpack. 'Yeah . . . Five minutes sounds reasonable . . .'

Engulfed in the ghosts of stale bidi smoke outside the apartment on the first floor, where he and his mother lived, Aman could still hear the voices of his classmates—*He just can't speak . . .! But he can* surely *cry!* Those words had torn open old wounds and snatched away the last shred of his dignity. The moat he'd built brick by brick had been breached. His meticulous planning before every move, his scrutinization of each situation for possible pitfalls, his overthinking every decision—it had all been for nothing. His armour had been undone.

But since he was the male child of an army family, his mother would not look kindly on his tears, so he wiped his face before knocking on the door. Aman told himself it would never get better for him. Society would never let him escape the ghosts of his father's sins.

He took a deep breath. 'Maa! Open up!' he said, knocking for the third time.

Eighteen-year-old Aman Chandra didn't really stand out in a crowd. He was just another gangly teenager, nothing but sticks and hinges: tall and extremely thin. Dark, with dishevelled, dusty hair, and a slouch to his walk, almost as if he wanted to be closer to the ground, away from anyone's line of sight.

At that moment, what Aman did not know was that he and Prakash would never meet again. But if you had happened to tell him so, he would have been too angry to care. *C'mon, open up!* He clenched his jaw and kicked a pebble down the dimly lit hallway.

Aman heard footsteps getting louder, and then the door opened, revealing the yellow paint of the small apartment.

'You're back early,' Upasna Chandra said. She was wearing a faded sari, which had once been bright red. She held out her thin arms, offering to take his schoolbag. 'It's only four.'

Aman charged in. He had so much to say but didn't know where to start. He stormed across the room towards the steel almirah and slammed its doors open. He fished out his phone—an eight-year-old refurbished Samsung Galaxy S5 that lasted fifty minutes per charge—and started to scroll through it.

'What's wrong?' she asked.

He refused to look up. All he could think about were the innumerable times he had been shunned, by others, by his classmates, by everyone who sooner or later learnt of his last name.

'What happened at school, Aman?' she asked.

His mind raced until he snapped. 'Why *us*? Why *me*?!'

'Sit down, *beta*.'

'No, today I need answers,' he said. 'You say that they lied about Papa. That in reality he did not betray this country . . . that he didn't betray us . . . Then why am I called a "traitor's son"?'

Upasna looked at her feet.

'What exactly was Papa accused of?' he asked, his voice getting louder.

She shook her head and took a step towards him. 'All in good time, *beta*.'

'None of this makes sen- . . . I don't understand . . .' Aman said, waving his arms about, walking in circles. 'Don't want to live like this . . .'

'But you have to believe,' she said. 'That thread around your wrist is a blessing from the gods. Your life *will* turn around.'

'Mother, stop! Not again,' Aman said. Frustrated, he yanked the thread off his wrist. 'This thing didn't work in the fifth or sixth grade. And it definitely didn't work today. These useless superstitions have only ever given me false hope,' he said. 'Hope that maybe I will be able to speak normally to a friend one day . . .'

She met his eyes as if about to say something but then looked towards the floor. 'Can't . . . I can't,' she said with a catch in her throat. 'I wish I—was that the door?!'

Aman stopped pacing.

And there it was again: a faint but impatient knock.

They both looked at each other in surprise. They couldn't remember the last time they had visitors.

Aman walked to the door and unlatched it. A four-foot-tall, pot-bellied man pushed past him. His hair was in a bun on top of his head and the rest fell in dreadlocks, all the way down to his arms. His teeth were yellow and his eyebrows bushy.

The colour drained from Upasna's face as she stepped forward. 'Namahkrita, Sanaka.'

Namahkrita? Aman thought. *What does that even mean?*

'Namahkrita, Upasna!' said Sanaka. 'You've been in my thoughts. Both you *and* the child.'

Aman stared at this dwarf-like man. He had swept his dreadlocks aside, exposing his left forearm where a tattoo faintly glowed—no, not a tattoo—a blue design, a series of unbroken rings between his elbow and wrist. When his muscles flexed, and the intricate and busy pieces appeared to move, Aman realized that the image was of a blue serpent with large scales that encircled the man's arm.

'What brings you by?' Upasna asked.

'Only one thought. I have much to tell you, Upasna,' the man said to her. 'But before I do . . .' he stopped mid-sentence, raising his eyebrows as if to signal something.

'Oh, yes . . . uhh, Aman. Excuse us, please,' she said.

'What?'

'Please, Aman. The balcony.'

Aman stood his ground. 'Who is he?'

'Aman! We just need a minute or two,' his mother said. She escorted him to the small area outside they called a balcony and locked the door behind her.

He was alone. This, however, wasn't his first time on the balcony. Aman instantly ducked and put his eye to the keyhole. Now he could see them, but he could only hear a faint mumbling; the spinning fan drowned out what they were saying. *This guy is so weird,* he thought.

It was only much later, when the voices were raised, that Aman caught something that made his blood boil: the mention of his father.

'. . . to decide is for *you*, Upasna. No longer Avi,' the man said sternly.

Aman bared his teeth.

'Hah! My decision?' He heard Upasna scoff.

Then, suddenly, instead of responding to her, Sanaka turned around and looked straight into the keyhole, his gaze locking on to Aman's.

Aman jolted back with a start, his heart beating fast in his chest. He couldn't dare to return to his vantage point. So, he sat on the floor with his back against the railing of the balcony, looking up at the sky's twilight colours.

Ten minutes later, Upasna opened the balcony door. But she wouldn't meet his eyes and refused to turn around to face him. Aman didn't need to see her face to know she was crying.

Sanaka had clearly left—the front door was wide open. Aman's thoughts were in turmoil—between what he had failed to say in class, what Prakash had said later and what the strange man might have said, everything bunched together into one unhappy cloud above his head. Aman had reached his breaking point. He clenched his fists and looked at his weeping mother. The man had surely thrown more insults his mother's way and made more attacks on his family name. Any other day, perhaps, he would have let it slide. But not today.

I am going to kill him. He made a break for the door.

'Amaaan! Where are you going? Ama- . . .' Upasna's voice faded into the background as he ran down the hallway.

He couldn't find the man. Sanaka was nowhere to be seen. Upon his return a few minutes later, Aman found his mother sitting on the floor, her hands covering her face. Her eyes were swollen with tears that had smudged the kajal she wore.

'Who was that?!' Aman demanded.

She sighed, removed her hands from her face and looked at him. 'I am sorry, beta. I am so sorry.'

She knew why Sanaka's visit had enraged Aman. After her husband's treachery and demise had become the subject of TV news channels, her son had been unable to fathom what was going on. Their acquaintances and occasionally even strangers found new ways to put them to shame. The verbal volleys sometimes gave way to physical displays of derision—stones had been thrown at them when they were moving out of the army quarters; there would be heavy knocks on their door in the middle of the night; and anonymous callers would ring their phone number and shout expletives. There had even been one local policeman who had started turning up to pronounce that only his protection could fill the gap of a missing male figure in their lives—at a price, of course. Whether Sanaka was like them all was a riddle that remained unsolved.

The only peace Upasna ever found was in the embrace of her son, Aman. His very name meant peace. But his steadfast support, too, seemed to be straying away from her.

'NO!' Aman shook his head. 'Tell me! Who was THAT?'

Upasna clenched her jaw. 'Why are you always so self-absorbed? Have I ever had a supporting hand from YOU?' She tried to pull herself together. 'But you're right,' she resumed, wiping her face and standing up. 'I was hoping to wait until next year, when you turn nineteen, but you are an adult already. I can't hide things from you any longer,' she said, walking towards the wall adjacent to the front door. She ran her finger down its yellow plaster. 'You deserve to know . . .'

She took a deep breath. 'Avi Chandra was anything but a traitor. I don't know why the army said . . . Aman, he was a good man. It's just . . . his final job, the orders that eventually forced him out of our lives—I don't know why, but he was gone for a long, long time.'

'How do you know all this? I've seen the one letter they sent. Were there other letters?'

'I know because a friend of his, a fellow soldier, paid us a visit a year after his death. He told me a story that I refused to believe. Until he showed me Avi's belongings. His notes. His photos from the mission. I doubt you'd remember Uncle Deepak, beta . . . but you need to hear it from him. Maybe when you see those things, you'll believe it too. In fact, we should go first thing tomorrow.' Her eyes lit up. 'We can take the morning bus to Agra. It'll only take a couple of hours. But in the meantime, I *do* have something to show you.' She continued examining the wallpaper. 'Grab your cricket bat for me.'

What? Aman hesitated, but then said gently, 'Ma, have a seat. I'll get you a glass of water.'

'Just get me the bat, please! That's all I need.'

Aman gave her a bewildered look but obeyed. Upasna grabbed the bat from his hands. Turning around to face the wall with the yellow plaster, she closed her eyes for a second and then, as if with new-found purpose, raised the bat over her head and brought it down on the wall with all her strength. Surprisingly, it wasn't the crack of cement but the thud of timber that echoed around him. Aman's heart stopped momentarily. Upasna aimed at the same spot and swung the bat again and again. Eventually, an opening appeared. The plaster was ripped apart, and the wooden plank behind it broke into pieces.

2

Upasna

Upasna put her hand through the hole in the wall and kept removing the pieces of plaster until there was just enough space for them to enter.

When she pointed the flashlight inside, it lit up a room Aman had never seen—it looked like a storage space with shelves. 'What's happening?' Aman coughed as they brushed away spiderwebs and entered. The room stank of mice droppings.

Upasna stepped over cartons and moved them around, rummaging about with purpose. Going to some shelves in a corner, she pulled herself up to the topmost ledge. Her fingers turned a cardboard box around until it came half off the shelf. Aman jumped to help, and the box slid into his arms. It felt heavy and the contents rattled.

Upasna and Aman climbed out of the storage space with the box and took it to the dining table. Upasna gently wiped the dust away and opened the box.

It didn't seem to contain much: a few photographs, a small string pouch, a jar and—tucked to one side—heaps of palm leaves tied together. Aman pushed the photographs aside to look at the palm leaves, and his mother stifled a scream. Her eyes widened in panic. 'Wait, Aman!' she said. 'Hmm . . . this is too dirty. Let me go and clean this properly . . . umm . . . outside. I'll be right back!'

Before Aman could react, Upasna took the box and walked out to the hallway.

What is on those palm leaves? What is she hiding? He wondered if this Uncle Deepak they were going to meet would be able to shed some light on all this strangeness. Aman suddenly felt weary with all the thoughts in his head. Curiosity about the contents of the box swirled around his mind, along with thoughts of his father and the events of the day at school.

It was well past Aman's bedtime. Upasna returned after an hour, with the cardboard box thoroughly dusted. Her eyes shone with tears as she ran her fingers through his hair, leant forward and kissed him on his forehead. She then left him with the box and went to the kitchen, which was nothing more than a stove and some utensils at the edge of the room the two called home.

Aman opened the box and dug out the palm leaves first. Were these the notes his mother had mentioned? He wanted to study them thoroughly. He pulled out the bundle and untied the string that held them together. They were filled with scribbles and drawings of all sorts, but all in Sanskrit. Aman was unable to decipher more than a couple of words that read 'The Preservers'.

'Ma?' he asked. 'Can you help me understand—'

'Uncle Deepak may be of help tomorrow. I don't understand it myself. That reminds me, I will phone him and let him know we'll get there early,' Upasna said, adding sugar to the steaming pan in front of her.

Aman looked at the pan and grimaced. He had to drink a glass of milk before bed every day and despite the extraordinary events, today seemed to be no exception. He turned his attention back to the box. He noticed that the photographs were of his father and a group of men—all bare-chested and clad in orange dhotis—standing beside a humongous tree, the likes of which he'd never seen. Aman couldn't bear to look at his father—he missed him too much, the man he'd known anyway—so he quickly put the photographs away.

He opened the string pouch last. Inside, he found coins made of stone. They had rough edges, and unpractised carvings of images of the sun, trees and flowers.

'That's enough for tonight,' Upasna said, holding out the glass. 'Finish your milk.'

Aman gulped it down in one go. She waited until he was done, switched off the lights and said, 'Go to sleep now, beta. We have to take the bus to Agra early in the morning.'

As he prepared to go to bed, Aman couldn't recall the last time he had felt such anticipation. He could tell that his life was about to change forever. His feelings of resentment against his mother had dissipated. She'd finally taken the lid off the box of secrets about Avi Chandra, quite literally, and handed it to him.

So, the last thing he wanted was to continue keeping his own secrets. But he had one, buried deep in his bag. He waited for his mother's light snores to begin. After a while, he expelled his breath and slowly stood up. He tiptoed to his school bag and pulled out the gift Prakash had given him.

He looked at his mother once more and slowly flipped the book open. One thin cannabis cigarette and a matchbox were neatly tucked inside a rectangular hole at the centre of the pages.

He collected the items and put the book back into his bag. Stealing into the balcony, he peered over the railing to make sure there was no one below. And then he let go: the joint and the matchbox soon fell from his hand into the darkness of the street.

I was right to reject it earlier; now I will never touch it again, he told himself.

Aman went to sleep, feeling lighter than he had in years. He didn't know it then, but he would later tell many of his dream that night. In the dream, he was on a cliff in the middle of nowhere and jumped off it against his will. But instead of falling, he only rose up, until he was above the clouds. Somehow, he was flying over a dark forest, and he could see a valley below. It seemed as though God had sculpted the ring of mountains that hid the valley within the woods. In the middle of it lay a lake. The moon shimmered in its rippling waters, and the lake's shores glowed with extraordinary vitality.

The wind gushing past his face, Aman looked to his right: a cloud floated away into the distance. When he got closer, the fog below had thinned, and he caught sight of a tree towering in the middle of the valley. It was vast in size and width, and a thousand stars glittered on its branches. The entire valley, Aman was sure, was deserted: there was not a being in sight.

Just then, he saw a movement from the corner of his eye. A figure emerged from the shadow of the massive tree. It was a man with a white cloth wrapped around his waist, which flapped in the wind behind him. He lifted his head and looked up at Aman. Aman looked back at the man's strangely twinkling eyes. He felt a prickling at the nape of his neck, the hairs on his arms bristled, and then his entire body convulsed with a jolt.

The cloud that had been silently floating by him started barking. Yes, like a dog. And just like that, the cloud dissolved, and Aman woke up.

He opened a bleary eye. A dog on the street below was barking its lungs out. *Stupid dog.* He scowled. It was early in the morning. Aman had woken up away from his rug on the hard floor, drenched in a pool of sweat. He rolled over to his rug to find it no softer. His mother was sleeping on a mattress close by.

Aman's eyes scanned the room and watched the creaking fan send the cobwebs on the ceiling aflutter. He stretched and stood up. A cool breeze rolled in from the balcony, which made him recall fragments of the dream he had just had. But the more he tried to remember it, the more it slipped away, like a fistful of sand. He felt queasy.

He opened the door and staggered down the hallway, not able to walk straight. He was heading to the shared bathrooms on his floor. He felt nauseous and light-headed— so he picked up speed. Just when he was about to turn left and enter the bathroom, he slipped in a puddle, banging his left knee against the threshold. With a sickening thud, his chin hit the floor, pushing his teeth into his tongue.

Aman's belly heaved and his tongue felt sour. Somehow, he picked himself up and made it inside the bathroom, where the flickering of the yellow bulb above caused painful flashes behind his eyes. He touched his left knee, and it clicked awkwardly. He had to make it to the washbasin. But when he stood up, a sharp pain vibrated through his left leg and his eyes filled with tears. He plodded forward, limping and clenching his teeth, and just before he reached the tap, his body jerked and vomit shot out of his mouth. A discharge with yellow chunks fell into the basin.

But I didn't even smoke the joint! What's happening?

Aman splashed water on his face. He pulled down his cheeks, and as he stared at himself in the mirror through bloodshot eyes, the events of the previous day came rushing to him. *The type of person only a mother could love,* he thought, wondering if he would ever be seen for himself, as someone other than a traitor's son.

Trying to ignore his splitting headache and stiffening knee, he pulled himself together. They had to leave for the bus stand in less than an hour. He couldn't risk his mother calling off the plan. He made the journey back to his room, the nausea slightly better after he had expelled the contents of his stomach.

'Up early? You're awfully excited.' His mother was folding up his rug as he entered.

'Hmm.' Aman slipped his phone into his pocket. He tried his best not to limp.

'Don't carry anything unnecessary, Aman,' she said. 'Take only the cardboard box. Uncle Deepak will explain the palm leaves.'

Half an hour later, through torturous pain and with a spinning head, Aman followed his mother outside. He held the box and walked cautiously down the paan-stained staircase. They were greeted by a red-black sky, the horizon almost completely hidden behind smog, and were soon on a bumpy autorickshaw ride to Kashmere Gate bus station.

The morning traffic made the ride seem endless. For over fifteen minutes, they waited 500 metres from the bus station in a traffic jam, surrounded by cars that honked for no reason other than to assert their presence. The nausea had returned, and Aman was drowsy. He had almost fallen asleep with his head on the cardboard box in his lap.

When they reached, Upasna paid the autorickshaw driver, and they went into the bus terminal. Aman struggled to keep up with her. His head, ears and injured knee were throbbing. His vision was blurry.

'Wait right here,' she told him. 'I'll go buy the tickets.'

Aman was relieved for the break. His knee had been stinging, and he felt as if an odd bone was boring a hole in his skin. He had to make it to the bus somehow. Then he could sleep till they arrived in Agra.

The air was humid, and the announcements overhead were loud but unclear. When Upasna returned with the tickets, they walked towards the buses, zigzagging between people sleeping on the floor.

'Seats seventeen and eighteen!' she said as they entered their bus, which was almost full.

Aman felt like he was dangerously close to blacking out. He moved as fast as his knee would allow towards his seat, which was by the window, and sat down. He could still hear his heart pounding in his head and feel a pulse on his frontal lobe. Aman tucked the box into the space between his feet and the seat in front.

'You didn't sleep on time, did you?' Upasna asked.

'I did! But . . .' Aman yawned. *What's happening to me?*

'Anyway, I have a Disprin here somewhere,' she said, unzipping her handbag. Then she paused. 'We don't have any water. I'll go buy some from one of the stalls.' She got up. 'Be *strong*, beta.' She looked at him and smiled.

Aman saw his mother go to the bus exit and have a quick word with the driver before getting out. Aman tried to sit up straight, but his head was heavy, so he rested it against the window. He could see his mother. She stood at the bus stand, far away from any refreshment stall—the only stationary person in a place teeming with people. She was looking at him intently. Her face was red, and she covered it with her hands.

The bus honked. It was time to leave. But Upasna did not move—not an inch. It was as if she wanted to stop time.

Aman's vision stayed blurry, his eyes shut and his world went black. And when the bus started rolling out of Kashmere Gate bus station with a jerk, Upasna waved goodbye to her sleeping son, whom she hadn't let out of her sight for eighteen years.

They would never meet again.

3

Idhika

Not too far from New Delhi, near the northern tip of Uttarakhand, in the lap of the Dronagiri woods, lay the valley of Vanyasa. It was divided into three parts: jungle, lake and land. The ancient jungle, known as Aranyala, sprawled across the western part of it and ended at the shores of Pandayam Tal, the lake.

Idhika sat on the thwart of the boat, imagining her father seated across from her. It had been many years since she'd talked to him. Rishi Ajan had been revered for his extensive research on Vanyasa's scriptures. That was until he stole the one thing considered most valuable in the valley.

Idhika pulled the paddle out of the water as the boat floated towards the shore. She recalled what he had told her about the lake, sitting in this very boat.

'Pandayam Tal, you see, is unique, *bacche*,' her father had said. 'Its bottom harbours springs.'

'How deep is it?'

'That's a secret.'

'A "secret"? One too many, Father.' Idhika still didn't know why she was called the 'Child of the Valley', the only soul born within the Seven Hills that guarded Vanyasa. Her father had never explained. 'Pray, tell me!'

'Many nights before I reveal that, bacche. For now, enquire about the lake.'

'Fine . . . Do demons dwell in its depths?'

'Monsters? None.' Rishi Ajan laughed.

'And if I drank the water?' she asked.

'From Pandayam Tal? Why drink the lake water when you have *neer*, water from the springs?' he said and handed her the *kamandalu*, waterpot. 'These springs from where we get our water are magic—full of minerals gathered after a journey over slopes, under rocks and free-falls, touching nothing but wind, sun and earth. Remember, bacche, the valley owes its health to this neer.'

It had been over thirteen years since that chat with her father. She both missed him and despised him. Banished from the valley, he'd written to her many times, but she'd chosen not to respond, and couldn't even think of visiting him.

The boat came to a halt in front of trees with high tops. She stepped out, flung the rope that fell from the sculling notch over her shoulder and moored the boat to the edge of the lake where the forest, Aranyala, started.

Gurukul is only a few nights away, she reminded herself, determined to succeed today. Idhika wanted to be ready before the other Souls of Samsara arrived from the plains.

The sun was setting and, with it, her mood. Sunset in Vanyasa meant *Suryast*, the holy hour. It used to be Idhika's favourite part of the day, when her father taught her meditation. But now, the memory was too painful.

Idhika knew her anxiety would evaporate once the dark hour of Suryast was over, when the earthen lamps in Vanyasa lit up the edges of huts and paths. Every evening, their light, collectively powered by meditation, brought the valley back to life. *It truly is magnificent after dark.*

She entered the woods. Aranyala was a limitless labyrinth, but Idhika knew its secrets, and so she walked its trails without hesitation. When the time was right, she abandoned the main path and pierced the thick forest. Dry leaves started to crackle under her feet as she thought about her home and how secluded it was from the rest of the world. *Pity that plain dwellers never learn of its beauty.*

Her father's exile from Vanyasa had come early in Idhika's life. After he'd left, alone in the valley, it took her years to figure out why she was the only one her age to be born here. Her mother had been the second-to-last Eka and her father one of the ten Souls of Samsara in that decade. But she had never been able to understand how exactly her mother had died on the Mahayatra.

Idhika walked deeper into Aranyala, past a bright-feathered peacock that didn't flinch at her approach. The air became cooler. She was now concealed inside the forest under a canopy that blocked the sunlight. She could have been anywhere. But it didn't matter. Today, she'd come to the Clearing, a place of peace.

Time was running out. She needed to practise and be ready. With bright scarlet flowers giving her company, she started a combination of *asanas*, yoga postures, by bending forward. She shifted her weight to her palms and arched her back until she looked like a downward-facing dog. Only then was her *yog* ready to be taken to the next step.

Idhika sat cross-legged and straightened her back. Next, she closed her eyes, rested her knuckles on her knees and formed a *jnanamudra*, sacred hand gesture, with her fingers. Taking a deep breath, she began to meditate. *Just as Father taught me,* she noted wryly. Her mind kept thinking of Gurukul—if the new Souls bested her at anything she would never be able to live it down. So, she focused on her breathing, until there was nothing but the sensation of *Vayu* passing through her lungs. *In from the nose, out from the mouth.*

When Idhika was close to the moment she awaited, she was disturbed by a tickling on her thigh. It took her a while—her eyes still shut—to realize that it was a caterpillar inching up her skin, annoyingly keeping her away from her yog. She felt guilty when she moved her hand and brushed the caterpillar away. But it paid off, as she soon found herself slowly receding from the edges of her physical body. The world surrounding her was inviting, and she felt the familiar weightlessness that signified a deep meditative state. *Here we go.*

She was finally within reach, but the need for a companion remained. It couldn't be done alone. Idhika's atman, soul, searched with warmth, approaching a butterfly that wouldn't let her in, a ladybug that flew away at the request, a mongoose that was too far away. She was ignored by all those she approached.

Then she remembered the caterpillar. Idhika couldn't see it but could hear the slightest movements of its prolegs against a tall leaf in front of her. With eyes closed, navigating through the world of sound, Idhika's atman approached the caterpillar speculatively.

Namahkrita, she greeted it.

As soon as the insect responded, Idhika leapt— summoning every bit of her willpower, she pushed for that final step. Darkness surrounded her. She felt as if she had shed her skin; for a second, her bones went limp, and then her soul was set free from between her eyes.

It drifted towards the caterpillar—and pierced it.

Idhika had achieved *Atmayog.* She now occupied the insect's body, its skin, flesh and consciousness. The caterpillar acknowledged her command, stretching and contracting its tiny muscles at her bidding.

When Idhika finally opened her eyes, she had twelve of them. You'd think an insect with twelve eyes would have good eyesight, but as Idhika looked through the caterpillar's eyes, she could only see a blurred image of her own physical body sitting a little away, her back straight and eyes shut in tranquillity.

Idhika had seen herself in the reflection of Pandayam Tal before, and she realized that she emanated more power in her yogic stance with her eyes shut. When open, they were beguiling: warm, amber, soft. But in reality, she had a hard competitive shell, resistant to change or anything new— befitting a solitary Child of the Valley.

Her human form had a cotton dhoti wrapped around her waist and an upper cloth covering her chest. The *Deh* on her forearm glowed green—the intricate pattern of the graceful serpent mingling into her blue veins. The fine details of her face were hidden behind curly black hair, but every now and then, a breeze swept her locks aside to reveal her intense expression, while her chest arched in and out to the drumbeat of her breathing sequence.

The caterpillar bit into a leaf and bitter starch flooded Idhika's mouth. *Yuck!* She instantly spat it out, but the spittle only got as far as the corner of its mouth, appearing like a thread of silk hanging off it.

Eating leaves was not Idhika's aim today. She craved a sense of liberation, of exhilaration. She wanted another companion. Luckily, another ideal being had presented itself. The caterpillar's senses pricked up. Through one of its twelve eyes, Idhika spotted the shadow of the hunter, her next companion, closing down on her caterpillar self.

As soon as the startled insect jerked its prolegs, severing their connection, Idhika felt a sudden recoil as she was pushed back into her own body.

Her soul had returned, but she kept her eyes shut. *Wait . . . listen for it.*

Idhika was ready. The instant the Himalayan bulbul landed near the leaf and pecked at the caterpillar, she jumped. The connection solidified instantly, and the taste of the caterpillar she had been moments ago filled her mouth.

Crunchy. Idhika felt the bulbul's actions as her own. She shook her feathers ever so slightly, flexing them out and feeling the minuscule adjustments of the wind that was her constant guide. Then she spread her wings and took off, with difficulty at first, but after a few hard flaps she managed to rise high enough to ride the thermals, elevating her tiny body.

She rose until she left the forest behind and flew past the lake towards the huts. The sun had begun to dip, but Idhika the bulbul did not tire, circling the sky endlessly.

Orange turned to brown as the last light in the sky died behind the mountain, Sarp-poonch. And as soon as Suryast began, it was as if the valley below ceased to exist. Not one hut or tree was visible—the land hid behind a curtain, safe from the eyes of outsiders.

Just like that, it disappears, Idhika thought, flying over her home for the first time. The huts had concealed themselves in shadows and the trees within the dark slopes of the mountains. But Idhika could hear the strains of the collective vibrations rising from the huts below—the same vibrations from the meditation that enabled Suryast. They hit her in waves, one at a time.

Finally, silence took over, apart from the calls of blue whistling thrushes and the comforting hush of the wind.

Then, as Suryast ended, the dusk retreated—the trees straightened their backs and the mountain wind gave way to flickering oil lamps, reigniting life in the valley. The din picked up, and residents emerged from their huts. Moths gathered around lanterns for warmth and light. Pandayam Tal, however, remained dark, save for the one lamp in the boat-hut at its far-east corner.

In a momentary lapse of concentration, Idhika's vision went pitch black. The coloured spectrum and broad vision of the bulbul were no more. The bird fell from the sky as if without life, zigzagging at the will of the wind.

Idhika was pushed back into her physical body. She gingerly opened her own two eyes. Her legs collapsed when she tried to stand up. It took her a few stretches to shake off the stiffness in her feet. She watched the bulbul fly away into the distance. *Thank Indra, he's alive.*

She rowed back across Pandayam Tal and then walked the Chakkar that lined the lake's banks and ringed the entire valley, connecting its different sections. Her insides pumped with confidence—everything around her seemed brighter than usual. Although this was only her third successful attempt at Atmayog and she had much to learn, she knew she was finally ready for Gurukul.

Her eyes never left the reflection of the stars.

4

Aditya

Aman drifted in and out of sleep throughout that day. The first time he woke up, for just a few seconds, he realized he was still on the bus. It was dark outside, with only pinpricks of village lights as they zoomed past. *Has it been an entire day?*

The second time he woke up was for a full minute, the longest minute of his life. Between his pounding head and blurry vision, he recalled his mother waving goodbye at the bus stand. He turned around to inspect the bus. *Maybe she's sitting in a different seat.* That was when he saw that all the other passengers had left—it was just him and the driver.

Aman's stomach heaved—like a punch to the gut. His mother had chosen to leave him. He had no idea what had happened and what it meant. *No . . . no, you're getting it all wrong,* he consoled himself, frantically looking for her.

He tried to fight back tears. His breathing quickened when he imagined fending for himself in an unknown place. *How will I reach Uncle Deepak's house?* He looked out of the window as if the answers were there. The bus was puttering along the steeply curved shoulder of a mountain.

But there are no mountains on the way to Agra, he thought, wiping his sweaty hands. He still felt drugged. Staring at the empty seat beside him and feeling the bus taking him further and further away from home, Aman felt sick, as if he was in freefall, and soon passed out again.

The third time Aman woke up was because of the bumpy road the bus was on. He looked out the window to see that they were no longer on concrete. The bus seemed to be in a forest, traversing over fallen pine cones and large rocks. *How long has it been?*

After what felt like an hour of being jolted along, the bus slowed down. He opened the window to let the sweltering heat in, as though Aditya, the sun god, had decided to pay a visit. The unadulterated, crisp breath of the Himalayas coursed through the trees and broke against Aman's face. He spotted deer and birds with glittering feathers in the foliage around the bus.

The bus came to an abrupt halt in front of a small, moss-covered bridge.

'Oh, no no no . . .' the bus driver cursed. 'This is as far as I go.'

'Give me some water,' Aman said, looking at the swelling on his knee—now the size of a tennis ball.

'That bridge will collapse if the bus goes on it. Out, boy. Now!' the driver yelled at Aman.

'Where are we?' Aman asked him.

'You have some nerve!' The driver turned off the engine and stood up. 'I've brought you here as asked. Now quit wasting my time.' He stomped down the aisle, pulled Aman up by his T-shirt and, with little care for the boy's injured gait, pushed him out of the bus. Then he got the cardboard box from under Aman's seat and chucked that out as well.

'Wait!' Aman shouted, but the driver got behind the wheel and prepared to leave. The bus soon rocked out of sight. Aman gathered up the palm leaves that had fallen out of the box. 'Is anybody there?' he shouted repeatedly into the deserted forest. His phone's battery was dead. He was by himself in the middle of nowhere.

Not knowing what else to do, Aman approached the moss-covered bridge, which smelt of rot and was aged in layers of dead leaves. The water below was calm and clear. He climbed the bridge to get a better look at his surroundings and find a way to get to the stream.

On the bridge, despite the heat that surrounded him, Aman shivered because of the sense of desolation he felt. His left knee was heavy and the box in his hands seemed even heavier. He felt paralysed. Time had slowed down. He closed his eyes and wondered why his mother had abandoned him. He hadn't the faintest idea. He was as alone as one could be, in the middle of nowhere, with no family or friends.

Aman made his way down to the other side of the bridge, trying to avoid the patches of mould. But he slipped on one and felt the back of his head hit the crest of the bridge. He fell unconscious, not waking up even when the clouds above gave way and poured themselves dry on to him.

Much later, a four-foot-tall man arrived and stood next to Aman's fallen body. 'Plain-dwelling piece of filth,' he murmured as he checked his vital signs and examined his knee. Reassured that the boy was still breathing, he lifted him on to his back.

He tried to evenly distribute Aman's weight on his own body but was secure in the knowledge that the closer he got to home, the stronger his arms would get. He walked with lengthening steps, skipping over boulders when required. It was an impossible path to discern, but Sanaka never second-guessed himself as he cut across the dense forest. Aman was still asleep, and his limp body started to flap like a piece of cloth against Sanaka's calves when he started jogging.

Aman woke up yet again. Sanaka had taken a large leap—and his heel had collided with Aman's head. As he jerked awake, Aman realized his world was upside down. Drool from his mouth had pooled in his eyebrows, straining his vision. He tried to pull himself up and almost managed to wring his way out of Sanaka's grasp.

'Stop it!' Sanaka snapped, redoubling his grip.

'Is that—I know you!' he said, still hanging upside down. 'There has been a mistake.'

Sanaka refused to let go of him.

'Umm . . . Thanks for the ride!' Aman protested. 'Put me down now.'

'No, not even upon divine request,' Sanaka said hotly.

'I need to get back home!' Aman said.

'It *is* home where I'm taking you,' Sanaka said. 'Home to all the Souls of Samsara.'

'Souls of what?' Aman was confused. 'Just let me go!' His right hand formed a fist, and with all his strength he threw a punch into Sanaka's thigh.

Sanaka didn't even register the impact. When Aman pulled away, he snapped, 'Delusional fool! No idea of the bigger plan of the gods, have you? We have a religion to save, you and I! I am only acting as per your mother's wish.'

Aman thought back to the conversation and realized something he should have long ago: Sanaka obviously knew his father. Before he could think of a befitting reply to the insanity Sanaka spouted, he remembered something with dismay. 'Papa's box!' Aman suddenly said. 'We left it on the bridge. All his notes . . .'

Sanaka almost stopped for a split second. But then he picked up his pace and said, 'No time to turn back!'

Aman remembered. 'The Preservers . . . What does that mean?'

'Watch your words!' Sanaka instantly tightened his grip around the boy's knees.

I am considerably taller than him. How is he even carrying me? He swung his arms in protest, but Sanaka ignored him. Aman gave up, and the rhythm of the man's stride lulled the boy back to sleep.

Sanaka walked all day, and it was only close to sunset that he put Aman down on a patch of grass. Aman woke up from the impact. His forehead was purple and all the blood that had collected in his face slowly drained back to the rest of his body. His knee was still numb.

Aman looked up to find the most unusual banyan tree he had ever seen. He could see its leaves and canopy but not the trunk. Vines fell from its branches, wide and thick, and entangled with the roots on the ground to create a barrier, a curtain of snakelike drapes, around the tree.

'Trees have feet too,' Sanaka said, walking up to the vines.

What? Aman stared hard at Sanaka.

'Listen closely,' Sanaka said. 'You're already late for Adwaita, so listen well. Today I reveal the secret of the valley's entrance. The Song of the Valley is key. An offering to the great Nandana, this tree that stands between us and home . . . He's wise and requires the hymn . . . And only then, through the Song, will you find his feet, to which—of course—you must bow and pray and hope that he shows the way.'

Aman was still trying to wrap his head around 'trees have feet'. But Sanaka paid no heed and continued: 'Only if Nandana detects within you the purity will he present his feet. You must own the Song, know its variations and arcane pronunciations, for each syllable will tell you how to place your steps, how to walk—with your head down, of course— to the beat of the song. Watch and, more importantly, listen, as I sing the Song of my people, the Vanyasis—soon to also be . . . your people.' He ended with a distasteful look.

Sanaka then started singing in what sounded like a version of Sanskrit with a faint crescendo:

Tucked within brambles that may.

He walked to the song's rhythm, circling the tree, only turning around and going the other way when the next line started.

Shielding boughs and keeping at bay.

The tune echoed hauntingly, and Aman felt dormant energy rise from within the tree.

> *Every* dashak *centres a blue rose,*
> *Scent of which dale invariably knows;*
> *Watered, it riots by the nights,*
> *Sheeny, eliciting awe from sights.*

Aman could understand little of these words. All that the song did was to make him feel hollow, like he wanted to weep. The birds around him grew silent in agreement. The incomprehensible lyrics evoked in him thoughts of his mother, his home and the familiarity of his rug.

> *But in the valley fortified by the one that slithers,*
> *For the sake of home, that flower must wither.*

Sanaka ended with a poignant note in his voice. He now stood on the other side of the tree, in front of the curtain of vines.

'Namahkrita,' Sanaka said to the tree with downcast eyes. He then lay on the forest floor and gestured to Aman to follow him.

Aman hesitated, looking at the mounds of mud that Sanaka was deep in.

'Get down!' Sanaka grabbed his arm and pulled him down to the ground beside him. *Thud!*

'Arghh!'

'Shhh . . . focus!' He was impatient. 'I know your knee's hurt. But it's nothing that Chitra cannot fix. For Agni's sake, just hold on until we get in.'

And then, there was a shift in the atmosphere. The tree seemed to be stirring from a deep sleep. Its roots crackled and the vines started to part ways.

'Oh, great sage, Nandana,' Sanaka said, folding his hands over his head, which Aman emulated. He looked up to see dark shadows looming through the gap.

'No way the tree is moving . . .' Aman said, looking at the sight before him that defied all logic. Maybe none of it was real. *Am I really in a jungle, or is this all a dream?*

'Keep your head down, you stupid boy!' Sanaka was furious and pushed Aman's head into the mud.

Only when the crackling of the roots stopped did Sanaka say, 'Up.'

Aman was trying to stand up, bearing the pain in his left knee, when tentacle-like vines shot forward from the tree and wrapped around his heel.

'Uaaaaahhh—noooooooooo!' Aman yelled. The vines were unyielding, and he was pulled up into the air. Aman was upside down again. He couldn't believe it.

Sanaka's face betrayed surprise, but he was quick to react. He leapt at the stringy vines, jumped over a set of thick bundles of them in the air and ripped apart the prop roots. 'ARANYANIIII!' Sanaka yelled—not at the tree, but at the goddess who controlled the forests. 'Why are you doing this?!' Sanaka said as his bulging arms swung uncontrollably, tearing through the different vines that were reaching for Aman.

'RUN!' Sanaka's voice roared. Flocks of birds flew away at the thunderous tone—in fact, even Nandana appeared to have been rattled. The vines recoiled and momentarily let Aman go. He fell on his face and fumbled around, his knee in excruciating pain, his heart pulsating faster than ever.

Aman began running for his life. His chest pained as he scurried without direction in the mud. The land under his scampering feet was laden with small mounds of mud, and he had only made it a little way when his left foot got caught awkwardly in one of the burrows. Instantly, his body yanked back and his left knee twisted completely while his heel jammed into the ditch. He cried out in pain, clutching his leg, with tears streaming down his face.

Steeling himself, Aman pulled out his foot, but it was too late. He couldn't feel his leg any more. He was sure it was broken. The kneecap seemed to be out of place as it bulged awkwardly from the back of his leg, almost tearing through the skin. He clung to his thigh and saw his misshapen leg.

As he looked to his right, Aman spotted the longest of Nandana's vines coming for him. They reached him before he could react, enveloping his arms, embracing his body. Aman didn't even bother resisting. The vines lifted him high, well out of Sanaka's reach, and then started to twist and entangle around him. His legs alone hung limply from his waist as if separated from his body.

Suspended in the air, Aman saw the prop roots circling down his rib cage, waist and eventually enwrapping both his legs. They slowly made their way up to his neck and even around his throat until every inch of skin was covered. Aman felt throttled. He tried to scream, but that required him to have a breath in him. Aman was frozen, suffocating, locked in an unrelenting coffin.

Somewhere down below, he could hear Sanaka struggling, perhaps to break free from another set of vines. Aman was sure he was going to die soon. His body quivered. Would it really matter? Who would mourn his death?

The vines started to tighten even more around his left knee, targeting his injury. They further compressed his knee with crushing force until Aman tried screaming, but no sound escaped his throat. A few seconds after that, he fainted.

5

Nandana

It was the loud, painful click of his knee that woke Aman up. He saw a branch softly unwrap itself from his knee and retreat. It seemed like the tree had adjusted his kneecap back into its socket. There was no bone sticking out any longer, and blood finally flowed into his left foot. The vines lowered and gently undid themselves, setting him on the ground. Aman stretched out his leg, unable to believe that there was not a trace of pain in his knee.

Sanaka walked up to him, brushing leaves off his arms. The tree looked like it had settled back into sleep. Its prop roots hung dormant, drawn apart like a curtain that had a wide opening at its feet, welcoming them in.

'Enter,' Sanaka said.

Aman panicked. He looked around to identify the route that would lead him back to the bridge and his father's abandoned box. *Who knows what the hell is inside that tree?* He had had enough of this unreal world. Giving Sanaka a determined look, he began running.

It was strange that Sanaka did not try to stop him, and Aman heaved a sigh of relief—but it soon became clear why he hadn't bothered. Aman had run just about 100 metres and come up in front of the largest living being he'd ever encountered: a spotless white elephant with golden tusks. It trumpeted angrily and swayed from side to side. Aman noticed not one but five trunks hanging off its face. Its ears fanned out wide and the legs began to move but the eyes stayed locked on Aman.

Gasping, he stopped and took several steps back. Suddenly the prospect of entering the tree didn't seem too bad at all. He turned and began running back towards Sanaka, but the elephant's charge was swifter. In no time, the beast had gained on Aman, who ran as hard as his body allowed, knowing that he was moments away from being trampled.

The sharp edge of the elephant's tusk met the flesh of his back. But for some reason, he felt no pain. In fact, he couldn't move a muscle. He couldn't even turn around to see that the elephant too had frozen into a statue. Everything had turned black and white, and the wind had died.

Sanaka walked past Aman and, with a quizzical look, examined the elephant, murmuring, 'So far from the sky.' Then, with an exasperated sigh, he grabbed Aman's collar and pulled him away from the elephant. He dragged Aman back to Nandana and stepped inside the dark mouth of the tree.

Colour returned to the world, and Aman saw the elephant resume its charge. But the tree's vines closed just in time, shutting out the tusker, leaving it behind in a world that was no longer his. They were now tucked into the space between the tree trunk and the vines. Aman's eyes struggled to adjust to the darkness.

'Sanaka?!' Aman called out, but there was no response. It was all too quiet. He could hear the slithering of tiny creatures. 'Uhh . . . you there?'

'The path is clear; the destination ahead in a circle,' Sanaka said and smacked him on his head.

Aman's eyes had adjusted to the darkness, and he saw Sanaka going down rough-hewn steps into a tunnel under the ground. 'What is this place?' he asked as he followed, looking at their interlocking shadows cast by the lanterns on the walls.

'Shreyan's Tunnel—this is one of the few entrances. The first of the plain dwellers who found the valley, Shreyan, built it. It took him a year to dig his way in. Some of the others also entered this way.'

Aman was dumbfounded. Every answer of Sanaka's threw up a million more questions in his mind. 'There are others?' he asked.

'Indeed. The other Souls of Samsara.' They had reached a passage after their descent.

'Sanaka, what does that mean?'

'You see, the valley has a divine tree, bigger than even Nandana. And all valley dwellers meditate under its shadow. Some of them compete with one another to meditate for the most number of hours. In return, the tree connects with the best of them, who become the Tapasvis. It uses the thoughts of the exceptional yogis to find like-minded individuals in the plains, who may or may not have a relation with the Tapasvi.

But it matters not, for these Tapasvis are never allowed to meet the Souls. My task is to bring these Souls to the valley.'

'My father!' Aman recalled the gigantic tree in the photograph from the cardboard box. 'So he was one of the Tapasvis?'

Sanaka scoffed. 'Who? Hah! To enter Vanyasa is not simple. To be a part of the abode of the sages is an honour only the Souls of Samsara receive.' They reached a fork and took a right. 'It's difficult, however. Not easy for men of the plains. Ahead of you is a life with no friends, no love and few celebrations. A hermit's life. Do you think you can live that way?'

Aman smiled politely at Sanaka, who was clearly unfamiliar with his life to be asking such a question. *Have I known any other way of living?*

The passage stopped dipping further into the earth. They seemed to be near its end and drew closer to the exit. Ahead of him, the tunnel seemed to be glowing. Before long, Aman found himself standing in front of a shining gateway, at least thirty feet tall. In fact, the light emanating from the structure was blinding to the extent that all Aman could make out was a man on its right pillar and the shape of a snake on the left. Before his eyes could settle, Sanaka pushed him through the gateway and into the open expanse which signalled the end of the tunnel. Right below him, a series of large, moss-covered steps disappeared into a blanket of clouds that stretched until they met tall mountain peaks. *The valley must be beneath.*

Just then, a draft passed by Aman, and he heaved as if he were breathing for the first time in his life.

'Sanaka!' Aranyani said. 'What have you done?! This is sacrilege!' Her green eyes surveyed Sanaka's hut.

Sanaka sat cross-legged on his rug, unaffected by Aranyani's sudden charge inside.

The hut was minimally furnished with objects made of pine branches. Sanaka sat flaunting his usual state of undress. A lantern in front of him cast a shadow which could have belonged to a fat child.

Aranyani asserted herself. 'You risked it all, even the health of Aranyala. Only the worthy find Vanyasa, Sanaka. Father would have never allowed it. I'm telling you: that boy cannot breathe any more of our air. Put him back where you found him.' Despite her demeanour, she gave him an injured look. It was incredible that she was the same person who had sat with the ancient yogis who established Vanyasa a few thousand years ago.

Sanaka refused to acknowledge her complaint. How could he possibly be indifferent to Aranyani, a deity? But offending one deity for another was never a solution, so he raised his hand and said, 'There's no showing disrespect to the ritual of the holy herb. You know this: once initiated, the process has to be completed without digression.'

That's when Aranyani noticed it: a flat stool in front of Sanaka with green buds of cannabis.

Sanaka pulled out a cloth from under his thigh and used it to clean his serpent-engraved chillum. Examining it as if it were a rare stone, he raised the largest of the cannabis buds above his head until it caught the sunlight shining in through the window. Sanaka placed the nug in the mortar and pressed down hard with sheer determination. He took his time to empty the mortar's insides into the chillum and then finally used the blue flame in his lantern to bring the pipe to life.

'The boy is not going anywhere.' Each word expelled thick white smoke from his mouth. The hut filled with a milky vapour.

'But he isn't one of the Souls,' she said.

'He *is*, Aranyani,' Sanaka lied.

'Then who is the boy's Tapasvi parent?'

'Nandana let him in, didn't he?'

Aranyani seemed to be waging an internal battle. 'We already *have* ten souls, Sanaka!'

Sanaka avoided the question by placing his chillum on his lips and taking in a lungful of kush. 'Why scare the child? What did you get from using Nandana so violently?'

'I fixed his knee, didn't I?' Aranyani said. 'Why are you dodging my question? What is it that you are not telling—'

'He's the *Eka*. I am not blind to this aberration, Aranyani! But with the threat of Chayan looming, when all the Souls have failed Adwaita, the eleventh might be the answer. You know better than anyone that we are useless without a leader for these recruits.'

'What? Him?!' Aranyani said, surprised. 'Sanaka, you continue to forget that we need not bring on this anomaly. We have, every decade, recruited only the nine Souls. Don't you remember when Kautilya had failed his Adwaita, it was the usual tenth, the Child of the Valley who is always overlooked, who took on the role of the Eka? And since Idhika is immune to Madhu and cannot have her Adwaita, it must be *she* who takes on the mantle this year. There is no other way!'

'No other way?' Sanaka scoffed. 'Why, of course, there is. The most obvious one. The boy, Aman, must be the Eka. We certainly cannot rule him out until his Adwaita. That's the only way to know. Your father would have agreed, correct? We need to question rules that have been set in a different time, Aranyani. Perhaps we can recruit more than we always have. I say this, again, because Nandana let him in, and although I do not know his Tapasvi parent here in Shambhala, it doesn't mean he is unfit for these seven walls.'

It was with much vigour in his dilated pupils that Sanaka tried to sound respectful when he softened his tone and continued, 'Devi Aranyani, I do really think there's a chance that this boy could be the one to lead the Mahayatra at the end of the year.' He picked up a tiny, arrow-shaped leaf from a wooden bowl beside him and popped it into his mouth.

'Then I must see the boy for myself. *I*, not Chitra, will conduct his Adwaita, to be sure.'

Sanaka smiled as he exhaled. 'You'll see.'

He suddenly realized the gamble he'd taken. But in that moment what mattered more was that the ritual had been respected.

6

Prithvi, Ujal and Fayza

Archery requires thumbs. But when Prithvi took her position, her back unbending and eyes fixed on the target, she pulled the string with only her index and middle fingers. The *teer-kaman*, her bow and arrow, was a part of her as much as any other limb, and she found comfort in the thought that it would be cremated with her. It was the way of her people. As was living life with a severed right thumb—an ode to their ancestor, Ekalavya.

Prithvi and her twin, Ujal, were Bhils from a tribal belt in Madhya Pradesh, perfect Souls of Samsara for an angst-stricken Vanyasa that could definitely do with a few more archers.

The tension of the string tightened around Prithvi's index finger. The *twang* of her bow brought her solace, it reminded her of home, of her parents and of Bhavesh—so she let go.

TWISH!

The arrow whirred endlessly and just about missed the falling leaf. *Did you take the wind into account?* Bhavesh's words echoed in her head.

SNAP! A twig broke somewhere behind Prithvi. She whipped around. Then she heard leaves crackling under scurrying steps. She ran after the sound, diving through thorny bushes and going past the clearing from where the noise had come. But she only caught sight of their boots before whoever it was hared off.

It was a man wearing shoes . . . like people in the plains! she thought. *And why did he run?*

That was when she saw the freshly felled tree. When she approached it, her eyes caught the glint of something lying in the grass beside it. An axe.

Her body froze. Although it was her first time in Aranyala, Prithvi knew that cutting trees was against Vanyasa's laws. She glanced around nervously to make sure no one had seen her. Thinking about the punishment for such a crime, Prithvi stumbled a couple of steps back and began running. Her legs carried her out of Aranyala, on to the Chakkar by Pandayam Tal, and to the huts where she knew she would find her twin brother.

Ujal barged out of his hut and almost bumped into her. He had leathery black skin, and his upper body bore cuts that are the hallmark of an archer. He had a thin frame and wide forearms, and he too was missing his right thumb. The twins' faces looked similar—with sharp, beak-like noses, black lips and dark circles under their eyes—but they were built differently. While Ujal was big and tall with a mild stubble and an ever-shaved head, Prithvi was small and slender with her long hair tied into a ponytail. The other distinction lay in their abilities—Ujal would never accept it, but his twin was indeed the better archer. 'Where *were* you?!' he asked.

'I-had-gone-to-practise-but . . .' She struggled to catch her breath. 'There was someone and he tried to run away.' She paused to drink water from the kamandalu. 'I found an axe and a tree sliced in half. Also, I am telling you this man was wearing rubber shoes on his feet!'

Ujal rolled his eyes. 'Hah, *shoes* you say? And let me guess, he was wearing clothes too, like people in cities?'

'Ujal!' she snapped at him. 'I'm serious. I saw him run into the bushes.'

'Prithvi!' He tightly grabbed her arm. Baring his teeth, he said, 'Don't forget that you are a Bhil.'

She looked deep into his eyes, unwilling to flinch despite the pain. She was used to his intensity and bursts of temper.

'Remember what we decided?' he said. 'We would brave whatever this place threw at us and eventually bring Amma and Baba here. That means you can't get into any trouble. It hasn't even been a *week* for us. And what you just said sounds false. No one will believe you.'

Prithvi and Ujal had been spirited away from their pre-Vanyasa lives by Sanaka, like most Souls of Samsara that showed any form of resistance. But now that they had seen Vanyasa, they wanted to stay. Someday, they wished to create a home for their parents in the valley.

However, Prithvi had another goal. She wanted Bhavesh. Ujal would never have guessed where their motives diverged. He had no knowledge of the parts of her mind Prithvi kept secret. 'Aren't we one, sister, as we once were in Mother's womb?' he would pronounce to her time and again. But even before they came to Vanyasa, Prithvi could never have confided in Ujal about Bhavesh. And because of this, despite the fact that they shared the one goal of succeeding in the Mahayatra, their destinations differed.

'So, what are you suggesting?' Prithvi's eyebrows knit in disbelief. 'That we don't tell anyone at all?'

'Precisely. Or the blame will fall on you. We could be kicked out of here before we even get started,' Ujal added. 'So don't go to practise in the forest any more. There are tons of other places.' He paused. 'Listen, Prithvi, I'm sure there is a temple for the wind god here too, like in the tribe. Go there right now and pray that we succeed.' He picked up a brass kamandalu and poured some *sura paniyam*, a strong alcoholic drink, down his throat. 'Meanwhile, I'm going to see if I can find more of this *charas*, hashish. It's magical!'

Prithvi stormed out of his hut and headed towards hers. On her way, she ran into a group of girls.

'You, Prithvi!' The taller of the girls walked up to her. The other followed. Prithvi noticed that unlike the other female Souls of Samsara who wore a single cloth wrapped around their body, fastened with a jute belt, this girl had torn her gown into two pieces to make upper and lower garments, which showed off her toned abs. She'd even fashioned a small, pouch-like bag with the torn cloth, the jute belt making an appearance as the strap slung over her shoulder.

'Namahkrita,' Prithvi said.

The tall girl pulled out a small metal cylinder from the pouch. She twisted it open and applied bright red colour to her lips. 'Lipstick?'

Prithvi stared at her.

'Wouldn't suit those dark lips anyway,' the tall girl said. 'I'm Aarti. Brahmin.'

'I'm confused. Which one is it? Aarti or Brahmin?'

'That's her . . . her caste, adivasi!' Half-chewed chunks of banana sprayed out of the mouth of the broad-shouldered girl beside Aarti. 'I'd advise you to sh-show some respect,' she said, moving towards Prithvi menacingly.

Prithvi looked at her and touched an arrow in her quiver. 'I really don't know whether to be scared or laugh at you.' The second girl flinched, backing away a couple of steps.

Aarti rolled her eyes. She pulled out a box from her pouch, from which emerged a stick. 'The last one.' She shook her head. Using a small device, she lit the stick and started spitting out halos of smoke. 'Forgive Payal. And listen. We've already tried to find a way out of this place, but there's a wall above these hills, in case you're wondering. We're all stuck here for now. And to play their game, we need a leader— what they called an "Eka". So, I'm stepping up by virtue of my caste, and I need your support in—'

'If I may,' Prithvi said. 'There's talk of an eleventh Soul being recruited, because, as you said, the Adwaita has failed to produce an Eka. What's to say that person doesn't—'

'It's crazy, this place,' Aarti said, holding up the burning tip of her cigarette. It had a blue glow. 'Fire isn't red here— whether it's in a lantern or in this.'

Payal kicked up dust. 'I'm going to see if I can find a phone signal on the other hill today. I don't have too many tries left.'

'That can wait,' Prithvi said. 'I know a way past the wall over the hill.'

Unlike most Souls of Samsara, Fayza had been allowed to say goodbye to her parents. They couldn't fathom what was happening when they found out their daughter would be taken away. Many plans were made to run away and hide her. But a friend of Fayza's grandfather, a sage from Rishikesh, had convinced her parents to let fate have a say. He had heard of Vanyasa. 'It's an honour she must not dismiss,' he said. 'And you don't really have a choice; you're lucky they're informing you at all. They're being polite, I don't know why. She'll be kidnapped if you resist.' The sage was a trusted friend of the family, so he convinced the parents of Fayza's destiny and offered to help her prepare. In the month leading up to her arrival in Vanyasa, the sage lived with the family and taught Fayza the legends of the valley and ways to survive its trials.

On her first day in Vanyasa, Fayza was shown to her hut at the base of the mountain Kalanag, at the eastern edge. It was to be her home for the next year. 'You'll have to furnish it yourself,' she had been told. 'Based on what you earn in the bazaar.'

The hut's windows were uneven holes in the side plaster. The insides smelt of dead animals. The floor was littered with feathers, and a rug gathered dust in the far corner. The residents of Vanyasa clearly did not enjoy the luxury of beds. Fayza got to work scrubbing the mud walls of her hut and sweeping the clay floors. She used a fibre broom to dust the roof, which was made of dried dung and hay. And only after a week, when her monkish room was clean, did she stop.

Over the course of that week, Fayza found out many more things about Vanyasa. Chief among them: who not to be friends with.

'That's weird!' Aarti's voice startled Fayza. Fayza looked up at the girl standing at her hut's entrance. Aarti shot her a wide smile. 'That really *is* weird!'

'Hi, I'm Fayza . . . And what is so weird?' She extended a handshake.

'I know your name, Fayza.' Aarti's folded palms clashed with Fayza's extended hand. 'Namahkrita.'

'Oh. Of course! How could I forget?' Fayza retreated her arm and bent in mutual respect.

'How was your Adwaita?' Aarti asked.

'As magical as I'd always imagined. But I'm not the Eka,' Fayza said.

Aarti smiled. 'I thought as much. You're the last person the lord is going to—'

'What do you mean?' Fayza cut her off. 'He could have looked at me as much as anyone else.'

Aarti let out a snort of derision.

'I ask again. What is so "weird"?' Fayza said.

'Oh, it came as a bit of a surprise to me . . . how clean your hut is,' Aarti explained.

'What are you implying?' Fayza asked.

Aarti stayed silent.

Fayza was caught off guard, but it was nothing she hadn't been subjected to before. Experiencing discrimination in Vanyasa was unexpected, though. Wasn't it supposed to be as she had been told—'a home to equals, in confluence with all faiths'?

Before Fayza could press her to come out with what she was thinking, Aarti left. Fayza tried to put the unpleasant interaction out of her mind, forcing herself to think about the life that lay ahead in Vanyasa. 'What's the first thing I should do when I'm there?' Fayza had asked her grandfather's friend before she left.

'I'll tell you,' the sage had said. 'When in doubt, always go to the Temple of Indra on top of Kalanag.'

'What's Kalanag?'

'One of the three *parvats* around Vanyasa. Although there are many mountains, the giants are Sarp-poonch, Kalanag and Rohini.'

'Which one is the tallest?' Fayza asked.

'That'll be Sarp-poonch. But it's further away, beyond the forest called Aranyala. The other two are beside the village. Kalanag is on the eastern edge and Rohini in the south.'

Fayza could see Kalanag behind her. The steps which ran up to the holy shrine of Indra started not too far from the edge of her cottage.

She started climbing the stairs, the sage's words echoing in her head. *'But that bread, Fayza. Up there, yes, at the Temple of Indra. Guru Amrav's recipe comes from the King of the Gods himself. Do you know that they sing tales about that bread in Rishikesh?'*

As she climbed, Fayza spotted several stone cairns adorned with triangular orange flags, and before long, she had arrived within sight of the temple. When she reached the crest of Kalanag, she was taken aback by the force of the wind.

The top of the mountain had a rectangular stone structure raised a few inches above the ground. Behind it was a simple room for the priest which appeared to be built of hay. Tall, thin weeds swayed in the wind around the shrine.

She circled the temple until she was face to face with the valley. With dishevelled hair and crinkled eyes, she looked down at her new home. Vanyasa was bigger than she'd imagined. There were endless squares of farming fields carpeting the floor of the valley, and trees of all kinds, dark and thick, their branches untamed. But the tree that caught her eye was the largest she'd ever seen, towering in the middle of the valley. Its trunk was as wide as her school auditorium— it zigzagged its way up to the branches that sparkled like stars.

Fayza removed her glasses and used the hem of her gown to clean the lenses. In the distance, she saw minute figures labouring with bent backs. Moving mounds of hay distinguished the female farmers from the men. Gamblers exchanged oddly shaped coins, squatting on the edges of beaten footpaths, and deer chewed grass near the caves on the opposite side of the valley.

Fayza caught sight of cows and goats, probably mooing and bleating, but there was only silence where she stood. The glistering blue of Pandayam Tal was the cornerstone of the valley, surrounded by clusters of huts of all shapes and sizes, made of earth, straw, hay and reeds—homes, halls, fields, barracks, small and big. White smoke billowed out of their carved windows. The mud walls and thatched roofs put forth a sturdy facade. Some huts were tucked into the hollows of big oaks. Fayza spotted at least seven tea stalls dotting the paths.

'Breathtaking, isn't it?' Fayza hadn't noticed when the man had come to stand beside her. He was looking at the valley with enchanted eyes. Standing in polished wooden sandals, he wore a white dhoti and sported a tika, which extended upwards from his forehead and disappeared in the curve of his shaven head. The cloth over his shoulder, as well as his long white beard, swayed in the wind. 'These hills that cradle Vanyasa, even the Tal, and Pataan below that hollows the mountain you stand on, are all a blessing. I've lived here my entire life, but I'm still a stranger to these lands.'

For a second, absorbing the vastness in front of her, Fayza felt weak and alone.

As though he had read her thoughts, the man said, 'Indra is the first of all gods, which means he is bored in the company of most. It also means that he is a lonely god. The presence around his temple will do that to you. Make you contemplative and miserable. Don't let him bother you.'

Fayza was taken aback by the way the priest had mentioned the lord—in such a casual manner. 'You're Guru Amrav!'

'Yes, my child. And you're one of the ten. Tapasvi's Souls.'

'Yes, Namahkrita, guru-ji.' Fayza bowed.

'Namahkrita,' the man said gently.

'Guru-ji,' she said, 'I've heard a lot about your bread . . .'

The guru shot her a smile and walked back to the priest's room, holding his dhoti up with his hands. He came back carrying a circular loaf of glazed bread. 'Have a bite.' He pushed it towards her. 'And take some for later. The last thing I want to do is get rid of this week's produce. To throw away Indra's blessed food is blasphemous. I can only have so much, you see.'

Fayza broke off a piece and put it in her mouth. It was harder than she'd expected, getting stuck in her throat and betraying its staleness. Fayza got a whiff of something sour, and when she turned the loaf over, she saw a thin layer of fungus on the surface.

'Oh, no! There goes another batch,' Guru Amrav said. He took the bread from Fayza and tucked it under his arm. 'I'm sorry, beta. These get stale too often now in the summers— and I haven't had a visitor since the winter month of Pausha.'

Fayza's insides warmed at being called 'beta'. 'But I was told that this bread was much sought by everyone.'

'Different times, my child, different times.'

'I've heard some things, but none of it makes any sense to me. How do you mean different?' she asked.

Guru Amrav looked around to make sure they were alone. 'The threat of Vanyasa's old enemy, Chayan, now looms stronger than ever. Rumour has it that his army is poised to journey up the Seven Hills and steal into the valley any day. Under no circumstances can we allow that to happen; Chayan of all people knows the secret to cripple our millennia-old establishment.'

'And what's the secret? Surely the powerful in Vanyasa can defend it?'

The expression on his face turned dark when he said, 'No. Not even Lord Indra's intervention would help if Chayan found Madhu, the source of the valley's strength. Its reserves are key. It's why you're here too, to sustain its supply. Wisdom lies in understanding that our *only* hope is Sanaka. Irascible and despotic he may be, but Sanaka is a true lover of this land. He will die before anything happens to Vanyasa.'

'Sanaka is no saint,' Fayza said. 'Kidnapping us. Tearing apart our families. With absolutely no regard for our hopes and dreams.'

'Despite that, the righteous Vanyasis don't question his methods of recruitment,' the guru said. 'Do you know why, why they continue to turn a blind eye to his crimes? Because the villagers know that recruitment is essential to Vanyasa's survival. That's right; we're hypocrites. It's the natural state of the mortal mind. Even plain dwellers keep grain out for pigeons and at the same time pay to butcher chickens. Rest assured, once the recruits enter Vanyasa, they are given the utmost attention. The first task is Adwaita. Sure, it's a way to find the Eka, but what they don't tell you is that Adwaita is also a ritual to cleanse your vulnerable souls of the power of Chayan, the only yogi in the subcontinent who can Atmayog into humans.' Guru Amrav continued, pointing to some huts on the opposite side, near the low-lying hills, on an elevation near the spring. 'That's the Assembly, where the Sabha and Samiti meet every turn of the moon. Today, the worst is upon us. Our last hope lies in what is happening there right now.'

Fayza nervously cleared her throat. 'What's happening?'

'The last recruit has arrived. Never in my life have I seen an eleventh.' Guru Amrav shook his head. 'Save us, Indra. We haven't found the Eka yet.'

Fayza's eyes widened. 'There's only one recruit left?!' She had been told of the Mahayatra and its importance to the survival of Vanyasa. 'How long will it take to get there?'

'Don't bother.' He closed his eyes and took a deep breath. 'Just take all of this in before it fades away.'

But Fayza had to know. She bowed to Guru Amrav and started to run back down the hill, skipping steps as she jogged. Her eyes occasionally left the path to look at the phalanx of birds that filled the sky. She caught the flight of an eagle. There were forktails, sparrows, flycatchers and bulbuls. Some glided while others darted; a songster zoomed past Fayza, chirping an anxious tune. They were all going the same way as her, to the Assembly.

It took her around thirty minutes to reach the home of the council. The cottages were as large as halls, and at the centre was the colossal structure of the Assembly, where people had gathered in large numbers. Birds sat on thatches above, their silhouettes blending into the edges of the hut. As Fayza tried squeezing through the crowd, she could feel the anxiety in the air. Vanyasis prayed, some with eyes closed, hoping for the recruit inside to be the one who would lead the Mahayatra.

But before she could make it to the antechamber, let alone the threshold of the Assembly, she heard crying and wailing inside. The others gathered outside heard this too, and many broke down, some of them falling to the ground. Fayza knew the danger was getting closer.

7

Adwaita

'Adwaita is the initiation ceremony,' Chitra, the *vaidya*, practitioner of medicine, said. Her hands moved deftly as she poured a liquid into a clay goblet and handed it to Aman, who lay warily on a *charpai*, cot. 'A cleansing of sorts.'

The chalice contained a sticky yellow sap. 'What is it?'

'Madhu.' She nodded reassuringly. 'Go on.'

The liquid carried a smell and a taste, like a memory, perhaps of when the Earth was created. And with each gulp that Aman took, his head felt heavier. He tried his best to stay up, but it was as if some magnetic force was pulling him towards sleep.

Before his eyes shut, he was suddenly aware of voices around him and was shocked to see a barrage of people flooding around him. *Why have they come in?* They looked at him and spoke softly to one another. They had perfect teeth and flawless skin, which made their poorly trimmed beards and tangled hair look even starker. The whispers died out when they began making way for an old woman who emerged from the crowd.

Chitra bowed. 'Namahkrita, Aranyani.'

'By the sun! Have you fed him already?'

'I . . . I apologize, Mother. Was I not supposed to?'

The matron, who looked older than time, walked past the vaidya and towered over Aman with a stern expression. Aman fought the weight of his eyelids as he scanned Aranyani. She was the colour of seasoned boughs; her wrinkles made her delicate arms look like crumpled brown paper, with blue veins running over them like roots. Small brown insects crawled over her skin, but she paid them no heed. Despite her dark circles, her eyes, with calm exuding from deep green pupils, eased his nerves. Aman spotted longing on her face. The rest of the people, too, looked at him eagerly. He had figured out by now that something massive was expected from him. *Don't pin your hopes on me!* He'd never been a hero and he wasn't going to become one today. He knew he'd fail them, whatever it was they wanted him to accomplish.

Aranyani closed her eyes and stayed that way for a while. Aman noticed the faint green glow of the tattoo on her forearm. She opened her eyes and touched Aman's forehead, and he plunged into a deep sleep.

When he opened his eyes, he was in a dream sitting cross-legged on a reed mat that ran around the inside edge of an oval hut. The bright lights hurt his eyes. He looked to his right and left, and saw ten people sitting with banana-leaf plates in front of them and a lavish spread in the centre. Every plate had a flickering blue flame swimming in a bowl of ghee. *Looks like a celebration,* Aman thought. *But for what?*

The four women and six men appeared to be in high spirits, gossiping and filling each other in on recent discoveries. To the side, a scribe cleaned his *pankh*, a peacock-feathered quill, and beside him stood two servers. Aman heard the men and women call for drinks and look on approvingly as their chalices were filled with sura paniyam. He saw the women cradle their hands over the fire on their plates, remarking on how auspicious this moment was. Three of the men appeared to be clan chiefs—their words were measured, and they had quivers on their backs. Two sadhus, with weathered bodies and long matted hair, sat silently, absorbed in contemplation. The odd one out in this gathering—apart from Aman—was the female child who sat on his right, wearing a milky-white gown, clearly uncomfortable in this gathering of adults.

From the corner of his eye, something got Aman's attention. He had to turn and look again. Two plates away, right beside the little girl, at the head of the gathering, sat a man with four arms. Two of the arms emerged from his back; they were cupped together and, in their centre, sizzled a deep blue flame.

Aman looked down at his own banana leaf and spotted the same blue fire.

The man with four arms was draped in silk and adorned with many necklaces. On top of his head sat a black-and-gold crown with a crevice—this had another blue spark dancing in mid-air. Vine-like hair fell from under the crown on to his shoulders. The young girl nestled close to him—they seemed to have a filial bond.

Are they gods? Aman had never really given any kind of god a thought, let alone had dreams about them.

Aman heard one of the women boast about how she'd meditated for a couple of centuries at a stretch. Others responded with claims of their own.

The chief deity spoke. 'You'll really like that one! That one called apupa.' He lifted a dish from the spread using one of his arms and placed it beside the girl. 'It's a barley cake sweetened with honey. Sautéed in *kaccha* milk and ghee.'

Aman observed that the food included dates, gooseberries, mangoes, lotus stalks, cucumbers, jujubes, water chestnuts, even wheat stew. But he was most intrigued by the sight of a large bowl with a yellow beverage, sprinkled with seeds of all shapes and sizes. The young girl, too, seemed to find it curious. 'And that one? The yellow soup in the middle?'

'That isn't soup. That's *saktu*, a powder mixed in water. It's an accompaniment to a meal.' He added, 'The mortals misheard and now they call it "sattu".'

Laughter rang out among the gathering. Even the solemn-looking rishi on Aman's left let out a snicker, his protruding belly shaking, but the young girl laughed the loudest. Aman saw her eyes for the first time—a familiar green.

The conversations and banter continued. Gifts were presented to the deity with four arms—both verbal and ornamental. This went on for a while. Aman wondered how long he would be here. His thoughts began drifting away as he seemed to have no place in the gathering. *Where is my mother? Why did she let me be taken away like this?* But he had to snap out of this self-pity when he noticed a palpable shift in the atmosphere. Everyone had fallen silent as the deity stood up. 'Let us satisfy Agni and pray from the Rigveda

before we eat,' he said, holding out his two arms that
contained the fire.

Everyone got up, carrying their bowls, and sang along as
he recited a hymn:

> *This is the hidden name of butter:*
> *'Tongue of the gods', 'navel of immortality'.*
> *We will proclaim its name;*
> *Sustain it in this sacrifice by bowing low . . .*

The deity locked eyes with each member of the hut one by one
as if bestowing his appreciation. But he skipped past Aman as if
he didn't exist. Even though he had no idea of the significance
of this act, Aman was aware of the sense of deep neglect he felt.

> *These waves of Butter flow like gazelles before the hunter;*
> *Streams of Butter caress the burning wood.*
> *Agni, the fire, loves it and is satisfied.*

With the final strains of the song, a strong draft burst into
the hut and extinguished all the flames in the bowls. Silence
swept over the gathering, and tense faces turned towards the
four-armed deity. But his smile remained, and the flame in
his hands burnt strong, licking the air.

Within moments, all the bowls slowly found fire again
and relit themselves. Everyone cheered. The feast commenced
and the accolades resumed. The deity sat down and served
the little girl some apupa. One of the sages turned to him and
said, 'Oh, Lord Indra. We are so grateful to you for fire.'

'The mortals have long deserved it,' Indra said. 'They will be able to keep themselves safe from the dark, and it'll allow them to cook.'

Another rishi spoke. 'The true gift that you have bestowed upon us mountain dwellers is the deceased body of the snake-demon, Vritra, which will provide unparalleled protection through its large lifeless body. The valley will need it.'

'The snake will indeed do you good and keep this land secluded,' the deity said in a gentle voice.

'Oh, King of the Gods, my people thank you for the grass of *kusha*, for now we have something to feed our land. The soil will not erode, and we can consider settling down,' one of the clan chiefs showed his gratitude. 'And of course, the earliest of the sacred texts, the Rigveda. Its importance shines above all.'

The deity, equanimous in the face of such outpourings of gratitude, gave a slight nod.

'Forgive me and my brothers, lord,' said the oldest of the four Kumars, 'for the long and incessant questions over the past century. We transcribed the Rigveda as fast as we could.'

A smile formed on the deity's lips. 'That's enough praise for me. Don't overlook the divine Kalpavriksha and the power that the shade of its bower lends.' He gestured outside, and everyone turned to look. They could see the zigzagging trunk of an enormous tree.

The deity with the four arms closed his eyes and was soon lost elsewhere in his meditation, leaving the others to turn their attention to the feast. They dove into the food with gusto. Some called for seconds of the sura paniyam while others filled their banana leaves with food. Once they were sated and had washed their fingers on their plates, conversations resumed.

'On this full-moon night, let us discuss the valley,' someone said.

Aman heard them mention the boundary of Vanyasa, the panchayat, the seasons and the Kalpavriksha. They also spoke about the valley's residents and the ten Souls who were allowed to enter it every decade.

One of them proudly said, 'Brahmins will be stationed under the Kalanag, and a contingent of Kshatriyas will be forever posted on treetops to keep a lookout. The responsibility for cultivation will fall on the lower castes. No society can run without their dedication to upper-caste men, Mahajan.'

'Valid input. I concur and do not forget to note that down.' The man they called Mahajan turned his head to the scribe who sat to his side, noting everything down with his pankh. 'And if I may add, the Vedas are to be reserved for the Brahmins. No other human is to know Lord Indra and experience moksha.'

There were nods of agreement. One by one, each member of the gathering proposed more rules, and they were all written out on parchments. The deity was silent all this while, firm in his meditative stance.

A yogini stood up. She wore a simple white sari with an embroidered gold border, and white mogras braided neatly in her hair. 'What is a woman but a worshipper of her man? The husband is to be her god. No other god for her, really. This god—even if he is a sinner—is nonetheless to be forever listened to. How else is she to reincarnate as a high-caste man and more importantly—'

The sound of the deity's heavy breath cut her off. His meditation had ended. He roared, 'Perchance!' Lightning flashed outside, and Aman heard thunder. Rain began falling in thick sheets. 'That is *one* way to conduct yourself. *Or* we can let this land be a land for all. Mortals will time and time again be subjected to their destruction, but the valley is and always will be pious. It should provide shelter to all beings equally.'

The deity continued shouting at the sages as the scribe scribbled away. 'Mankind's manipulation will not fester the privilege of a few. Women can and should be entitled to knowledge as any other being. In fact, any new faiths that arise besides ours will be equally accommodated. That being said, your species, mankind, will not rule. If we are to create an ideal world, the land will belong to all creatures that crawl upon it—birds, flies, snakes, trees and everything that draws breath.'

'But, but . . . you surely cannot mean Anuloma and Pratiloma? Inter-caste marriage is *just* not a thing of our—'

'And?' Aman heard Aranyani's voice as soon as he opened his eyes. She sat on the charpai beside him. There were more people in the hut now, all of them staring and waiting for his response. Aman felt as cornered as he had in his classroom a few days ago. Or another lifetime ago.

'. . . and?' He repeated, confused.

'Did he look at you?!' The woman asked.

'Who?'

'Lord Indra? You couldn't have missed him. The man with four arms? Please tell me he noticed you, *talked* to you.'

Aman shook his head. 'He was about to, but he didn't.'

His words produced extreme reactions. As if he had brought news that the sky had fallen. The woman on the charpai broke down and wailed. Many ran out of the hut, which emptied within minutes. Even the birds screeched and flew away.

That left Aranyani and Chitra. The graceful old lady maintained a staid face, but the green in her eyes had paled. She remained silent for what felt like an eternity before finally speaking. 'Despite what has transpired, the boy is to stay and train and be one of the Souls. He has seen enough of our valley and tasted Madhu. He *cannot* be sent back.'

Chitra blurted out impulsively, 'But he can be, right?!' Her head fell as soon as the words left her.

Aranyani's face turned dark. 'Explain yourself, vaidya.'

'Mother . . . Aa- . . . I-I j-just meant he can always be stung by a *lal bicchu* and sent back,' Chitra said.

'Child! Didn't your training teach you that the lal bicchu's effect *only* takes place *after* the sting, not before? Don't you think centuries of trials with the Souls would have been significantly easier if the lal bicchu could simply make the past, and not the future, elusive?'

Chitra looked ashamed at being reprimanded this way. Aranyani paid her no heed and stood up, slowly, and saw herself out.

'My head hurts,' Aman told Chitra. He was wearing the same T-shirt and jeans he'd left Delhi in. His phone was still

in his pocket, nothing but a useless piece of metal without
any charge.

'Here, chew on this,' Chitra said, handing him a neem
twig. 'It's bitter, but it'll fight the sweetness of Madhu and
help you with the dizziness.' She studied him curiously and
leant forward. 'So, what did you see? In the dream?'

The twig came out disfigured from his mouth as Aman
said, 'There were lots of people and we were sitting around so
much food and—'

'Hmm . . . in the hut with the fire in the middle of your
plate, right?'

'Yes, exactly!'

Chitra turned around to retrieve a parchment. She wrote
something down.

'Is mine a common dream?' he asked.

'The commonest of all.' She looked unimpressed. 'And
honestly, this kind of dream has birthed very few Ekas.'

'What is an Eka?'

'The most important of all the Souls. But like I said, in
your particular dream, called "The Founding of Vanyasa",
rarely does the lord look.'

'Are there other kinds of dreams? How many are there?'

'Many,' she said. 'I still remember mine. I got "The
Shadow of the Kalpavriksha"—another common dream.
There's also "The Crusting of Vritra". There are more than
one can count. Some have only occurred once. But it doesn't
matter which one you see—Lord Indra needs to make eye
contact, which is the most important bit. That's how he
decides the Eka.'

Aman was trying to absorb all this new information coming his way. 'What did I do wrong?'

It took a second for Chitra to understand his question. Then she walked up to him and put her hand on his shoulder. 'It isn't your fault. Given how things are, they just need someone to blame, and since you joined last, it's easy to pin it on you.'

'What's different about me?'

'Well, for starters, we usually have one Child of the Valley and nine new recruits, making a total of ten Souls. So I guess everyone was just expecting a lot from you—as the unexpected eleventh.'

Chitra's words were little consolation to Aman. He just wanted to wake up from this never-ending bad dream.

8

Maidaan

Aman had failed his Adwaita, and Sanaka was displeased.

'Useless child!' He arrived moments after Chitra left and smacked Aman. 'Aman Chandra! Are you sure the lord did not look at you? What a waste of Madhu.'

'Does this mean I can go back now?'

'Sure, if you survive the Mahayatra.' Sanaka dragged Aman out of the Assembly. Then, pointing across the valley to a small hut, he said, 'Now, go! There! Find your roof, and sleep it off. Report to the divine tree at the sound of the conch shell in the morning. In the correct attire. And don't be late!'

The Madhu's effects on him hadn't eased, and he had no memory of how he reached his destination. He stumbled into the cottage and spent the night drifting in and out of a fevered, uneasy slumber.

He was up early the next morning, well before the sky had filled with light. The dew had left everything damp. Aman lay on the uneven floor of his hut, his head resting on his folded arms. Staring at the ceiling, he found it hard to put into words his current state of mind. He had been pushed into a new world he had no information about. Tears rolled down his cheeks. He could still see his mother standing at the bus station as the bus pulled away. *How could she?* He alternated between anger and grief as he thought of that moment, but he knew he would abandon all the anger if he could just return home. How was he to do that, though? There was no escaping. Even if he found the way back through Shreyan's tunnel, Nandana's vines would not open to allow him out of the valley.

Despite the self-pity that he afforded himself, somewhere in the depths of his soul a part of him was warming up to the idea of a new identity, a chance to live a different life. One where he wasn't known as a traitor's son.

A cold wind swept the valley and the empty stretches of land that surrounded it. It entered his hut and made him shiver. He heard a loud conch somewhere and was shaken out of his reverie. He had to do as Sanaka had told him.

He found a worn-out *matka*, an earthen pot, tucked into a corner, right below the window sill. Aman used a clay mug to first fill himself a glass of water to drink, then again to wash his face and hands. He took off his T-shirt and jeans—tucked them under his rug, along with his phone—and tied a long cloth he found around his waist, like a dhoti. He took a deep breath and wished for an easy day.

Aman wondered how he would find the divine tree. But as soon as he stepped out of his hut, he knew where to go. Standing tall above him was a maze of branches that seemed to be extending from a large tree that covered, like an umbrella, almost a third of the valley. Far off into the distance, he could see the upper half of the tree's trunk, zigzagging its way to the heavens. Aman stepped back momentarily, his back straight and mouth wide open, to ascertain that it was indeed no more than one tree. He'd never seen anything like it. Despite the circumstances, he felt an unexplainable surge of joy: it was the same tree as the one in the photographs with his father—which were probably still in the cardboard box he had left at the moss-covered bridge. There was no doubt in his mind now that his father had indeed been here, and, perhaps, Vanyasa had been his final mission. But why did Sanaka deny it? Why wasn't he telling him the full story?

As Aman walked towards the trunk of the tree, he was amazed at the vision of nature's bounty that surrounded him. There were squirrels and snakes and yellow palm-sized spiders. Fruits of contrasting colours hung not far from one another. He looked to the left, to the southern branches, and deep within them he spotted many bird nests. As he watched, a flock of sparrows burst forth, sailed rhythmically and landed on the faraway boughs of the western edge of the tree.

Even upon reaching the base of the divine tree in Maidaan, where the colossal tree met the earth, it was a bit of a walk to the other side. Realizing he was probably late, he jogged along the never-ending breadth of the trunk and only stopped where two thin branches shot down from the leaves and intertwined a few metres before the ground to create a raised podium. A crowd of people with clueless faces sat facing the podium and the tree trunk. Sanaka was nowhere in sight.

'Praise the lord! Finally, our saviour, the Eka, has arrived,' Aarti pronounced upon seeing him. Payal laughed.

All right then, Aman noted. *This is going to be no different from school.* He didn't know them yet, but in the front row, close to the podium, sat Idhika and the bespectacled Dhara, both looking ahead intently, unaware of each other's presence. Fayza sat farthest away, at the edge of the glade, increasingly sceptical of her place in Vanyasa. A few paces away from her were Jagrav and Savitri, chattering away. Ujal sulked by himself, twitching, eyeing his sister, Prithvi, who sat with Aarti and Payal, like sycophants, by the podium, a little away from the Child of the Valley.

Aman thought it best to sit away from Aarti and settled beside Fayza.

'Don't worry,' Fayza whispered in Aman's ear. 'She's playing mind games. Aarti's as clueless as you or me.' Macchli, a brown-furred dog, bounced over to Aman, wagging her tail, and sniffed him. Fayza flinched, but resumed, whispering, 'The only one who isn't clueless is the Child of the Valley— there's always one native among the Souls of Samsara. She might truly be the Eka.'

'Who? Then why put me through Adwaita?' he asked.

'Because there is no way to know for sure,' she said, eyeing Idhika. 'The Child of the Valley was born here. She's immune to Madhu, so there can't be any Adwaita for her. Only time will tell if she'll lead our Mahayatra.'

'Huh?' Aman recalled the Mahayatra as something Sanaka had mentioned.

'Okay. You're clearly more clueless than I am. The Mahayatra is why we're here. It's the final test to determine if we are fit to join this place as permanent residents, obviously notwithstanding whether or not we want to live here at all. Some actually do. I believe the tribal twins as well as your biggest supporter, Aarti, want to excel here; she's set to step up as the Eka.'

Aman and Fayza sat close together, their knees only separated by the breadth of a needle, touching every now and then. He found himself stealing glances at Fayza. It had been so long since he had had a genuine conversation with someone his age. He constantly grounded himself, not forgetting he was destined to be an outsider.

Fayza asked, 'So . . . what's your name, Eleven?'

'Aman.'

'Tell me, did you have someone special in the plains?'

That was out of the blue, and although this was the first time they'd met, something about her reminded him of the past. Aman mustered up the courage to meet Fayza's eyes. He saw the small mole on her temple half-hidden behind the frame of her glasses, the thin scar at the end of her right eyebrow, her eyes which looked like pools of honey. He tried to think of where else he'd seen the same mole and scar. He felt a gush of comfort and found himself wanting to tell Fayza about his whole life, and his trip to the valley—from the moment his mother had left him on the bus to when he passed out on the bridge. But he stayed silent. That just wasn't him, the speaking kind, the trusting kind. So, he chose

not to mention any of it, not even the cardboard box he now
so desperately wanted.

'Namahkrita,' said the man who limped into the glade.
He was easy on the eyes, with neatly parted hair, a chiselled
jawline and broad shoulders. Setting his walking stick against
the base of the trunk, he prepared to climb the podium.
Aarti instantly shot up, ready to aid him, but the man
shook his head. 'I've been doing this for a long time.' Using
only the strength of his biceps, he pulled himself up. Over
the decades, Acharya Ashwini had excelled at welcoming
newcomers to Atmayog. He would be their first teacher,
leading the first six months of their year-long preparation
for the Mahayatra. 'Servants of Samsara, your body is not
yours. You are not flesh, bones or blood. You are, in fact,
very light, weighing no more than a pinch of cotton. All you
are is a soul. Each of you. Your body is only the chariot to
the rider that is your soul. And that's how the real you, the
spirit, can inhabit temporary bodies through reincarnation.
Seven bodies to be exact.'

What is he on about? Aman thought.

Acharya Ashwini looked up at the sky. 'You see, in
reality, there is no heaven. There is instead a large ocean of
souls there called Brahman. It is where existence originated.
And when your soul came to the earth, it joined a cycle called
Samsara, being reborn again and again seven times. After its
liberation, also called nirvana or moksha, it will break free
and become one with the eternal ocean, Brahman. I know
some of you don't want to be here. You'd rather be in the
plains. But you're all in your final birth, the seventh. And if

you're to reach Brahman, you must renounce the material world and cleanse your soul.'

Hysterical laughter came from somewhere. 'Hah! So all of us have had six lives before this?' Aman turned to see a boy roughly his age lying on the grass. He wore an oversized pair of black trackpants and a white hoodie, and Aman saw that he hadn't even taken off his chains, bracelets or diamond ear studs, which were clearly fake. 'What?!' he barked at Aman, styling his blonde hair simultaneously. His name was Yuvan, as Aman later found out.

'Acharya,' Fayza said, 'you mentioned Brahman. I thought he was one of the deities. Are you implying that the gods are real?'

'Shut it!' Aarti shouted at Fayza. 'What do you know of our gods?'

The acharya ignored Aarti. 'Yes, of course, they exist. But not in quite the same way as the plain dwellers see.'

'Okay.' Yuvan raised his arms theatrically towards the sky. 'Tell me, then. Who's the strongest of them?'

'Tricky question,' the acharya said. 'Many new recruits over the years have asked me this. But I ask you what you mean when you say "strongest". Is it he who wins a battle? Or he who has better powers or can lift heavier objects? Bear in mind that the Vedas, Puranas, Ramayana and Mahabharata collectively mention many deities. Some of you may say that Krishna or Vishnu is the strongest. Or Shiva or Ram. And the truth is that all of those answers are correct. The presence of gods varies from region to region. But here, under the divine Kalpavriksha, where the Vedas were written, the old gods, the omniscient and original ones, rule the lands as far as the eye can see. And their king, the old and forgotten leader of all gods. Almost just the way he wants it. Indra. Lord of the sky and thunder. He is above all. An entity that has always existed, taking on different forms.'

'Really, old man?' Yuvan scoffed. 'Have you heard of science?'

'Don't differentiate between the two. The gurus that worshipped the gods were also scientists. That's even by your modern certifications. Some of the foremost Western scientists that ever lived believed in god. The Upanishads have been credited by Schrödinger and Heisenberg. Lord Krishna in the Bhagavad Gita described the contemporary study of modern polarity, the negative balance of the subatomic realm, even the superstring theory. In fact, our study of planets and the sky has helped astronomers throughout the centuries.'

Aman's sceptical mind took these words with a pinch of salt, though he wasn't as vocal about it as Yuvan. He'd heard about godmen as silver-tongued as Ashwini who were full of hot air.

The acharya took a deep breath. 'Our lesson for today. The ancient art of Atmayog is a privilege, a gift from the gods that allows us to understand his other children. It's the ability to master your external distractions. And although its boon offers much, it also entails sacrifices. The smallest of these sacrifices is luxury. For it, one has to befriend discipline. With that in mind, your first session of Gurukul will see you sitting cross-legged.' He waited until each of his students, even Yuvan, was sitting in the correct posture, with their backs straight, and then added, 'But in order to succeed, this physical stance you currently occupy, with your eyes closed, cannot deter. Not slightly, no peeking or twitching . . . not until I ask you to.'

The instructions were clear: shut your mouth, shut your eyes and shut down all movement. Acharya Ashwini stood up and smiled at the unseeing faces of his nascent yogis. All eleven of them had their eyes closed.

For the next twenty minutes, Aman sat still, trying to stifle his yawns. It was getting difficult, but he was determined not to be the first to give in. *At what point does this cease to be meditation and start becoming a nap?*

Aman gingerly opened one eye. As he looked around, he saw that the other ten still had their eyes shut. The acharya was nowhere to be seen. Finally, Aman succumbed to the strain in his back and let go of his posture. Fayza had opened her eyes as well. Before too long, Aarti and her entourage, too, noticed the absence of the teacher and relaxed.

'That's Jagrav—don't look—who's approaching us right now,' Fayza quickly whispered to Aman. 'His father is some stinking-rich industrialist from Mumbai. And the person he was just sitting with is Savitri, a national-level boxer from Haryana.'

'Have you two seen my smartwatch anywhere?' Jagrav said. He had a big, shiny beard which, along with the wide frames of his designer glasses, hid most of his face. He didn't bother waiting around once they gave no response, heading towards Ujal. But before he could reach him, Savitri's strong arms had pulled him back to where he was sitting.

'What use is it without battery? Here!' Savitri drew Jagrav into a friendly yet firm headlock until his eyes were an inch away from her analogue wristwatch. Aman felt scared for Jagrav. Savitri had rugged arms that looked like they could strangle a boar. Her eyebrows were bushy and her skin pale. A ponytail fastened by fluorescent and red rubber bands ran to her hips. 'Can you stop searching now, Jagrav?!'

'*Puh*-lease! I'd like to,' he said. 'But you'll have to find me a chair, a charging port and—this is the truly important one—some mosquito repellent. Cause I'm going to be honest with you, Savitri; I was looking forward to going to New York this summer, not this crappy village.'

Idhika, who sat in the first row, still had her eyes closed and her face revealed no sign of exhaustion. She was at peace, for she alone knew that the acharya wouldn't return until Suryast. Her curly hair was tied into a large bun and its weight seemed to aid her posture. Somewhere by her side, Aarti shut her eyes again and pretended to compete with her.

Eager to learn fast, Idhika longed to impress her gurus. She craved to taste the world outside the valley, to see her father and find out if he missed her mother. Atmayog could take her places, and she knew that the more she practised, the closer she'd get.

An hour passed, but Idhika refused to break her concentration and kept her eyes shut. Macchli returned to Aman and Fayza after a stroll. She looked like a deadly mountain wolf but had the friendliness of a Labrador.

'I don't understand why she keeps following me. Back home, I stayed away from street dogs and they stayed away from me,' Fayza said, making a face. With no Acharya Ashwini in sight, they both were lying on their backs on the grass, staring at the sky through the canopy of the divine tree. They could see a white cumulus breaking up like cotton balls to give way to milky streaks. The sun had finally pulled up above and a cool breeze raked the fields. Fayza continued telling Aman about her past life and her grandfather's friend who had prepared her for Vanyasa.

After a few minutes, she fell silent, sitting up to look nervously at Idhika. Aman stayed where he was. In the east, the mountain Kalanag cut the view and in the south stood Rohini. As he scanned the landscape, he only saw tall mountains on all sides. The valley was in the shape of a wide bowl. *What if it rained for weeks and the Tal overflowed? Would it fill?*

All of a sudden, a giant object caught everyone's attention. Aarti stopped pretending to meditate and looked up. Aman locked his eyes on the creature as it soared out from above Sarp-poonch, the peak adjacent to Aranyala, and flew towards them. It seemed to be drifting over the divine tree towards the hills on the other side. Only when it dove under the tree and hovered in circles over Maidaan, right above their heads, did Aman realize that the creature was a majestically large bird. 'Fayza, look,' he said.

'No, you look.' Fayza's stomach lurched as she pointed towards Idhika. The Child of the Valley was radiating a powerful energy which was almost palpable. Her eyes were still shut, and the serpent tattoo between the elbow and wrist on her arm glowed brightly, even in the daylight. The bird was briefly forgotten by all the Souls.

'Are those scars glowing—'

'It's a tattoo, you dumbass,' Dhara said.

'. . . -hawt- . . .' Yuvan croaked.

'Deh. Remind me to tell you about it later,' Fayza whispered to Aman.

Aarti was fuming. She stood up, stormed towards Idhika and knelt in front of her. 'A fine yogini indeed.' She nodded sarcastically. 'STOP SHOWING OFF!'

Idhika was unmoved.

'How are you doing this?!' Aarti grabbed Idhika by her shoulders and shook her with all her might—her sole intention to snap Idhika out of her meditative trance.

Idhika fell on her side and fainted.

Shocked, Payal put aside the buttermilk-filled kamandalu. 'What have you done?' Dhara exclaimed. Aarti instantly stepped back. Everyone froze, unable to understand what to do, but something stirred inside Aman. He knew picking a fight with Aarti wasn't going to help him make friends, but maybe because he knew what it was like to be bullied, he jumped up and ran to Idhika. His knees slid and halted right before Idhika's body, which was gasping for air. Her body was shaking. Aman held her shoulders with both his arms, but he couldn't make the convulsions stop.

The large bird had been high up in the air when it suddenly lost life and started to fall. It looked unconscious, as if it had been shot. It gathered speed as it plummeted to the ground. As it got closer, Aman saw that its beige wings had a span wider than his body, and it was coming straight for him.

THUD! Aman and Aarti only just managed to step aside in time as the creature hit the ground, very close to Idhika. Clouds of dust circled Idhika's body, her twisted limbs mirroring the awkwardly wrapped legs of the bird and its sunken beak. Then the bird's eyes started bleeding and streaks of red rolled down its fur.

Feeling queasy at the sight of blood, Jagrav scurried off into the bushes. Ujal and Prithvi loosened the grips on their bows, now assured that the bird would not attack. Aman tended to Idhika, whose hair was white with dust. Everyone gathered around her.

'Finally!' Savitri noticed first. 'Acharya Ashwini is on his way back.'

Aman spotted Fayza running towards them from the eastern end of Maidaan. He hadn't known when she left to fetch their teacher. Acharya Ashwini limped alongside her and Chitra. Macchli, too, was with them, orbiting two identical, seven-foot-tall men, whom Aman later got to know as the Alok brothers, Ghanisht and Ekram.

'Step back!' Acharya Ashwini said. 'Give her breathing space.'

'Will she be fine?' Fayza asked.

'There's hope,' the acharya said. 'She's not lost yet. You found me in time.' A cotton string ran over his shoulder and back down to his waist, and on it was suspended a small matka. Acharya Ashwini lifted the clay plate from over it and used it to pour a yellowish liquid between Idhika's lips.

Idhika spluttered, coughing most of it out, but before long, her eyes blinked and her chest heaved with life. She slowly lifted herself but turned her head downwards. 'I'm sorry, guru-ji. I failed. And instead, this is what has come of it. I thought I could Atmay- . . . I have before . . . I don't know how I lost my concentration.' Tears rolled down her cheeks, and she struggled to meet the eyes of the bird's cold body.

'Retire to your huts—Gurukul is terminated for the day.'

Maidaan cleared of all the students, Aarti faster than the others. Chitra accompanied Idhika to the vaidya's cottage. Soon, only Aman, Fayza, the acharya, the Alok brothers and the lifeless bird were left.

Aman and Fayza had offered to help, but the Alok brothers bore most of its weight, standing on opposite ends with the bird on their powerful shoulders. The brothers' movements were stiff and slow, and they had an identical, sharp, stained tooth hanging around their necks. Together, the lot of them walked to Mukti, the cremation ground, which sat on the farthest end of Pandayam Tal, where the plateau was slightly sunken and the beach grey with ash.

Pandit Kanwa was the lone caretaker of Mukti and a devout disciple of Kala, the deity of cremation. 'Oh no, oh no!' He skipped towards them, holding up his dhoti. 'Yama, you *foolish man*!' Then he cleared his throat and corrected himself, 'Forgive me, lord. I get carried away.'

Antyesti, the last rite of passage, was a duty that fell on him. Air, fire, earth, space and water are the five elements that make the physical body, and it was Pandit Kanwa who would send these elements back to their origins.

In no time, all the prerequisites had been completed—sesame seeds in the vulture's beak, the pyre sprinkled with ghee, and the three lines in the sand around the heap of wood signifying Yama, Kala and the dead. 'We'll wait for Suryast to reach its conclusion,' the pandit said.

When the final light of the sun fell behind the peak, they waited patiently, ready in their positions—Pandit Kanwa with an unlit torch, Aman and Fayza beside Acharya Ashwini, the Alok brothers on the other side of the pyre, and the winged beast bedecked with logs from dead trees.

The valley filled with a beating sensation that grew louder and heavier by the minute, and soon all the lamps flickered on. The torch in Pandit Kanwa's hand, too, blazed blue, and he started singing under his breath, 'Burn him not up, not quite consume him . . .' He lowered the torch, lit the pyre from the end and started walking around it. '*Agni*, let not his body or skin be scattered . . . subject to the will of gods . . . with all thy members.'

Before long, Aman had to step back because of the heat. The fire licked the air and sparks shot up. He hardly believed himself when a bright ball, no bigger than a grape, escaped the pyre and slowly drifted up as all heads lifted. Perhaps what the acharya had told them earlier was true. *I wonder, when my time comes, if my soul will be as bright,* he thought.

Birds gathered and many flocks sailed in the sky. Finally, a silhouette of another, slightly smaller, Himalayan griffon vulture screeched and circled above them against the last red of the heavens.

Having made its way up, the atman was eventually lost in the twinkling of the stars.

Antyesti means 'last sacrifice', and today it shaped itself in the untimely demise of a vulture. Idhika may have suffered the same fate had Acharya Ashwini not intervened.

This was the sacrifice that entailed the magic of Atmayog.

PART II

9

Bazaar

Every day that passed without an Eka seemed to diminish Vanyasa. The leaves had grown a touch yellower, the animals' gaits were slower, the days somewhat colder. Aman carried out his duties mechanically as one week moved into the next following the Himalayan vulture's death. He was learning more about the ways of the valley, and perhaps even warming up to the idea of god, but he wouldn't admit it to himself just yet.

Over the past month or so, Aman had successfully avoided Sanaka, who was often seen walking around Vanyasa, flanked on either side by the towering Alok brothers. Gurukul took place in Maidaan as usual, with a focus on perfecting the recruits' asanas and yoga poses. After a few lessons, each Soul of Samsara had to choose a weapon that they would use in their training. Aman picked up a sword. Jagrav had been difficult in this regard. 'Don't we get cool weapons like the never-ending quiver of Arjuna or maybe a one-of-its-kind spear?' But these inquiries were met with a disapproving look from the acharya, and he had to settle for an ordinary *gada*, a mace.

Their meals consisted of simply cooked fruits, vegetables
and grains. In Aahaar, the dining hall, Aman often got his
favourite: a dish consisting of cottage cheese and red chillies
with fried bay leaves and honeyweed rice. He would purposely
go at odd hours to avoid being seen sitting by himself.
Occasionally, his solitude was broken by Fayza, who would
insist on sitting with him and making conversation, filling
him in on the social dynamics of the other Souls. Aman rarely
responded. He nodded and hummed and ate, but Fayza cared
less as she was filled with thoughts that wanted out. Over
time, he found himself eating with Fayza more and more.
But apart from Fayza, he got along little with the other Souls,
and his brush with Aarti, it seemed, had made any hopes of
making friends in Vanyasa a fanciful dream.

Fayza told him that Yuvan had rejected Aarti's offer
to join her group, which Prithvi was a part of now. Yuvan
kept to himself and spent most Gurukul classes lying lazily
in the grass, but Aman, who also sat in the back of the class
along with Jagrav, Savitri and Dhara, could sense a carefully
concealed restlessness in Yuvan. So he wasn't surprised to learn
that Yuvan had been caught sharpening a knife, and when the
weapon was eventually confiscated—like all other possessions
the Souls of Samsara had brought from the plains—he ran
away. He had managed to cross the wall over the Seven Hills
but could get no further, and had collapsed due to hunger.
He was found by one of the Vanyasis two days later.

Two days before Yuvan's attempted escape, Aman had
paid Fayza a visit and was surprised at the changes to her
living space. Her hut had a small stool, a carpet beside it, a

charpai and two matkas. 'That one was ten, the charpai was eighteen and this carpet used to belong to the diya-maker, so she sold it for only three danas.' Fayza was beaming. 'I've been busy earning enough danas to make sure my hut is better.' The table before her had heaps of palm leaves.

'Have you been studying?' he asked.

'Eleven, I have to, don't I? To prove a point to everyone. The days will progress, and the journey at the end of the year will arrive before we know it . . . And honestly, more importantly, between how Aarti treated me in Gurukul and how far ahead the Child of the Valley is, it is clear that we need to study more if we are to learn Atmayog—we could study together!'

Aman was aware of how weird he felt talking to someone his age, let alone a girl. It wasn't like he had had any kind of social life back home, and now he actually had a friend he was dropping in on. Not that things could progress any further between him and Fayza, for celibacy was one of Vanyasa's rules for the Souls; romantic engagements were strictly prohibited—except for any formed by the Eka.

Every day after the Gurukul session ended, Aman would take the central Chakkar to the bazaar—the marketplace was the only area in Vanyasa which felt similar to the plains, and it was where he felt least trapped. The bazaar was no more than a collection of thirty huts with display stalls, broken up by trees full of cawing crows. Dana was the currency, and although he had only just learnt the names and differences between each of the stone coins, Aman remembered the pouch full of them in his father's cardboard box. He was more convinced every day that his father had indeed been in Vanyasa for his final mission.

Aman had received six danas for raking a section of Maidaan before Gurukul each day over the last month and had found another dana in the grass behind his hut. He was sceptical of the plan he had in mind and reconsidered it as he strolled through the bazaar.

'Three matkas for twenty danas!' a potter shouted from his hut.

'Fresh, extremely fresh from the recent harvest! A bag for a dana.' He heard the tobacco trader and then saw Aarti talking to him. She had taken to rolling her own cigarettes these days.

As if the sight of Aarti wasn't bad enough, in the middle of the bazaar was a large white sculpture of an elephant with five trunks, serving as a sudden, not entirely pleasant reminder of Aman's eventful entry into the valley.

As the day's trading and bargaining continued, dust flew, shoulders brushed past each other and people argued over prices and objects. Aman had to be inconspicuous. This time of day was perfect for him because he could easily lose himself in the crowd if his plan didn't work out.

Most of the salesmen looked too approachable. He walked further into the bazaar and came across a shop on his left, a little off the main road, where mats of different sizes hung from the roof. Upon entering, he saw a man sitting with sewing implements, tending to a half-finished grass-and-reed rug.

'Thinking early, young man? Smart. Very smart.' The trader stood up in a welcoming gesture. 'If the cold floor bothers you now, wait until the winter months of Magha and Phalguna.' He tugged slightly at a mat, and it came tumbling down into his hands. 'Buy this! Protect yourself.'

'I'm actually looking for something else,' Aman said, and stopped to register the man's reaction.

'Oh . . . who told you?' the seller said with a sly smile. He leant in to whisper, 'I *do* also have a special rug. Made from the fibres of the Kalpavriksha himself. Most don't believe me, but six years ago a dead branch *fell* on me when I was walking in Maidaan. I swear to Indra. No one else was there—so I picked it up. It had the hottest strands I've ever seen, each as thick as a stem. And the mat it made, I tell you, it is the warmest. I used it for long myself. But only now am I willing to part with it—wait, do you have enough danas?'

'Not rugs!' Aman said. He whispered, 'I want information, and I have seven danas here.' He waved the coins in the man's face, but the mat trader didn't seem impressed. 'And in case these aren't enough, I also have an extraordinary device from the plains,' Aman lied.

'Information?' the vendor said. 'You do realize that I too came here from the plains, right? Was a long time ago, though. I figure things have changed down there. What information do you seek?'

'I need to know the way past the wall.'

The man studied Aman with a disdainful look. He had been baiting the boy—he knew very well that all items from the plains were confiscated. 'What's your name?!' He inched closer to Aman and made a sudden move to grab him. Aman ducked and ran out of the hut as fast as he

could. The man shouted, 'I'M GOING TO SANAKA!
THIS IS MUTINY!'

Good going. Against his better instincts, Aman had asked
Yuvan about the way out of the valley but, after his spectacular
failure, Yuvan was less than inclined to help anyone else.
The mat trader had been a desperate attempt. And although
Aman's plan had not been successful, he was still determined
to find a way back to the moss-covered bridge where the
bus had left him. That's where the cardboard box was—his
father's palm leaves probably wet now, if not stolen.

Running, as he neared the end of the bazaar, Aman
thought he saw Idhika. She hadn't attended Gurukul since
the incident with the vulture. She stood facing a stall, with
a basket strapped to her back. Aman approached her and
tapped her shoulder.

The Child of the Valley turned around and, when she saw
that it was Aman, smiled. 'Aman, today, I speak your name in
respect and gratitude. Indra be praised that you intervened on
the first day of Gurukul or I might have lost my soul.'

'I too speak your name in . . . you're welcome?' Aman
said, taken aback at her warmth and effusiveness. Her manner
of speaking set her apart—but she wasn't a plain dweller, so
that was understandable. 'But don't thank me too soon—
Aarti is still a menace in Gurukul.'

Idhika looked at him and laughed. 'The concern that is
Aarti is no longer mine because . . .' She didn't say anything
further and searched Aman's eyes, wondering if she could tell
him more.

'What are you doing in the bazaar?' he asked.

She swung her shoulders around and the basket rattled with wood. 'Trees. Once they die, I pick them up and sell them here. After my father's exile from the Seven Hills, my food and water come from these earnings.'

'Ever been outside these hills?' Aman asked.

'Not really. Only until Pataan. But I long to see the world outside of this valley,' Idhika said. 'Take the plains, for instance. Tell me a little of them, would you, please?'

Aman did. He told her of skyscrapers and pens and space expeditions and computers. 'Among all these "nations" and "cities", my home is in Delhi, far from here.'

Her eyes were bright. 'Sounds glorious. Vanyasa pales in comparison to the outside world.'

Aman nervously looked over his shoulder, hoping the trader he had run from wouldn't show up. 'But . . . you don't have pollution and diseases. By the way, I've been meaning to ask: How . . . your arm was glowing . . . why did the vulture listen to you?'

'No, no. The vulture and I were one. These are the fruits of years of practice. You'll learn how to do it yourself soon enough. Your arm too will develop the Deh, which shines only when you're in Atmayog.'

Idhika wasn't the only one on whom secrets weighed heavy. Despite this being the first time he was speaking to her properly, Aman felt he could confide in Idhika. 'Honestly, I'm not sure if Atmayog is for me.'

'What do you mean? You want to go back?'

'For the moment, my only concern is some belongings of my father that I left outside these Seven Hills. They contain the last of his memories. I was hoping you could tell me the way.'

'Only trouble will come of that. Unspeakable creatures circle the valley, Aman, feeding off the leftovers of the Kalpavriksha's vibrations.'

'I have to try. It's all I have left of him.' He lowered his voice. 'Believe it or not, my father was here in the valley a long time ago. I don't know how but he had managed to enter. Ever heard of "The Preservers"?'

'You put no thought before speaking.' She looked cross. 'That is in the realm of the impossible.'

'No, Idhika,' Aman said. 'I can prove it. I have pictures of my father standing beside the Kalpavriksha.'

'Others have mistaken different trees for the Kalpavriksha. Look, Aman. Does this bazaar seem at all of the outside world? There is, and simply cannot be, any movement in and out of here. Don't you figure I myself would have ventured a trip to the plains?'

Aman could have mentioned the string purse full of danas—also in the box—but he could see Idhika would not believe him.

'I dearly miss my father too, Aman, and there can be many paths to your goal.' She paused dramatically. 'I might be able to help you. But it'll be a while before I'm ready.'

'I knew you'd come around,' Aman said.

'Nothing can be done yet.' She wanted to let him down gently. 'Can I entrust you with the uncommunicated? Not one Vanyasi other than me and Aranyani knows this secret for now; not even Sanaka.'

'What is it? I promise to keep it to myself.' Would this information help him with his aim? He waited eagerly for her to speak.

'The reason Aarti is no longer a concern for me in Gurukul,' she said, 'is because Aranyani is teaching me in private. News of the incident with the vulture travelled through the threshold of her hut, and that is where I have spent the majority of the last month. I'm getting better at Atmayog. I won't be resuming Gurukul with the other Souls for a while.'

'Why is that?'

'For the transparent grounds before us. I'm the Blue Rose. Aranyani herself informed me that I'm the Eka, just as my mother was. And rightly so. From what Father had taught me, it is not a simple task. Since I feel responsible for the valley, and know most about our ways, it is only sensible that I lead the Mahayatra.'

Aman realized he would no longer be blamed for failing Adwaita. 'You have to tell everyone! The whole valley is waiting—'

'No! Swear to Indra you will not mention this to anyone,' she said. 'In return, when I can Atmayog to different locations—even outside of the Seven Hills—I will find your father's box—'

'Idhika, run!' From the corner of his eye, Aman had spotted the mat trader in the distance, making his way towards them through the shuffle of villagers.

She was startled but realized the import of his words. They squeezed past people, through the crowds, and by the time the trader got to where they had been standing, Aman and Idhika were well on their way to the village.

10

Suryast

'Thank Indra that you reminded me,' Idhika said, running faster than Aman, leading the way to her hut. 'It's almost sunset, and we don't want to be caught outside during Suryast.'

Aman was relieved he wouldn't have to explain their hasty exit from the bazaar. When they reached her hut, Idhika led him in and gestured to the cold floor. It dug into his ankles as he sat beside Idhika in the centre of her hut. He exhaled and straightened his back. *Time to meditate.*

Idhika had already shut her eyes, but not before saying, 'If you really want to contribute to Suryast, then try and Atmayog to the Kalpavriksha. Only when all Vanyasis collectively do so does Indra's gift of light find the valley.'

As the minutes passed, the faint chatter of the outside world subsided. The residents of Vanyasa had retired to their huts, and only the sound of crickets chirping remained. Aman struggled to fence his thoughts—he was constantly worried about the mat trader finding them. He sat up straighter, trying to emulate Idhika's posture, but the calm in the hut was disturbed all of a sudden by the furious patter of running feet.

'Help . . . they took her . . . forced Prithvi!' Ujal had darted in. He stopped and caught his breath and shifted the bow slung over his upper body.

'Who?' Idhika broke out of her meditation and stood up.

'Aarti and Payal!' Ujal spat out the words and then pointed his finger at Idhika. '*You!* She's hell-bent on besting *you* in Atmayog. That is why Aarti led them to Pataan,' he snapped. 'I've been following her—all of them—for days . . . and they've only just slipped out. You have to take me.' His eyes begged for help.

Idhika paused before answering. 'To that land beyond the Seven Hills, no sane soul goes. And you don't need to worry about those that have already: the girls will be punished when they—'

'*If* they return. I know of Pataan, Idhika. Don't try and tell me she's safe.' Ujal paused. 'I really don't understand. What did Prithvi and I ever do to deserve this fate? You kidnap us and bring us here . . . like we belong to you. All the more reason for me to protect my own. I *will* go after her, no matter what.'

'Aren't we restricted to the huts at this time?' Aman asked.

'No! In fact, we should be on the move right now,' Ujal said desperately, inching back out towards the threshold. 'It's already halfway into Suryast.'

'He's right . . .' Idhika said. 'It seems Aarti waited for the ideal time. The sun has just dipped, and the lamps are yet to come to life. This is as dark as it gets. Perfect time to sneak out.'

The three of them abandoned their duties and rushed out into the moonless night. There were oil lamps everywhere but none were ignited at that time. In that darkness, it felt like the tiniest of wicks would be akin to a crater full of light. 'Faster!' Idhika led the way by the side of the huts, ensuring even their silhouettes would not be visible.

Aman was having trouble seeing the path in front of him. As they jogged in single file, he forced himself into the middle. The trio muscled through the fields of tall grass until they found the central Chakkar and trekked to the base of Kalanag in no more than fifteen minutes, the mountain towering before them. Aman couldn't help thinking about the goal he had left his hut with that morning. *After we find Prithvi, I could try to locate the moss-covered bridge.*

They were about to start climbing the mountain when an abrupt bustling in a hedge close by halted them in their tracks. The three of them exchanged looks, unsure if they should proceed. Someone leapt out into the path ahead of them and stood in the shadow of the steps that zigzagged to the top of Kalanag. Idhika and Ujal dispersed instantly, but Aman was slow to react; he crouched down in the middle of the road with his hands over his head, bracing himself for the worst. Idhika had to rush out and pull him into the set of brambles where she hid. Near them, Ujal stealthily readied his teer-kaman and pointed it towards the shadow.

Aman thought his rapidly beating heart would give away their hiding post. *No one is supposed to be outside their huts at this hour,* he thought. A thorn dug into his bare back, but he bit down on the pain.

The figure finally stepped out of the shadow. 'Eleven?' It was Fayza. She walked closer to them with a glance that was both enterprising and veiled. 'You wouldn't sneak out without me?'

'We're only going to the Temple of Indra,' Idhika said, stepping out of the bushes. Ujal put away his bow.

'No, we're not,' Aman corrected Idhika, who instantly made a face at him.

'I know you guys are going to Pataan; I saw that narcissist and her gang leave with his sister,' Fayza said, tilting her head towards Ujal. 'And I have business there too. Guru Amrav of the temple on top had mentioned Pataan earlier. But he's been missing for a few days, and it is vital that I find him.'

Being left with no option but to let her accompany them, Idhika filled Fayza in on the plan, and the group of four began climbing Kalanag. Not too far from the Temple of Indra, just when the path dipped down towards the jungle outside, they encountered a barrier. A twelve-foot wall snaked around the Seven Hills of Vanyasa.

'Now?' Aman asked.

'Aarti found a way,' Ujal remarked, eyeing Idhika, hoping she would rise to the bait. Idhika knew Vansaya like no other Soul and was aware that everyone else knew this too. She had a reputation to uphold. With practised diligence, she found a loose brick in the otherwise smooth mud wall and pulled it out. Idhika stepped back to gather momentum, then charged forward—placing her right foot into the chink—and lifted her body up. Her fingers barely caught the top of the wall, but she managed to pull herself up.

The others followed, and with Idhika's help made it over the wall to the other side, where a less dense, less green landscape greeted them. The air was discernibly thicker, and the increased temperature felt like a stark change after Vanyasa. Aman felt his mood change instantly; his feet felt heavier and his mind lazy, unfocused, less intent on helping Ujal.

As they walked down the steep outer slopes of Kalanag, Aman spotted a cave a few feet below with bright orange streaks of light shooting out of it. The murmurs intensified as he jogged down the slippery, mossy steps as if hypnotized.

'Slow down, Aman!' Idhika followed him, skipping steps. Ujal and Fayza lagged behind. 'It's illegal in Vanyasa!'

'What's illegal?' Aman slowed down to ask.

Idhika had caught up. '*Sangram!* It pulls you. It's an addiction. That's why they only practice it in Pataan.'

11

Sangram

The four of them stood at the mouth of the cave for a second to brace themselves, and then entered. They were now in a tunnel, which twisted and turned in the belly of the mountain. Oil lamps—with their fires burning red, not blue—were nailed to both sides of the inner walls, revealing the sloppy curves and illuminating the insects and bat roosts that lined the ceiling. As he moved deeper into Kalanag, Aman was mesmerized by the sights—and the sounds. Even at this distance, through the rocky walls, they could hear cheering.

Eventually, the tunnel opened out into a big hall. It was topped by a large, dome-like ceiling in the heart of the mountain—its insides gnarled and cavernously echoic. The ceiling was panelled in a rough grey stone more than a couple of hundred feet above them. The majestic feeling of the place made Aman quail. He had never imagined anything like it and wasn't too sure he wanted to be down here.

'The mouth of Lord Kalanag,' Idhika said using a deep voice. 'A great cesspool into which the criminals of Vanyasa are drained.' The hall was swarming with yogis of all shapes and sizes who had given up grooming themselves ages ago by the looks of their frizzy hair. Multiple chillums puffed out wisps of smoke that rose and collected near the roof of the dome.

Up ahead, all the yogis huddled around the centre of the dome, trying to catch a glimpse of the action. Stakes were raised and bets were made. A tall, thin man carrying cups of sura paniyam snaked his way towards them through the cheering crowd like a warm knife in butter. Ujal ignored the beverage, for the only time perhaps, and dove into the mob. He had to find his sister.

'Keep a lookout for the caretaker of the Temple of Indra, Guru Amrav,' Fayza told Aman moments before he was pulled ahead by Idhika to catch the spectacle. Curious to see what had occupied everyone's attention, Aman moved blindly past the bare-chested, sweat-soaked bodies. Despite the throng of people closing in on him, he felt a cold touch of dread. *What if Sanaka finds out I crossed the Seven Hills?*

In the front, Aman and Idhika had just enough standing room. A strange sight greeted them. 'The games of Sangram. We're in time for a new round!' Idhika said. There was a muddy, circular field with a rope running around its boundary, and on either end were two yogis raised on ornate pedestals. A full-sized rooster casually strolled the arena, and facing it was a king cobra, its flattened hood floating sideways. Blackness felt complete in the cobra's shiny scales as it braced itself to put on a stunning spectacle.

The loud voice of a commentator roared: 'By my troth! Next up, if the Gods will it, is none other than the devout servitor of Lord Indra, the Light Seeker himself—GURU AMRAV!' The crowd jumped, screaming at the top of their lungs and wriggling their shoulders, which Aman realized was the Vanyasis' way of celebrating. Fayza eyed the old man who had pretended to be righteous but ruled here as a favourite in this illegal sport.

The light reflected off Guru Amrav's shiny bald head as he sat on the pedestal to Aman's left, right behind the cobra. Supported by a cylindrical red pillow, he lazed on his side, supported by his elbow. His chin sunk into his chest so that his beard dropped down to his belly. Silver dishes laden with fruit were stationed within his arm's reach.

The commentator continued, 'Who is this sorrowful soul who is to be his opponent and face his eminent WRATH?!' The man turned his head to face a girl, asking her to speak up and reveal her name, but the booing was too loud for it to be audible. 'Nope! I think not, young girl. A plague be upon you! Shoo away! Let other worthy competitors take your place!'

Aman craned his neck to catch a glimpse of the opponent. *Aarti!* She sat there, steadfast, shaking her head. She was not going to step down.

'What is an idiot really, if not this girl right here?' Idhika asked Aman. 'She carries with her an aura of irrational impulses.'

Aarti's pedestal looked ordinary: made of wood, with no expensive cloth nor cushion giving it personality. But she was unfazed, sitting defiant, determined not to be defeated by Amrav.

Something made Aman look behind him. His eyes met those of an eagle perched on the shoulders of a yogi who seemed most disinterested in what was happening. He neither laughed nor cheered. In fact, his eyes were closed and his eyebrows furrowed; he seemed to be in Atmayog, scanning the area through the eyes of his bird. Aman found himself admiring the strong white beak of the beast and its massive brown talons. No prey would have a chance.

The commentator continued, 'It looks like we *truly* are in for a massacre tonight. Amrav and the king *versus* Aarti and the . . . chicken?' He ended the sentence with a whimper and then shot Aarti an angry look. 'Nev'r! Quit wasting our time, girl. How does a recruit even have a hundred danas to wager?'

Aarti tried to answer, but the crowd drowned out her voice by clicking their tongues. That seemed to be how the Vanyasis booed. Idhika, too, joined the chorus of disapproval. Fayza was fighting an internal battle, not sure whether to support Guru Amrav or feel betrayed by him.

'Shanti. Shanti. Shanti,' the commentator shouted, instructing the crowd to quiet down.

Aarti had paid no heed to the hooting. She pulled out her lipstick from her makeshift handbag and applied a streak of red. She pressed her lips and closed her eyes in order to initiate the Sangram. Amrav did the same. A deep, reverential silence befell the crowd as Amrav and Aarti faced each other and reached out to their companions. Bettors started placing wagers on how long they thought Aarti's rooster would last in the pen.

Ujal moved past the yogis to reach Aman and Idhika. His forehead had a crease that reflected his anxiety. 'I still can't find her. I see Payal, but Prithvi isn't with her.' He left them to continue looking.

The chicken and the cobra had started roaming the field. The cobra scoped out its opponent, familiarizing itself with the territory. Suddenly, it straightened and, as if not itself, started to circle the chicken while jerking its hood back and forth.

The commentator's voice rose tauntingly. 'Vanyasa condemns the thrill that we just can't resist, which pulls us down here. But, my brethren yogis and yoginis . . . It. Does. Not. Get. Better. Than. *This*—Guru Amrav's mocking!' He said as the cobra continued to imitate the chicken and bob its head.

Aman leant closer to Idhika. 'Can he hear all these yogis cheering for him?'

'Who?' Idhika asked.

'That man . . .'

'Guru Amrav?'

'Yes,' Aman said.

Idhika pointed at the pen, indicating the chicken. 'Atmayog forces the human to forgo their own senses for that of their companion. So if Aarti manages to connect with her rooster, she will hear, see, feel the world through it.'

'I thought so too. But that's why I ask,' Aman started, 'because Guru Amrav's companion is a snake.'

'Oh, you're quite perceptive,' Idhika said. 'Cobras can't hear sounds. To think of it, this is probably why he's an exceptional Sangram dueller. Noises can never wreck his concentration. Astounding if true . . . because Guru Amrav has forever claimed that it is Lord Indra's blessings that enable his distinctive skills.'

The crowd was in a state of frenzied excitement. As Aarti's animal continued to idle around the pen, bumbling in one direction and then the other, pecking the ground like an ordinary chicken, it was clear to all that the rooster had yet to be located by the yogini. The cobra continued its dancing, circling, taunting, and then proceeded to slither forward and charge at the rooster. It hissed, fangs first, and buried them deep in the rooster's flesh.

The bird let out a cry. It had little fight left in it, and just managed to flap its wings and lift itself to safety before being bitten again. Aman felt scared for the bird and, by extension, for Aarti. But he couldn't look away.

The cobra soon cornered the bird. It coiled around the squealing and struggling chicken, biting it in quick bursts. The commentator joked, 'The Light Seeker is no longer fooling around. His cobra's keen to kill—or will it be elimination by displacement? By forcing the chicken out of the boundary line? Either way, this is soon to turn into a foul fight for the *fowl*.'

The astonishingly poor wordplay made one of the yogis behind Amrav laugh so hard that he toppled the dishes beside the dueller into the arena, and in a momentary lapse of concentration the snake loosened its grip and the chicken found some room. It managed to wring itself free and fly to the other side of the field, right by the boundary where it bled and limped slowly, roaming the edges of the fighting arena.

This time, Guru Amrav decided not to rush after the bird. Instead, as the cobra, he slithered to the chicken's blind side, and silently started to twist his way towards his target.

Of all animals these magicians can use to play the games of Sangram, why is there a flightless bird in the arena? Aman thought. The cobra had got closer, seconds away from victory. The chicken oddly refused to react. The Light Seeker appeared keen on headbutting the unintelligible bird in its underbelly and in a single swift swoop tossing it out over the boundary line—winning the Sangram by elimination due to displacement.

In one rapid burst, the snake moved with single-minded intent, but moments before the impact, the chicken flapped its wings in a powerful sweep to lift itself in the air. Aarti had finally completed Atmayog—her forearm had developed a red Deh, visible to all. The cobra, unable to control itself, tried to stop all movement completely, but couldn't help blundering out of the boundary line.

The cheering had given way to stunned silence.

Whispers broke out. The commentator's voice rose over them all, 'THIS SANGRAM IS OVER!'

Idhika scoffed and, on the other side, Payal screamed in joy. 'WE HAVE A MIRACLE! THE UNDERDOG HAS W—'

'Cheated! The underdog has cheated!' Guru Amrav interrupted. The sage abandoned his pedestal and stomped unsteadily towards Aarti.

The commentator intercepted Guru Amrav. 'With all due respect, Light Seeker, it was a perfectly fair round of Sangram. As long as there is no intervention of a third soul you have no grounds for objection. Or are we still copying those spineless pansies of the valley?' He looked up at the ceiling of the dome, towards Vanyasa.

In the middle of all this, Aman spotted the eagle—the one sitting on the yogi's shoulder—take off, swoop dangerously low over everyone's head and disappear into the tunnel.

Guru Amrav was still glued to his spot, lost for words.

'Ahh—HELP—ahh! UJAALL!' Everyone heard the girl's voice as it tunnelled in from outside and thundered into the hall. Her scream was punctuated by the sounds of a screeching bird.

All stood frozen. They tried to comprehend the repeated rise of the girl's frantic cry in the distance. By the sound of it, she was out of reach, probably at the mouth of the cave, out on the ridges of Kalanag.

Ujal ran into the tunnel with little hope as Prithvi's voice grew distant, carried away by the eagle over the Dronagiri woods outside the valley.

12

Kamandalu

Aman, Idhika and Fayza immediately followed Ujal as he rushed off in pursuit of Prithvi. They sprinted as fast as they could towards the mouth of the cave, from where they had entered, and when they emerged, a faint silhouette of the eagle could be seen in the distance, holding on to a struggling figure.

Within minutes—though it felt like hours had passed—Guru Amrav, Aarti, Payal and a few of the yogis joined them out in the open.

'This is on . . .' Ujal could only whisper at first. He paused and then stepped up to Aarti. 'This is ON YOU!' He readied to launch an attack, but Payal brushed him aside.

Ujal wasn't the only one furious at Aarti. Idhika's list of grievances against Aarti had grown. She still wasn't over the incident with the Himalayan vulture, and Aarti's recent antics made her undeserving of the place she called home. She had to be taught a lesson.

Idhika moved forward. In one swift move, she brushed past Payal and dealt Aarti a hard slap.

Aarti froze. She dared not react. Not in front of everyone. Instead, she put on a bewildered look—much like the chicken whose body she had occupied earlier—and mumbled uneasily, 'She chose to follow us. We didn't force her.'

'Tru-truly,' Payal agreed.

Ujal turned to Guru Amrav. 'Help me, Light Seeker.'

'Son, your sister has disappeared beyond the river and is now in the clutches of those that roam the valley's surroundings. Only those within Vanyasa can help you now. But know that secrets don't cross between the valley and Pataan. So be mindful of that; don't let anyone learn that you crossed Kalanag and waltzed down here, no matter the cost.' His tone was full of foreboding.

'To hell with that. I'm telling all of Vanyasa! I don't care who wakes up—'

'Shhhh,' Guru Amrav snapped.

'In fact, I'm going to blow the conch and wake up the ENTIRE village!' Ujal's eyes were brimming with tears, and the bow that slung over his shoulders swung in frustration. 'They *have* to send out people to find Prithvi.'

'All right,' Guru Amrav said in a pacifying tone. 'Sanaka will have my hide . . . but . . . I'll send out a search party myself.'

He considered the yogis who had stepped out with him. When they realized what was on his mind, many of them tried their best to blend into the background and become inconspicuous. They squabbled over who deserved to sit out this expedition, but eventually, fearing the Light Seeker's rage, six yogis left brandishing weapons of all sorts.

Within moments of the search party's departure, Payal and Aarti prepared to sneak away, sheepish looks on their faces. They were as unwilling as the yogis to feel a smidgen of responsibility and edged towards the steps that ran up to Kalanag and into Vanyasa. Aman, Fayza, Idhika and Ujal had no energy to reprimand them, and let them go. The four of them kept their eyes on the sky for any sign of the eagle. As time wore on, Aman, Fayza and Idhika lay worried on the edge of the cave, making sure none of them fell asleep. Ujal sat beside them, his face digging into his palms. How would he ever face his parents if his sister did not return safely?

Their uneasiness grew as the night progressed. Hours later, the search party returned, but there was no Prithvi accompanying them. Without revealing details, they delivered the unfortunate news and rushed back into the valley.

From that moment on, Ujal did not sit. He stood at the edge of the cliff, looking in the direction of the Dronagiri woods, where the eagle had disappeared, where Prithvi was most likely to be. Fayza went to console him. Every now and then, Aman noticed, she would push her glasses up her nose. He watched the strong wind play with her hair as she encouraged Ujal to keep his spirits up.

Not far off, replaying the events in her head, Idhika realized how Aarti had carried out her plan to perfection. Not only had she learnt Atmayog in less than a month, but she had also bested one of the greatest Sangram duellers. Most importantly, she had kept her wits when Idhika slapped her and not retaliated. In contrast to her composure, Idhika seemed too impulsive, not a trait the Eka should possess.

As dawn approached, Ujal's eyes stayed hooked to the sky, which was now a palette of orange and red. 'Worry not. We'll find her,' Idhika said as she put her hand on his shoulder. 'A plan, a risky one, forms in my head. But for it, we need to approach one of the gurus . . . preferably Acharya Ashwini.'

'Okay, we tell him. And then what?' Aman said. 'What's the plan, Idhika? Surely we can't go after the eagle.' His words betrayed his fear of the Dronagiri woods, but the possibility of retrieving his father's box was too tempting. 'Umm . . . Where exactly is this . . .? As in, is it in the same—'

'There we go again,' Idhika snapped. 'No, Aman. It *isn't* in the same direction, so don't go searching for it.' She remembered Aman pestering her about the box.

Ujal didn't care for the tangent the conversation had taken. He brought them back on track. 'Telling the acharya is a gamble. If Sanaka finds out, we will be expelled.'

Idhika spoke with a weight of finality. 'I have thought about it. Acharya Ashwini cares for us, and if we tell him this news in confidence, he might understand.'

It wasn't like they had a plan B. So it was decided. As they walked hurriedly through the early-morning mist, Ujal's head was still ringing with Prithvi's screams. He braced himself. *You're an archer . . . a warrior, Ujal!*

They hiked back over the high ridge and climbed over the wall into Vanyasa. The familiarity of home had no effect on their gloom.

That morning, oddly shaped clouds filled the sky, and the valley's residents remarked on their strangeness. But the four Souls had no time for such trivialities. Despite having spent the entire night near Pataan, they did not think about sleep as adrenaline coursed through their veins. They thought of Prithvi alone.

To reach Acharya Ashwini's boat-hut, they jogged the winding trail of the central Chakkar that cut through the farmlands, past the bazaar and across Maidaan. The turmoil in their minds dissipated for a second as they crossed the Kalpavriksha. Continuing on the Chakkar, they turned left and crossed Mukti to head towards the southern edge of the lake.

When they reached Pandayam Tal and began wading through the bogs, Fayza spotted an untied rowing boat moored to the shore. The sturdy, unpolished sail looked big enough for two, maybe three people. Aman, Idhika, Fayza and Ujal got on, squeezing into the thwart of the boat.

They took turns to row in pairs, and when they neared Acharya Ashwini's abode, Aman failed to slow their ascent, which led to the boat crashing loudly into the wooden ladder that dipped down from the boat-hut's threshold. Idhika climbed the steps up to the deck to talk to him. The other three stayed back.

All the while, the acharya's muffled voice grew louder and then came to a halt. He and Idhika stepped out together. The man limped to the edge of the deck, leant over his dwelling and looked down at them. 'You all violated Suryast! And then even dared to cross the Seven Hills and run to Pataan?! I just can't believe it. Never in the entire last century can I recall a more ill-disciplined batch of recruits.'

They waited impatiently for his tirade to end. 'It is because of your foolishness that I was grilled by Sanaka. He questioned whether I was fit to be the Pratham Sadhu. Apparently, I'm slipping too often to be the first teacher to the Souls. Thank Indra that Aarti and Payal had the sense to come and inform Sanaka of your mutiny—'

'What? Aarti told Sanaka?' Aman interrupted his teacher. 'Acharya, we don't have much time. Please listen—'

'You!' Acharya Ashwini turned red. He pointed at Aman. 'Oh, you're in hot water. I've never seen Sanaka so angry. I swear on the holy fire . . . Oh! How can I forget his orders? He specifically asked me to fetch him the "discernibly stupid boy".' With that, he started climbing down, as fast as his irregular step allowed.

Aman's heartbeat quickened and he felt flushed. But Ujal's crying stopped Acharya Ashwini's charge. 'Prithvi!' he sobbed. 'The eagle took her. She screamed and begged but it flew away over the mountains. The Light Seeker says it was the fiends around the valley who took her.'

'What?' Acharya Ashwini stopped midway down the ladder. 'Aarti never mentioned any of this to Sanaka.'

'And Guru Amrav even sent out people to look for her, but to no effect.' Ujal looked at his teacher with imploring eyes. The four of them chaotically recounted the events— first all trying to speak simultaneously, and then slowing down but still cutting each other off to fill in all the details.

Acharya Ashwini heard them out. Then he rushed back up to his hut to procure several items. Two kamandalus swayed from his bare shoulders on a string—neer, spring water, in one, and Madhu in the other. He got on his boat, and they rowed the two boats back to the shore. Macchli ran up to them, her tail wagging.

'Where do we start?' Ujal questioned. 'She could be anywhere.'

'We start at the edge of Pataan, her last known location. From there, we'll follow the eagle,' Acharya Ashwini explained.

There would be no Gurukul that day. With the acharya's permission, they went through a hidden gate in the wall above the Seven Hills, which was a ten-minute walk away from the section above Kalanag that they had used. Macchli tagged along, refusing to leave, and together they went into the Dronagiri woods. Thus began their journey, threaded with zigzagging, shrub-laden paths and mountain goats. The teacher guided them with fierce energy, walking briskly despite his impediment. He barely broke a sweat. His movement was silent and effortless, and his breaths measured. At times the path dipped and sometimes it climbed. Macchli started to lead the way, sniffing out walkable terrains.

'She's truly delusional, trying to take on the Child of the Valley,' Fayza said to Idhika, catching up with her.

Acharya Ashwini had overheard. He asked, 'Aarti?'

'Yes,' Fayza said. 'She's the one who led Prithvi to Pataan, which is why we followed her.'

The teacher absorbed this information and nodded. An hour had passed. 'We should pick up our pace,' the acharya said. 'Let us pause here, take one gulp of the spring water. It will refresh you.'

The cold water hit Aman's dry mouth, and he found it near impossible to stop after only one sip. Following this brief pause, without food or sleep, they were back on course, crackling dry leaves under fast feet. Thoughts of Prithvi were uppermost in Ujal's mind, and he was the quietest of the lot. He constantly murmured the names of his tribal gods and marvelled at how just the previous day the biggest thing on his mind was his desire to be the Eka. He would have been in charge, and Prithvi never would have dared to cross the Seven Hills. There was so much good, he believed, that could come about if only his sister listened to him. And, of course, as the Eka, Ujal could have as much sura paniyam as his heart desired.

By noon, it was clear that they were lost, having turned the same shoulder of the mountain three times. Hope was down to its final embers. Ujal voiced his concern, 'It is almost midday. We have to find another way to locate her.'

'But how?' Fayza asked.

'One more look in the direction the eagle disappeared is all we need,' Acharya Ashwini said.

'We could climb up this mountain and check,' Aman suggested.

'No, that'll take too long.' Acharya Ashwini stepped off the delineated path into the soft bed of grass. 'There is a faster way.'

13

Varunasmati

THUD! Prithvi woke up to the sound of a burning log giving way. She lay on patted cold mud, but it felt like a bed of nails. Her shoulders screamed in pain when she tried to move, and she saw streaks of dried blood running down her chest—injuries from the grasp of the eagle. One by one, as each of her senses awakened, Prithvi probed her memory for answers. Her head churned with images of Pataan, being carried by the eagle and flying over hills. Her bow and quiver had fallen below on her journey.

As she lay sideways, tears rolled down her cheeks. She had no idea where she was and if anyone would even come searching for her. She wished for Bhavesh to be her rescuer. There was no one she wanted to see more. She wanted to look at his face, tell him that she hadn't left him. Coming to Vanyasa hadn't been her choice; she had been abducted. She recalled the last time they had talked—over a month ago.

'Stop deflecting, Bhavesh!' She ran her fingers over his hand, his phantom right thumb. They lay in each other's arms, behind

*the brambles, across a river from their land in Madhya Pradesh.
'We are old enough now to fend for ourselves.'*

'Are we?' he asked.

*'You know what the elders say. The jungle is thinning, and
the city folk are now as close as the southern pond. There's no
future here . . . But in the city, we could do anything, any work
that would feed us. Think about it, Bhavesh; we wouldn't have
to sneak arou—'*

*'What's this?!' Bhavesh stared at the bruises on her arm.
'Who did this . . . Was it . . .'*

Prithvi nodded.

*'WHY? Punishment for breaking which rule?' Bhavesh said.
'No one knows about us, so it can't possibly be* that—'

*'It is! Your old friend still has his suspicions, Bhavesh. Or
have you forgotten when Ujal saw us together in the fields last
year? This is what I mean, love. It's getting increasingly difficult
for us here. You know what,' Prithvi was now joking, 'I will do
it. In the morning tomorrow, I will go to the southern pond and
wait for an hour at sunrise . . . and if you don't decide to tag
along, maybe I'll find myself a boy among the city folk.'*

*Bhavesh laughed. 'I guess then I have no option but to
join you.'*

They both knew that they could only dream.

Within a few hours of that rendezvous, when Ujal
and Prithvi went out hunting, they had been drugged and
kidnapped by the Alok brothers, thrown in the back of a
small truck, and delivered to Sanaka in the valley. But Prithvi
knew Bhavesh would have assumed that she had gone to the
city and followed her there.

She stood up, trying to ignore the pain in her shoulders. The hut she was in, with its considerably ornate interiors, was unlike any she had seen in Vanyasa. Ascetics of the valley only considered their homes as roofs over their heads, perhaps not more than a necessity—but this cottage was someone's home. Wax overflowed from candles that occupied every ledge and sill. A turquoise curtain served as a door and opposite it was a fireplace supporting a teapot.

She was alone. Prithvi knew she had to act fast. She decided against the main exit and went to the window. When she drew the pink-dyed curtain aside, light illuminated the interiors. The view was obscured by tall peaks coated green with vegetation, the result of recent rains.

She studied the scene and realized that she would need to walk through the dense trees, hike up the ridge adjacent to the hill on the right and make her way to the top of the mountain before she could hope to locate where Vanyasa lay. And who knew how many days it would take after that.

Just as she finished scanning a meadow that was right next to the hut, her eyes met those of an eight-foot-tall creature standing not too far away. He held a bucket laden with wooden blocks in one hand and an axe in the other. Behind him, perched on a tree, was the brown eagle that had abducted her. With a dastardly smile and a glimmer in his eyes, the man continued to look at her.

A chill ran down Prithvi's spine. She stepped away from the window and scurried around the cottage, looking for any sort of weapon. There was nothing she could use. She swatted aside the curtain at the doorway and darted out of the hut.

But she hadn't gone more than a few paces when a long, muscular arm, almost as wide as her entire body, grabbed her by the neck and lifted her up. The man stormed inside and threw her on the floor.

'Kirtimukha!' he bellowed, beating his chest. Towering over Prithvi, his lips bore a grim slash of contempt. The behemoth was naked apart from underwear fashioned out of linen. Large copper bangles curved around his swollen biceps and a larger golden one enclosed his neck. His eyes were large, and two small horns jutted out through the long hair that covered his entire face.

Prithvi had heard that name before. *Kirtimukha. Oh!* Only recently in Gurukul had they been taught of the fiends that plagued the valley's outskirts. Their name literally meant 'glorious face'.

The monster upset utensils and wooden stools as he ponderously walked to the fireplace and picked up the teapot, which looked like a toy in his hand. He then shuffled around in his wooden trunk, throwing mugs about, trying to find the right one. A tiny cup appeared. The lid cranked open and the teapot hissed. The kirtimukha poured some steaming tea into the cup and extended his arm towards Prithvi. When Prithvi shook her head, he pointed a plump finger at her.

Prithvi closed both her hands around the cup and saw that it contained a thick yellow liquid. *This isn't tea; this is Madhu.*

For a minute, there was absolute quiet—save for the sizzling of the fire and the kirtimukha's heavy breathing. When he glowered at her and then at the cup, almost as if he was going to bore a hole in it with his eyes, Prithvi reluctantly positioned it close to her lips but did not drink. It was only after the fiend stood up in anger that she let the liquid dribble on to her tongue.

She was instantly reminded of her first day in Vanyasa over a month ago, the day she had had her Adwaita. Fatigue overtook her and she fell asleep on the floor.

They could never have hoped to find Prithvi without the acharya.

'Exactly how are we to trace the eagle without actually climbing to the top of this mountain?' Aman asked.

Acharya Ashwini looked up at the sky in response, following the flight of sparrows, parakeets and monals as they flew through the wind. He stepped off the track and stomped his feet against a patch of tussock. Once it was flattened, he sat cross-legged on the grass and said, 'Keep me guarded.'

Acharya Ashwini weighed his body back and lowered his eyelids, and within a few seconds, they were all certain that their acharya was only physically with them, while his spirit soared somewhere high up in the winds.

At that moment, in Atmayog, the acharya was most vulnerable; it was vital to protect his rigid physical body, which was divorced from his conscious mind. Although they had Madhu in the kamandalu for any such emergencies, Aman, Idhika, Fayza and Ujal sat in a circle around their guru. Macchli rolled around in the grass nearby.

Aman wondered how far he was from the bridge and his much-coveted box. He considered if he could go retrieve it himself, but the thought of foraying out into the woods made him shudder.

The longer the Atmayog went on, the optimism grew, for the Souls felt certain their acharya must be on to something. After more time had passed, a flock of sparrows, among them one with Acharya Ashwini's soul, settled on the bough of the tree to their right. Not long after that, the teacher gasped for air and his chest resumed heaving in a normal rhythm. His students stared at him. He only nodded and stood up with intent, pointing eastward. 'That's where she is. Beyond the river.'

'What? As in, the Varunasmati?' Idhika asked, notes of panic in her tone.

Acharya Ashwini said, 'Don't you see? It is a way to draw us out—we have no option but to cross it.'

Aman, Ujal and Fayza didn't understand any of this, but they had seen the blood drain from Idhika's face. The Child of the Valley explained to them the belief in Vanyasa that the unknown land beyond the cursed river not only had rogues and monsters lining the outer banks, but was also a place that depleted the energy of Vanyasis.

But at least they had a destination now. The band resumed its journey, walking faster. Their shadows grew progressively longer, and they soon lost track of time.

'What did Prithvi do to deserve this?!' Ujal said in despair.

No one dared meet his eyes. 'Don't worry, Ujal,' the acharya said.

'Why did it take her? No, I mean it. I'm *asking* . . . Acharya? What exactly does the valley want from us? Why were we brought here?'

'Young man, impatience will get you nowhere.' He was going to say no more but Ujal's face conveyed that he had lost hope, and the acharya couldn't bear to see him like that. He didn't wish to further aggravate a vexed soul. 'I will tell you now if it alleviates your burden. You see, the Kalpavriksha in the middle of the valley is no ordinary tree. Only under its shade can Atmayog be learnt, which is why others outside the valley are keen on bathing in its blessings and will do anything for it. The tree is also the reason Vanyasa recruits ten Souls every decade. The nine most sincere devotees in the valley find like-minded individuals like you by meditating under the Kalpavriksha. The tenth, of course, is the Child of the Valley.'

'And what about the odd eleventh?' Fayza eyed Aman, who was really tired of this line of conversation. He already knew his Tapasvi parent—none other than his actual father. No matter how much anyone denied it, he had surely been in the valley.

'And this Mahayatra business?' Ujal asked. 'You say it is to get Madhu. But what is it exactly? Why can't the villagers get it themselves?'

'Madhu, or the Himalayan bee's honey, is nearly impossible to locate. It is found at the ridges of the high cliffs, and only the Eka can sniff out the location of the beehives. So, through the Gift of Instinct, eventually, when the time comes, you all must retrieve it for the sake of the Kalpavriksha's health. Don't take this task lightly, for many of the older Mahayatras,' he paused to look at Idhika, 'have seen horrible conclusions to their journeys. Of course, I could also tell you legendary tales of the successful ones . . . But the most important thing is that if you succeed in the Mahayatra, you'll be rewarded with a lifetime in Vanyasa, and permission to bring in one plain dweller.'

All this information was not easy to digest. They resumed walking in silence. Light gave way to darkness, and the tweeting of birds to the chirp of crickets. The landscape had thrown on an ominous cloak—and the nascent moon could do little to light their path. Every now and then, their ears caught a sudden shuffling on the forest floor, and once their eyes got used to the darkness, they could see squirrels and other creatures scampering down the hill.

Finally, after they had walked riverwards for a couple of hours, the Varunasmati flowed in front of them like a large blue snake, violently bisecting the path ahead. They stood before its might, clueless, since wading the stream wasn't an option. Any grumbling of their stomachs was muffled in the gurgling of the waters.

'What's that?' Aman asked, pointing. Not too far across the river, against the black clouds and between the trees, rose a thin grey jet of smoke.

'That,' Acharya Ashwini said with certainty, 'is our destination. The sparrow's flight allowed me to view it. Had it not been for the smoke, I would have never caught on to Prithvi's trail.'

They began searching for a way past the body of water in front of them. A little over an hour of walking upstream was what it took to find the narrows in the Varunasmati. There, a large tree trunk had decayed and fallen over the river's breadth at an awkward angle. It acted as a bridge over the heavy water that ran downhill, but it looked too frail to support their weight.

Before anyone could say a word, Aman uncharacteristically stepped up, his head held high and overconfidence in his stance. Frogs leapt out of his way from thickets of tall grass. He propelled himself on to the log.

Aman instantly regretted it: the tree dipped deeper into the river than he had anticipated—and the log was set loose. He had only just managed to step back to the banks before the trunk escaped down the river's path. *Genius move!* Aman cursed inwardly. The log spun uncontrollably—its edges chipping off—until it jammed itself somewhere downstream between a collection of rocks. And this time, it looked perfectly stable.

'Popular in school, were we?' Fayza asked, leaning in.

And back they went downhill.

'This time, I cross first,' the teacher said. He gently walked on the tree's trunk, cautious not to dislodge the calm edges.

Aman waited for Fayza and Macchli to cross before stepping on the trunk himself. Then Ujal and finally Idhika joined them on the other side.

They all knew that their stronger selves were behind them now, but none spoke of it. Aman was aware of the energy draining from him. A sharp pain shot up his left leg. It had also been a while since they had eaten, and their entry into this strange land brought the weakness caused by this into sharp focus. All they could do was drink neer from the kamandalu and walk towards the unknown.

The forest thinned out as they made their way to the spire of smoke. They trudged up an elevated glade that overlooked the banks of the Varunasmati. Beyond that, a belt of wide tree stumps ran on both sides, and in the far distance was the hut with smoke coming out of its top, through a chimney of sorts.

Drawing closer, they saw the yellow light that emanated from the structure and fell on stacks of felled logs surrounding it. More wood stock and tree stumps dotted the area.

Acharya Ashwini had only just started to speak when Macchli ran up ahead and started barking. An eagle flew out of the meadow and flapped its wings furiously. 'RUUUFF . . . WOOF, WOOF!'

Everything after that happened at lightning speed. A girl's scream was heard from the hut: 'AAAAHHHHHHH!'

Ujal recognized the voice. Before anyone could react, he ran towards the hut, drawing his bow and jumping over tree stumps. 'PRITHVVVIIII!'

Acharya Ashwini and the others ran after him.

14

Kirtimukha

The kirtimukha was furious. He stood silently, a storm brewing inside him as he observed the sleeping girl. He swung his arm with force, striking her face. 'Who's the Eka?' he said.

Prithvi sat up in shock. Her world spun in a frenzy, and her cheek burned with a searing pain. *He can speak?!*

He went on to slap her repeatedly, asking questions about her Adwaita and her first days in Vanyasa. When he realized she had no useful answers to give, he grabbed her by the hair and swung her over his shoulders. He was just about to carry her out of the hut when a loud barking was heard.

'RUUUFF . . . WOOF, WOOF!'

The kirtimukha let go of Prithvi, whose head came crashing down; she screamed in pain.

As the creature rushed towards the back of the cottage for his axe, Ujal charged towards the hut. 'PRITHVVVIIII!'

Prithvi's insides flooded with hope, for she knew Ujal's voice. But it wasn't Ujal who was there first. Macchli overtook him and entered, and only in the moments that followed were they joined by the rest. The dog had intended to dart

131

in and dig her teeth into the enemy, but one sight of the kirtimukha and she no longer growled—only whimpered—and kept away. With all of them in his cottage, the fiend stole a quick glance out of his doorway. Then, once certain that no more reinforcements were to join his enemies, he grinned and snarled at them.

Over the past month or so, the sight of the valley and the magic of Atmayog had pulled the rug from under Aman's feet, making him question everything he believed in. But the kirtimukha magnified his trepidation a thousandfold. He was terrified as the monster continued to study them with his charcoal-black eyes, the axe firm in his hands, which could have swatted them back to Vanyasa. His blood curdled and his brain shut down. He closed his eyes and prayed that at any moment he would wake up in New Delhi with the fan creaking above him and his mother on the mattress beside him.

'Kirtimukha!' the creature shouted, his head arching back as he drummed his chest with his left fist.

Ujal was almost at his sister's side, but just then, the kirtimukha intercepted him. He pounced on Ujal, seized him by his ankle, turned him over and lifted him. Upside down, the boy punched the air with his hands. His bow and quiver fell on the cottage floor.

All hell had broken loose: Idhika positioned herself between the kirtimukha and Ujal, and could only manage to kick the axe away before the kirtimukha pushed her aside. Macchli ran to rescue Ujal, and her mouth latched on to the kirtimukha's leg, but one swing was all it took for her to go crashing into the ceiling.

Fayza leapt on him, trying to choke him from behind, her body dangling from the ring that circled his throat. The kirtimukha still held Ujal and could only sway his body with force to rid himself of Fayza's grasp.

'ARGHHH!' the fiend grunted, his roar thundering in the hut. He let go of Ujal and turned all his attention to Fayza. Too far from his displaced axe, the monster held her by her neck, looking into her eyes and squeezing her as if she were a ragdoll.

Fayza's lips started to turn blue, and her body went limp. Her glasses fell off her face. Aman thought of the first day of Gurukul when he sat with her after everyone had laughed at him for failing Adwaita, when later together they helped Idhika after Aarti had disturbed her Atmayog. And he remembered how worried Ujal had been for Prithvi, who looked starved and beaten and, with those thoughts, rage filled him.

Aman's instincts took over. He gulped down his fear, grabbed the teapot that sat over the fireplace and brought its blazing red bottom with both his hands down hard on to the kirtimukha's arm. Fayza fell, clutching her throat and coughing. She moved as fast as she could out of his reach. Aman repeatedly struck the beast with the teapot—but all it did was enrage the monster, whose breathing started to grow heavy.

Aman backed off. But the kirtimukha had his eyes on him now. With blanched knuckles, he plodded forward, a few seconds away from crushing Aman's skull.

'So this is how it ends,' Aman murmured to himself. 'At least I won't have to face Sanaka if I'm dead.' He knew there was no point sprinting out of the hut because he could never outrun the beast. But he couldn't give up so easily. He had to try something.

As the kirtimukha wheeled forward, Aman held his ground. He lay unmoving until the monster was only a couple of inches away and then suddenly jumped and sidestepped him. The kirtimukha barrelled past.

Aman took in the whiff of reeking corpses as the monster ran past him—but the kirtimukha's flailing arm caught Aman and slashed a cut below his lip with his huge nails. It felt like a thousand knives had stung him.

The kirtimukha turned to face Aman. His shoulders heaved, ready for a second charge, but this time his arms were wide open, not to be dodged.

A line of blood dribbled down Aman's chin as he frantically searched for Acharya Ashwini, hoping for any words of advice, if not support. Their teacher stood silently to the side, clutching the nock of an arrow. He had drawn Ujal's bow in his hands. The arrowhead was aimed upwards, while the shaft fell in the middle of his face, and mumbled words escaped his lips as he prayed.

The kirtimukha's glorious face was now contorted with rage, and he drew closer and closer to Aman, moments away from blowing him out of his hut.

TWISSSHHH!

The arrow whirred, rippling the wind in a brittle clang, and caught the kirtimukha deep in his shoulder blade. The extraordinary strength of the dart penetrated the monster's flesh and then lifted him into the air, continuing to whizz to the end of its path. The arrow zoomed across and dug into the mud wall right beside the fireplace. The kirtimukha hung in the air, his body pinned to the wall and roaring in pain. Helpless, he tried and failed to snap the thin wooden arrow.

'We're wasting precious time. Let's get out while we still have a chance,' Acharya Ashwini shouted, adjusting the two kamandalus that hung by his shoulder. Fayza collected her glasses from the floor and followed him.

When Ujal and Idhika tried to help Prithvi up and out of the hut, she told them, 'Pick that up first.' She gestured to a parchment on the sill above the fireplace. 'Saw it earlier; it's of importance.'

Idhika quickly hurried over to pick up the rectangular piece of animal hide and tucked it away safely under her arm. The three of them exited the hut—Macchli behind them.

Aman lingered. A plan had formed in his mind. And moments before he executed it, he heard an alien voice penetrate his head: *'Don't do it, child.'*

Aman instantly backed away, startled, but slipped, toppling over a few lighted candles. His plan seemed to come to life by itself: the cotton tapestry that hung on the doorway suddenly transformed into a flurry of sparks, filling the hut with white smoke and fire.

Blood slowly rushed to Aman's ashen face. He ran out of the hut as the crackling fire and snapping twigs did little to cover the screams of the burning monster. The kirtimukha groaned and howled, and although the air was inherently disquieting, the Souls and their teacher felt relieved at that moment. Standing at the edge of the clearing, silently watching the fire, Prithvi's face shone golden in the reflection of the burning hut. Ujal walked over and hugged his sister. She did not resist.

Idhika had been trying to read the parchment she had found. She then handed over what she understood to be a letter to Acharya Ashwini. He took the piece of animal hide from her and held it up so it caught the light from the burning hut. The recruits tried but couldn't decipher the words.

He read it out loud, 'All our blessings will be upon you and rewarded for a dashak will be your gain. Find and ye shall overcome those who outcast you. Find the flower that is hued bright and blue; find the Eka and . . .' He stopped, suddenly aware of the Souls with him. He read the rest silently and shuddered as he reached the signature at the bottom. For the first time, they saw fear in the teacher's eyes.

They could sense the horror in Acharya Ashwini's mind, but he spoke of something else. 'There are Bhuts—in the trees behind you. Don't look them in the eye. They're servants of Yama and are pulled to places that have seen Death. We should promptly head back home.' He secured the letter between the strings on his body.

Home? Aman thought.

Walking out of the glade, Aman could see long, white strands of hair falling from the branches. *What happens if you hold up a mirror to them?* White bodies shuffled and whispered behind the leaves, but he made sure not to look at them directly.

Instead of six, seven beings trekked back over the Varunasmati and back through the jungles towards the valley.

15

Sanaka

Acharya Ashwini helped Prithvi while Ujal and Idhika trudged up ahead. Their teacher led them back another way that saw them walk south and head towards the entrance into the valley through Rohini. Aman walked by Fayza, looking up every now and then at the clear sky of stars, a sight he was still getting used to after Delhi.

The entire way back to Vanyasa, Aman was surprised at how easily his conversation with Fayza flowed. It filled his heart in ways he couldn't have anticipated. He found himself confiding in her about his time in Delhi. He told her exactly how popular he was back in the plains. Before too long, she knew the main points of his entire life. When he mentioned his father and the photographs he had seen of him standing beside the Kalpavriksha, Fayza raised an eyebrow. He hesitantly told her his theory of how his father was possibly connected to it all and what people in the 'normal' world thought of his alleged betrayal as an army officer. It had been hard to speak of the last part, despite how relaxed he felt in Fayza's presence.

'Pft! Really, Eleven?' Fayza said. 'You believe them, the army?' Fayza had always been taught to dig under the surface. First impressions rarely formed the basis of her opinions.

'Mother never let me.'

'And why will I judge you for anything your father may or may not have done, especially when you hardly knew him?'

Hearing those words felt nice. Was she his friend? He had hardly made conversation with anyone in the valley, apart from her and Idhika. He knew it was the Child of the Valley who could help him locate the cardboard box at the moss-covered bridge, but all he wanted to do was continue his conversations with Fayza. Things had changed; Aman had changed.

They kept walking. After a few minutes of silence, Aman said, 'How do you do it? Keep going despite knowing that the world outside the valley continues in exactly the same way without you? As if you never mattered. Do you think the police are looking for us? Ten people gone missing at exactly the same time?'

'I don't think so,' Fayza said. 'The twins are from tribal lands, so the police wouldn't know of their disappearance as no one would have reported it. My parents agreed to my departure, so they are unlikely to tell anyone. It seems your mother did as well. As for the rest, well, so many go missing each day in this country that our disappearance would be just another drop in the ocean.'

Dawn approached and a tinge of saffron crept up from the horizon. Acharya Ashwini sang the Song of the Valley to

Nandana so he would allow them entry. Without any of the dramatic events that had besieged Aman the first time he came this way, he and the others soon hiked through Shreyan's Tunnel in Mount Rohini, entered the glowing gateway, and emerged on the ledge overlooking their new homes.

With feet caked in mud, empty stomachs and spent bodies, they let the cool air hit them and basked in the early blessings of Aditya, the sun god. The enormous structure of the Kalpavriksha was a reassuring presence. Hope surged through Aman. Maybe his mother had wanted this life for him so he could have a chance to find the truth about his father.

Life in the valley hadn't changed while Aman and his travelling companions had been on the eventful journey. The disciples were in the middle of their usual duties, arranged by rotation, not emitting a whine or complaint about their work. Some had farming duties, while others had to bathe animals. Some stirred the cooking pots and cut fruits while others transported water from the springs. From up there, Aman spotted a woman sweeping a trail close to a path that led to his hut, near which small specks gathered at a tea stall. He took in the expanse of the valley before him, its complexity, and not to forget its ingenious location—an isolated vastness ringed by the Seven Hills, like a protective crown that both secured and honoured it.

Everyone stretched, finally getting a chance to rest. Aman stood to one side, rubbing his tired eyes and face. His lip hurt and his hand came back red when he touched the cut that was bleeding even hours after the encounter with the kirtimukha.

'Our souls are made up of the choices in our lives,' Acharya Ashwini said, not giving any context to the statement.

'If I may ask, Acharya,' Idhika steered the conversation in another direction. 'How much Madhu do we have left?'

'We have to exercise limited consumption. In this century, the reserves of Madhu have dwindled. Only Indra knows what we will feed the Kalpavriksha's roots once we run out. It's down to you Souls to help when the time comes or the valley's defences will fall, and so will Vritra.'

'Vritra?'

'The old name for the Seven Hills,' Acharya Ashwini said, touching the parchment tucked into his waist. 'If that happens, it would mean the end of Vanyasa, the end of everything meaningful in the world. It is in the valley alone that we live in harmony with our surroundings, and not in authority over other beings.'

Animals in the valley indeed roamed without fear; they had rights over it equal to other humans. Squirrels did not scurry off and sparrows pecked rice from human plates.

Their discussion was halted as two identical-looking tall men ran up the hill to the ledge of Rohini. Macchli ran towards the distinct forms of the Alok brothers, Ghanisht and Ekram. She started following them, but they ignored her. When they reached the group, Ghanisht said to Acharya Ashwini. 'Where have you been?! Ashwini! How dare you leave the Seven Hills without Sanaka's permission?'

'Watch your words. I'm much older than you two,' the acharya said calmly.

'Ashwini, we answer to Sanaka alone. Whatever your intentions, it doesn't rid you of your duty. Now, if you desire to continue serving as the Pratham Sadhu, you'll do well to follow us.'

'We don't need to trouble Sanaka over such trifles,' Aman protested, but was met with little attention.

Ghanisht and Ekram stood by and looked at the acharya menacingly till he agreed to accompany them. The acharya and the Souls hadn't even been back an hour, and now they were on the move again. Their knees grew heavier with every step as they walked the Chakkar, but before they knew it, they were at the door of one of the widest huts Aman had seen in Vanyasa. It was Bhandaaram, where essential items were stored for the winter. To Bhandaaram's right was Sanaka's home. The Alok brothers promptly left.

Aman was filled with dread. He had hoped to avoid Sanaka for as long as possible. 'I don't feel too well . . . maybe I should go and rest,' he muttered feebly. But the Souls pulled him along with them into Sanaka's hut.

The entire room was filled with smoke. First came a flurry of smoke rings, shooting like darts, and then, between shrouds of white milky vapour, Sanaka revealed himself. He sat right in front of a curtain of wooden beads, so no one could pass and see what was inside.

'Ah, the sweet herb,' Ujal whispered, playing with the nock of his bow, which the acharya had returned to him on their way back to Vanyasa.

Sanaka set his burning blue chillum on the floor and stood up, lifting his protruding belly, adding no more than a foot to his height. He said nothing—just looked straight at them, curiously and closely. He looked at Acharya Ashwini with the same contempt he offered the students. But when his eyes met Aman's, he started grinding his teeth. A bunch of odd sounds escaped his throat as he charged at him, pulled him down by his ear and started to beat him relentlessly.

It was only after Acharya Ashwini intervened, pulling Sanaka back—telling him of Aman's courage when fighting the kirtimukha—that he stopped. But Sanaka continued to swear under his breath.

Sanaka noticed Aman wrinkling his nose at the smell. 'Oh! Is it bothering you, Servant of Samsara? But don't you see, nothing should bother you right now or you might find that both the councils of the Sabha and Samiti learn of your escape from the Seven Hills.' Sanaka spat out the words. He took another drag of his chillum and blew smoke in Aman's face. 'What have you really taught them, Pratham Sadhu? These recruits are so far from accepting our ways. *This*,' he said, shaking his chillum vigorously, 'is a staple to us who have taken saffron.'

There was no saffron on him—just the dull beige of his belly above the white of his dhoti. Sanaka continued in an imperious tone, 'Now, explain yourself.'

Acharya Ashwini started to narrate to Sanaka the events that led up to the cremation of the kirtimukha, from the moment the students had arrived at his boat-hut to the log that allowed them passage past the Varunasmati.

Sanaka was silent at first. His rage was palpable, just simmering below the surface as he heard what they had done.

What followed was a moment of profound silence—strong enough to hush the patter of the bazaar, the trill of the birds, the rustle of the hay. The village seemed to have fallen quiet.

He gave them individual chilling looks, conveying each and every sinew of his fury, and thundered. 'I see no God-fearing eyes. Oh, Father, how shall they pay? Some of them don't even belong here.' He stole a glance at Fayza. 'LISTEN TO YOUR PUNISHMENTS: Utensil cleaning at Aahaar, raking leaves by Pandayam Tal, collection of cow dung and timber, and one of you—divide these tasks among yourselves—collect these for me every day,' he shook his bowl of woodsorrel leaves in their faces, 'FOR THE ENTIRE WINTER!'

Aman steadied himself. Prithvi looked down. Before Sanaka could add anything, Acharya Ashwini untied the parchment from his waist and handed the animal skin to the short man. 'It was beyond me too, Sanaka. All of it, the kirtimukha, the poor child snatched by the eagle'—he put his hand on Prithvi's shoulder—'until these Souls here salvaged this.'

Sanaka's expression was full of scepticism as he started to read the letter. But as he continued, it was evident it contained words of significant import. Eventually realizing he had an audience, he brusquely turned around with the parchment and went past the curtain of wooden beads. He shouted from the small room, 'How this abduction was contrived, we cannot tell. But your safety here relies on the thin stick that is self-control. I urge you, Souls, the lot of you, to consider the consequences if you think of overstepping the ring again, for the wild will have you alone this time without help. The Dronagiri woods are fraught with danger and infested by those you have only heard of in stories. Keep that in mind— Now off you go . . . Ashwini, you stay back.'

Aman followed his friends out of the hut, but through the millimetres of space between the beads of the curtain, he thought he saw something familiar. A cardboard box that seemed identical to the one Aman had left behind on the bridge. Why did Sanaka retrieve it? Why did he not give it back to him? Aman's head swam with questions and shock— the one clue he had that could lead him to answers about his father's final mission was so near, yet out of his reach.

16

Angithi

The wind outside Sanaka's hut carried the aroma of morning chai. Aman, Idhika, Fayza, Ujal and Prithvi hurried to Aahaar to catch the early hours of breakfast when the stew was hot and the fruits were fresh. Although the contents of the letter from the kirtimukha's hut played on their minds, they put aside their thoughts and ate to their hearts' content.

Despite the shocking possibility of his box being in Sanaka's possession, Aman too was assailed by hunger and the exhaustion of the journey. But he couldn't stop thinking about it. Why had Sanaka gone back to retrieve it from the bridge? Aman recalled him shrugging off its importance when Aman had said they needed to go back for it.

'The letter, Idhika,' Prithvi said. 'Whose signature was at the bottom? You managed a glimpse, didn't you?'

'Yes. More than a glimpse,' Idhika said, looking around. 'Let's get some chai at Sudama's? We can talk in private there.'

On their way to the tea stall, they walked past a fortune teller sitting on the path under a mature poplar tree. 'That's

Sadhu Agami,' Idhika whispered, 'a fine palmist in his time, but one that is said to be lately going crazy.'

'Stop there! Come here and take this, you pitiful soul . . .' Sadhu Agami called out, holding in his hand an amulet. 'I can see your future . . . Pri-Prithvi?'

That made her stop.

He said again, 'Take this, poor soul. You do not have much time to live. He's never *just*. Taking a soul in the spring of her life.'

'Take it, sister!' Ujal said. 'It's just like in the tribes.'

From between the sadhu's sticky fingers that were swarming with flies, Prithvi took the amulet and paid the man a dana. It was a rusted ring in the shape of a coiled metal snake.

'It's a Nagsutra. Live your life like each day is your last. And if Indra wants, this Nagsutra might save you,' the sadhu said to her with a smile and pointed out his other offerings to her friends—shiny stones, bracelets and beaded necklets, all for a dana each.

They politely refused and soon reached Sudama's tea stall at the edge of the bazaar.

Idhika, Aman had noticed, wasn't too comfortable around the twins, which meant that there hadn't been many moments when the five were together. The tea spilt over the clay cup's edges and turned the outer surface sticky, but Aman held on to it for warmth. He didn't feel too good.

'In Vanyasa, gossip over chai is tradition,' Idhika said, blowing into her cup. 'You see, separately, the buffalo milk, the tea leaves and the spices are almost ordinary. But together, over the relentless simmer of a coal-fuelled *angithi*, they produce a concoction that provides both energy and calmness, a harmony of our contradictory desires.'

Aman had tried the tea at the stall under the yellow neem by his hut, but Sudama's was worth the journey to the bazaar. He only hoped the mat trader he had tried to deceive wouldn't show up.

The five of them sat on stone slabs while the other Vanyasis around them talked and laughed over one another. Dogs barked and someone played the sitar, which was only audible during the loud vibratos.

'I feel odd,' Aman said. 'Light-headed. Everything is blurry. I didn't mention it earlier, but I've been this way ever since the fight with the kirtimukha. I was convinced it was because I hadn't eaten anything. Then I thought it was the smoke in Sanaka's hut. But it's only getting worse. My left ear hurts too from where Sanaka pulled me. Should I get myself looked at?'

'Aman, Chitra has a fix for all problems. This one time many years ago, I ate some stale kheer—'

'Idhika!' Prithvi snapped. 'We're here now. No one can hear us. Will you please reveal what the letter said?'

'Yes, yes,' Idhika said. She paused for a second and then began, 'I had only moments to read the parchment before handing it over to the acharya.' They huddled closer to her. 'I don't remember the letter word for word, but it was a battle cry for all beasts east of the Varunasmati to find and deliver the Eka of the valley. They are looking for me! And the kirtimukha instead took you,' Idhika said to Prithvi.

'Wha—'

'You're the Eka?'

'Yes,' Idhika said, unable to suppress her smile. 'It is only a matter of time until Aranyani announces it. I have already started my training.'

'I knew it.' Fayza beamed, hugging Idhika.

'Are you sure? Can you handle the responsibility?' Ujal said.

Prithvi rolled her eyes at him. 'She brought us back safely from the Dronagiri woods, didn't she?' she said, stealing a glance at Idhika. She remembered the kirtimukha had tried to feed her Madhu and had asked about her Adwaita. 'But why would anyone want to find the Eka? Whose name was at the bottom of the letter?'

'. . . Chayan's. Leader of the Mountain Pishachus and the only yogi who can Atmayog into humans.'

'The Mountain Pishachus?' Ujal stopped rolling his joint.

'They are indigenous to the snow-covered Himalayas. Fear of them has loomed in the valley for as long as one can remember. Unlike their leader, Chayan, none of them has been under the Kalpavriksha, so Atmayog is beyond them. Without reason, every Mahayatra, they attack the Souls going up to find Madhu. They murder without regret and take hostage any they can . . . And what better way to succeed this decade,' Idhika gulped, 'than to kill the Eka even before we begin the journey? I am scared. The Mountain Pishachus have never ventured this close to the valley before. From what I recall—'

Aman fainted before she could finish and fell from the stone slab. His lip bled uncontrollably.

'Eleven!' Fayza screamed. She dabbed Aman's lip with the hem of her garment, trying to stop the blood. Idhika splashed water on his face. He opened his eyes in seconds, looking dazed. Idhika and Ujal insisted on escorting him to Chitra's cottage, and they asked Fayza to go to Gurukul and inform the acharya of their delay. Prithvi headed back to her hut to get some rest.

With arms around his friends' shoulders, Aman was steered left and right to avoid the muddy puddles on the way to the vaidya's hut, through a path lined with rows of the most uniquely shaped red flowers and eucalyptus trees.

The vaidya's hut was a large circular cottage that housed clay pots and stacks of roots on its shelves. The containers were labelled in Sanskrit. Differently sized mortars and pestles sat beside them. Aman was most intrigued by the tree trunk that ran up the middle of the cottage, through the roof and spread out with leaves shadowing the hut. Inside the hut, around the bark of the same tree, was a circular working station for the vaidya.

'Namahkrita, Souls!' Chitra said, watching the Child of the Valley and Ujal help Aman on to the charpai. 'Before you leave, a word, Idhika? There's a boy among the recruits. Yuvan. Doesn't he know the laws of the valley? He needs to be disciplined. Flirts with me every other day.'

Idhika whispered something in her ear and left with Ujal.

After they had gone, Chitra offered Aman a measured smile. 'There are whispers that the Child of the Valley is the Eka. Now that we have a leader, I hope the villagers are no longer blaming you.' She took notice of the cut on his lower lip and her eyebrows rose. 'What happened? Got into a fight?'

'Yup,' Aman said with his chin raised, 'with a kirtimukha. I've been nauseous ever since.' Touching the wound, which hurt upon contact, he recounted the events east of the Varunasmati.

She looked impressed and examined the gash. 'Unusual. The wound isn't scabbing. You're continuously bleeding. I've only seen this before with . . .' Chitra stopped, stifling her words.

'With?' Aman asked.

'Yes . . . that's what it is! An infection!' The vaidya raved enthusiastically. 'The nail of that occult being has destabilized you, for his touch lies above our mortal realm. It will continue to volatilize you and render you off-colour.'

'You are not making sense,' Aman said.

'Okay. Little fragments of the divine kirtimukha now run in your veins. And until they are washed out by the churna I'll give you, these fragments will give you a slight edge over others. A sharpness, or an advantage.'

'That's good?!' Aman was confused.

'It is!' she said. 'All I can say is trust your gut for the next few days. That is if you manage to see beyond the nausea. Let your instincts take charge. Be intuitive. But I take no responsibility after that. This will'—Chitra extended her palm, in the middle of which was a brown palm-leaf packet— 'heal you within two nights of sleep.'

'What is it?'

'The churna. I ground a few roots and added a bit of the ever-potent Sarpagandha—the red flower outside the hut? Sparsely is it found. Better than anything routinely available in the plains.'

Aman remembered the last time he had met Chitra. It was during his Adwaita when Lord Indra had refused to meet his eyes in the dream. 'What was that . . . what you said to Aranyani right when she was about to leave?'

She shifted her weight from one leg to the other. 'Umm . . . I only suggested that she get you stung by a lal bicchu.'

'What? Why would you suggest that?'

'To help you!' Chitra said. 'While the Matriarch was right—you *had* seen too much—it could all have been avoided. She could have, or I could also have, found a lal bicchu, a red scorpion, in Aranyala when you first entered the valley—I think there are a few nests by the western springs. Its venom detaches your soul from your memory. Stops you from registering much with the exception of being able to perform practised routines and daily tasks, even answering rudimentary questions . . . My only fault then was to suggest this much after your Adwaita was over. You see, the lal bicchu doesn't erase the past. It only numbs your memory *after* the sting for around one day. Had it been done when you first entered the valley, it could have potentially allowed you to resume life in the plains.'

'So I would return and remember nothing of the valley?'

'Precisely,' she said.

'Do the villagers use the lal bicchu often?'

Chitra seemed offended. 'What Sanaka, Aranyani, and the Sabha and Samiti do is beyond me. I've only heard of a few exceptional cases of its use on villagers about to witness the cremation of a loved one, to alleviate their pain by removing any recollection of it.'

Aman decided not to press her. He opened the palm-leaf churna packet to see six smaller ones inside.

'Twice a day with water.'

Aman walked into Maidaan around noon. Acharya Ashwini sat on the podium under the Kalpavriksha, facing his students. Idhika and Dhara were at the front, and Ujal was nodding off. Aman grabbed a kamandalu of water for Fayza, who pressed her fingers to her temples, and sat down beside her.

Jagrav, whose beard now covered his face, said to her, 'Your headache, Fayza. It's because you're still wearing your glasses. Chitra told me that the Kalpavriksha heals our eyesight.'

Fayza couldn't believe she hadn't known this and that it was Jagrav who told her. 'Oh, I knew that,' she said, her face burning with embarrassment.

Aarti looked gobsmacked when she saw Prithvi saunter into Gurukul, arranging the arrows in her new quiver. 'How?!' Aarti jumped up. 'You're alive! I was so worried for you.' Payal nodded, putting on a sympathetic look.

Aarti went over to Prithvi and made a greater show of relief—on the way, she stepped on Fayza's hand, whether by accident or design, it wasn't clear.

'Ahh!' Fayza recoiled in pain.

Prithvi had seen this happen and it seemed like she had had enough. She pulled one arrow from her quiver and loaded her bow.

Jagrav, the peacemaker, was up in an instant. He positioned his gada between Aarti and Prithvi, but in the process, it accidentally brushed Aarti's face. The ever-loyal Payal heaved herself up and charged towards Jagrav. Her fist caught his temple, tucking aside an inch of the skin on his forehead and revealing blood-soaked flesh. Savitri, the boxer, pushed Payal aside and became part of the melee.

'Settle down, Souls!' Acharya Ashwini said, his calm tone in contrast with the physical blows he was witnessing.

'Oh man!' Yuvan said, disappointed. 'I would pay a hundred danas to watch Payal and Savitri fight.'

'Although I'm delighted to see you all carrying your weapons, pay heed to the necessity at hand. Conserve your energy. Chayan's army is closing in on us. The best way to save yourselves is to conquer the journey within and learn Atmayog.'

That evening, as Aditya made his way below the horizon, Aman found himself at the top of Kalanag, at the edge of the Seven Hills. He looked out into the woods. A cold draft rolled in and crashed against his face, triggering buried memories of his mother's embrace. He wondered if his mother missed him like he missed her.

He was a silent figure atop a silent hill.

17

Airavata

Ninda, Stuti, Haan aur Labh
(Chastisement, Compliments, Harm and Gain),
Ek samaan jo rehta hai
(the One who is unaffected),
Vo yogi Prabhu ka pyara hai
(is the yogi loved by the Omniscient).

Thoughts of the cardboard box in Sanaka's hut consumed Aman's thoughts. He was determined to get to the bottom of this mystery. It was no longer an escape route that he fixated on—he had to know his father's story. For that, he had to stay put in Vanyasa.

When he woke up the next morning, he soaked in the tweeting of birds and the veena music floating in the air. Even the cut on his lip was starting to heal. The nausea persisted, however. On the bright side, the circadian chores were effortless as luck was by his side. He pondered over what Chitra had told him—the universe did seem to be conspiring in his favour. He started to revel in his newfound gift.

Aman went to Pandayam Tal and drew water for a bath. But an irrational itch urged him to do otherwise, so he set aside the filled matkas and left early for breakfast.

Upon entering Aahaar, he saw that there wasn't much real food—just mounds of something red and chewy in the larger earthen pot. The other vessel held a curry with pebble-like mounds in it. He was about to leave, stomach still empty, when he overheard something interesting.

Sanaka had skipped breakfast. Not willing the specially cooked items to go to waste, the cooks saw Aman standing at the food counter and asked him if he was interested. So Aman walked to the sitting mat with the biggest smile on his face, carrying a plate laden with honey-dipped bananas, almonds, apple slices, jaggery and cooked sorghum.

When he returned to Pandayam Tal and his matkas, Aman found them hot to the touch as the sun had been shining heavily on them. He enjoyed a rare warm shower. There was no such thing as a calendar in his possession, and he had little idea then that the cold winds of Pausha were around the corner.

Later that day, in Gurukul, Aman was delighted when Savitri's ample form came and sat right in front of him, blocking him from Acharya Ashwini's view. The teacher had a habit of picking on Aman when asking questions.

That day, the acharya told his students about the impending winter: 'Assaulting winds are due to roll in from the peaks. In these times, the value of tolerance and the ability to control your body heat cannot be stressed enough. Don't forget, the journey lies within. You must know what it takes to conjure up the deepest of controls, meditate and, most importantly, seize command of your dress.'

Dress? What dress? Aman looked at the acharya through the gap in Savitri's bent elbow.

Acharya Ashwini continued, 'We are not our body. We are only the soul.' The teacher touched his forehead. 'But this,' he said with eyes closed, his index finger delicately covering his wrist to indicate his body, 'is merely a dress.'

Aman had started ascribing every pleasant occurrence in his life to the temporary power flowing through his veins—remnants of the kirtimukha. Later that day, for lunch, he wasn't surprised when he found grapes, his favourite, in the lunch packet he had picked randomly. He felt powerful, like he could do no wrong.

Of the five of them, only Prithvi had been given a reprieve from Sanaka's punishments. Idhika, Ujal, Fayza and Aman decided to choose their chores by randomly selecting twigs.

'So,' Idhika said, holding up four twigs of different sizes. 'I'll hide these until all four look the same. Then we each pull one. The shortest one gets the last pick.'

'What were Sanaka's four punishments again?' Ujal asked.

'Let's see,' Idhika said. 'One of us has to clean utensils. Another has to collect wood. The third chore is raking leaves. The final, and probably the most difficult, is to find the rare woodsorrel leaves for Sanaka.'

Idhika offered Aman the first go, covering the twigs with her fingers until they looked the same length.

Trust your gut. The prospect of having to visit Sanaka regularly gave Aman the chills. But this time luck was not on his side—he pulled the shortest twig. The group broke into laughter as it meant Aman would have to look for the woodsorrel leaves.

Ujal pulled the longest stick and chose to collect wood. Fayza was to rake the leaves and that meant that Idhika would be at Aahaar, cleaning utensils.

Clearly, Aman's good fortune was starting to flame out. But over the next week, he utilized it well: he searched and made a note of different clusters of woodsorrel leaves, allowing himself to pluck them fresh each day. For ordinary life without any powers was to resume soon, and when it did, it would be dull in comparison.

Thanks to Savitri's analogue wristwatch, which she had expertly hidden, Aman learnt of the turn of the year well in time and, on New Year's Eve, spent a night stargazing with Fayza. She told him about her family, that she was an only child and, because she'd been homeschooled her entire life, how happy she was to have company her age in the valley. Shortly after that, the cold temperatures peaked. Everyone could tell the weather had turned—the sweet kiss of autumn giving way to a wintery punch. It was in the bite of those raw and icy winds that Aman felt the days rush past.

The numbness of the cold tore through the Dronagiri woods until it pushed up the mute shield of the Seven Hills and spread through Vanyasa. Pandayam Tal, too, looked bluer. The trees were naked, stripped of leaves, lying bare like the residents of Vanyasa. The bazaar was buzzing as ever, fuelling industry through the sale of bags, clothes and bowstrings made from spun fibre obtained by hemp cultivation. The eleven students were regularly given lessons under the shade of the Kalpavriksha; there, they were taught arcane symbols and fighting formations from an ancient Vedic manual.

Stories of Indra, whether from the Rigveda, the Puranas or the Mahabharata, were recited to the Souls. Aman struggled with daily readings of the Upanishads, partially because his thoughts were occupied with the box in Sanaka's possession, and as each day passed, taking them closer to practising Atmayog, his worries grew. Of the students, only Aarti and Idhika had learnt Atmayog—and therefore had a Deh on their forearms.

'Materialistic satisfaction adds no value to your life. Your body is the only gift you need,' Acharya Ashwini would tell them repeatedly, touching his wrist every time, 'for not all souls have the good fortune to find a dress.'

It was true, Aman realized. The circular belt of the mountains kept out of this realm all forms of materialism. Ostensibly, to the outside world, there was no valley, but Vanyasa subsisted secretly, revelling each day in its esoteric spirituality. Banana leaves were used as plates, while clothes were a commodity many did not find necessary. When the hardened bottoms of the village's residents failed to find a charpai, their fortified attitudes urged them to sit on the floor. It was also as if the valley dwellers were oblivious to the decreasing temperatures and went about their duties as usual. The sun god Aditya was often eclipsed by Indra's clouds, which quelled any hopes for warm water, but the

Vanyasis' regular routine of taking daily baths, using neem for brushing their teeth, finding unfrequented hillsides for relieving themselves and using earth—not soap—for washing hands was not interrupted.

In the second week of the new year, the winds gained in ferocity, almost appearing to taunt and hiss at anyone who dared to step outdoors. There was an impending frost in the morning dew. The drops trickled through reeds and froze the muddy walls, sucking out any warmth from within huts.

One day, Aman was visited by a hare, which silently scurried into his hut. It had white fur that had been stained brown, but the insides of its tall ears were clean and bright pink. Tucked between the hare's teeth was a heap of palm leaves. It dropped one leaf and darted back out.

Aman read the message:

Lord Indra, once again, has chosen. It will riot, and sheeny will be its sight. For the might of the Eka, this decade, will reside in *Idhika, the Child of the Valley.*

Aman felt relieved. *Hopefully, now everyone can forget that I am the odd eleventh.* More than anything, he wanted to witness Aarti receiving her palm leaf. *If only I could Atmayog.*

Over the next few days, there was continuous rain, and deep puddles covered the paths. From the window of his hut, Aman would spend his days gazing at the darkened hills for hours, the dots of lamplight flickering in blue flames. Although his lip had long healed, the nausea hadn't left him entirely, and he often found his fingertips were purple.

When Aman told the vaidya of this, she had no answers or explanations, and would wave him away with yet another batch of some ground root.

By late January, the deafening noise of hail on the rooftops had been smothered by the deathly silence of snow. The chill permeated the far corners of the valley—tree branches turned white, and every blade of grass froze, rigid against any wind. Fayza found out that Aman did not have enough danas on him, so she bought him a mat from the bazaar, but it did little to keep away the cold. Aman visited Chitra at the vaidya's cottage and learnt that a fortnight ago, a snow leopard had strolled into Vanyasa, entering without anyone knowing how.

Throughout the valley, whenever fresh snow covered the hut roofs, the tea stalls became perpetually full, with yogis and yoginis jostling for the prime seats around angithis. In the daytime, the villagers went to the edge of Maidaan to catch the meagre sun and, after Suryast, swarmed the bonfires erected around Pandayam Tal. It was at these bonfires that legends were recited by old munis.

Aman sat by one such bonfire on a winter evening. Mounds of dead grass and crisp twigs crackled silently in the azure fire. The intense heat reminded him of his birthday ritual, when he and his mother would sneak on to the restricted terrace of their apartment and sit all night talking beside a makeshift bonfire. *Did I miss it this year?*

'Any tale requests tonight?' a man announced. He sported a bun and sat extremely close to the fire, as if immune to heat.

Savitri and Jagrav sat together, not far from Aman. Yuvan was by himself, nearer to the shoreline of Pandayam Tal. He was saying loudly, 'If cutting trees isn't allowed, how do we manage bonfires every night?'

Aranyani's voice came from somewhere, whispering like the wind: 'A keen observation indeed.' When Aman managed to spot her, he saw that she too sat close to the bonfire; her face shone in its blue glow. Glow-worms darted about over her head. 'We don't just rely on Aranyala, for *I* can only provide so much. And a society like Shambhala *needs* to search beyond the Seven Hills for dead wood and fallen fruit. It is the boon of Atmayog that allows us to gather from all over the Himalayas. This valley is unlike anything in the plains, child. It is layered with centuries of events, its sand having touched the feet of thousands of deities . . . Chief Bhrigu . . . why don't you tell us one of those stories? I think the Souls would do well to learn about Airavata.'

The head of the clans nodded and said, 'Yes, Mother. So be it.' Brighu paused for dramatic effect. 'The Curse of Airavata explains the purpose of each of us.' He stared into the flame, the stick he carried poking the fire. Blue-tailed sparks reached for the heavens and then fell as charcoaled dots. 'Three thousand years ago, at a time when very few lived in the valley, Airavata, the white elephant, was taking a cold bath in Pandayam Tal when a crocodile, Huhu, swam up from underneath.'

The white elephant was familiar to Aman—it had waylaid his initial entry into Vanyasa—but its mention stirred no one else. Everyone around him looked to the lake on their right; the Seven Hills and the fire were mirrored in the reflection of its unruffled waters.

'Huhu, the crocodile, bit the elephant with all its might, clutching on with sheer force. Airavata shook in agony, but the crocodile wouldn't let go. Legend has it that without any help from our ancestors, the elephant wept and trumpeted with all five of its trunks for over a year. For another year after that, he cursed the valley, saying that we too would be unable to move, not be allowed to spread the magic of Atmayog, bound by the Seven Hills—much like he was stuck to his spot in the silty lake. Since then, the secrets of Vanyasa have never left the walls of Vritra. But the story doesn't end there. When no help arrived for the suffering Airavata, it seemed he let go of his thoughts and offered himself to Death. Bhuts flew in and circled Pandayam Tal for months. Upon his final breath, in a last-ditch plea, the elephant offered a lotus to Indra. You see, Airavata was Lord Indra's ride. He held the flower high, lifting his trunk towards Svarga, heaven, where his master, the king of the gods, waited for him.'

Lord Indra's vehicle attacked me? Aman thought.

'Eventually,' Chief Brighu continued, 'the deity answered the elephant's prayers. Indra struck the lake with his lightning bolt and burnt the crocodile. Airavata was finally free, and he lay prostrate to thank the lord. But you see, it was only after the elephant stopped resisting death that he attained salvation. The muddy waters of Pandayam Tal are like the cycle of Samsara. They keep the soul trapped—by things materialistic and even sinful. These things are represented by Huhu, the crocodile, who will hold one down. Who can tell me what Airavata represents?'

'A yogi,' said Fayza from within the crowd.

18

Vritra

As winter dragged on, Aman had almost resigned himself to living with the constant nausea he felt. In stark contrast, Idhika appeared to be thriving—not only was she unaffected by the cold, but she had also started to condition herself to eat smaller meals in order to prepare for the Mahayatra.

'But that's over three months away!' Aman had said when she told him.

'As the Eka, I have to be ready.'

Aman, Idhika, Fayza and Ujal had been busy the entire winter completing the term of their punishments and were nearing the end. They would finally be free.

The dining hall, Aahaar, was the tallest hut in Vanyasa. Green chilli shrubs accentuated its edges, and a saffron flag flapped on its roof. It was where Idhika had carried out her punishment duties. With the constant background noise of the mess, she scraped fruit skins off banana-leaf plates and rinsed the clay plates. The water did turn cold in the ewers, but the steam rising from the cooking pots kept Aahaar warm and foggy.

Fayza, too, had done her task diligently, for she had imbibed the importance of keeping the valley clean. But she was used to overcompensating in whatever work she did, so she went the extra mile. She would keep aside the leaves she raked—from within dikes and under boughs and over rutted paths—to be used as mulch for farming. So by the time it was Suryast, the rhododendron tree by the Chakkar would boast under its bower a mound of leaves so tall that it reached up to its lower branches. Sometimes, just to annoy her, Yuvan would climb the tree with a fistful of leaves and throw them down one at a time, saying, 'You missed one.'

Ujal had been meandering through the valley with a basket tethered to his back—to find wood and collect cakes of dung. Cutting trees was prohibited, so he would pick up fallen cones and dead sticks from within the coppices of Aranyala in the early morning chill. To collect dung, he would roam the fold that stationed the cows in the late afternoon. One day, as he stood there stacking dried patties of dung, he was suddenly confronted by the giver of his pickings. It stood there, chewing grass, mooing on occasion. Then it lifted its tail and fresh droppings splattered wetly on the ground. That was the last time Ujal went to the fold.

For the woodsorrel leaves, Aman had to hike up to Kalanag every day. Whenever he plucked the leaves from the glade behind the Temple of Indra, he thought of the mountain on which he stood and Pataan under his feet. He would often go back to the day of Sangram and Aarti's victory over Guru Amrav. After Prithvi's abduction and all the events that followed, they had never dared to return to Pataan.

One of those days, on top of Kalanag's spherical surface, Aman thought to taste a woodsorrel leaf himself. It was then that he noticed something odd. At first, the heart-shaped leaf was utterly tasteless, only mildly cold because of the dewdrops over it. But when he chewed, wild sourness filled his mouth, making him pucker his lips, and the acidity rushed to his head. For a second, his body seemed to go numb; his vision waned, and he was forced to squint to see anything. When he looked at the Seven Hills, it revealed a different view: the shape of a long serpent.

The more closely Aman observed, the clearer he could see it. The ring of mountains that circled the valley and on which he stood curved sinuously and fell rhythmically. *'It is a true gift that you have bestowed upon us mountain dwellers. The deceased body of the snake-demon, Vritra, will provide unparalleled protection.'* Aman recalled the dream in his Adwaita when he'd seen the Founding of Vanyasa in the hut with the lavish feast and four-armed Indra.

Aman now turned to the other side of the valley, beyond Aranyala at the crest of the mountain, where a long tail jutted out into the tallest peak of Sarp-poonch. That's when he realized he stood directly on the resting head of a colossal lifeless snake, Vritra itself, now encrusted in grass and floral skin. Mount Kalanag. *Is that why Idhika called Pataan the 'mouth of Lord Kalanag'?*

He remembered the snake inscribed on Sanaka's chillum, and Acharya Ashwini's words rang in his head: *'Snakes are figures of immortality. They coil into circles, biting their own tails to spiral into the shape of eternity. Just like Atmayog allows you to cheat death and live to be over a thousand.'*

'I was naive enough to think I'm the only one who enjoys the view from up here.' Fayza appeared from the temple steps, the strong breeze teasing her hair. She brushed it away from her face.

'Have you been following me?' Aman's face turned scarlet.

'*I'm* the one who comes here after Gurukul. And *you* are intruding,' she said with a slight smile.

Without her glasses covering her face, Aman noticed that Fayza's nose twitched every time she smiled. The wind whistled louder in his ears. 'And I come here in the mornings . . . to collect these,' he said and bent down to pluck a woodsorrel leaf. *Don't make a fool of yourself.*

Fayza wore a thin white gown and the jute girdle around her waist was tied tightly. Her long black hair swayed in the breeze, which also made her gown billow.

'He doesn't hit you . . . does he? Sanaka?' Fayza asked, placing her hand on his shoulder.

Aman didn't respond, and they stood silently in the glade—from a bird's-eye view, they were no more than two black specks around a knot of low-lying shrubbery. But there they were, Aman and Fayza, flesh and bones. Aman wanted to speak, say something. Instead, the words, noiseless, escaped from between his lips in a foggy breath.

Somewhere in their plentiful interactions, Fayza had begun to recognize Aman's hesitation to speak at times when he really wanted to. She would never push him. That day, she looked at him encouragingly. 'The plains are behind us. This is a new life.'

Aman straightened his back. That was what he liked best about her. Like him, she too was fluent in the language of silence, and was content to just be with him. They stood there quietly, staring at the expanse of the valley and stealing looks at each other.

19

Chaturanga

Few had noticed, but the leaves of Vanyasa were turning yellower and the animals were moving slower.

Aman's anxiety grew when he learnt that Dhara and Yuvan, of all people, had joined the ranks of Atmayogis and, like Idhika and Aarti, developed a Deh on their arms. This anxiety added to his furious contemplation of how he would steal the cardboard box from Sanaka's hut. He'd tried convincing Idhika to help him, but she would just say, 'Oh drop it' in exasperation. He was alone in a web of his own conspiracies. But he was so caught up in his persona and his quandaries that he hadn't noticed that something was troubling Idhika—even in the company of the Souls, she had gone quiet, only speaking when correcting someone.

In Gurukul, with the turn of the seasons, Mata Uttari, the Dwitiya, second, Sadhu, had replaced Acharya Ashwini, the Pratham Sadhu. Mata Uttari spent most of the month correcting their meditation postures. 'In the hills, when the sages meditate for decades, sometimes centuries, by sending their atmans to the trees, it is important to sit in a way that doesn't take a toll on your dress, the body,' she reminded them each day before class. 'How else are we to learn the ways of immortality?

March had arrived with longer days and the thaw of Pandayam Tal, and one evening, Aman was at his usual tea stall under the yellow neem. Two middle-aged villagers were playing Chaturanga, seated opposite each other. They pored over an 8x8 checkerboard carved into the flat surface of a tree stump between them.

The first time Aman had seen Chaturanga pieces, he had thought they all looked identical. Only after the third match that he observed did he realize that each piece had a distinct line on it, which defined its character. Over time, he learnt the rules of the game and how different it was from any of its adulterated variations in the plains, even chess. Chaturanga was an arcane edition, the ancestor of all games of strategy. Each wooden piece embodied a different attribute of a grand stratagem. Aman liked the Mantri and Gaja pieces the most. These were the two whose moves he would follow as he observed players contemplating their next move.

It was on one such day that he'd been watching a Gaja for some time now, but however seasoned a player the woman may have been, she was overlooking an obvious winning move. Aman was overcome by a relentless urge to move the piece. 'Now!' Aman couldn't hold himself back. 'This is your chance. Move the Gaja and take down his Chariot.'

'Sacrilege!' the old woman jumped up. 'How dare you wreck my concentration? I will not have this! This match has lost its purity. There can be no winner here now . . .' She sat back down in frustration, her lips pursed, staring unblinkingly at the Gaja on the board. She picked up her clay mug and blew steam off the edges, but her eyes never left the piece. 'May I conclusively say, fellow Brother Chandprakash,' she said, picking up the Gaja and placing it right beside his Ashva, 'that my atman has lifted itself above yours today?' Once she had finished teasing her opponent, she stood up to face Aman. 'Who *are* you?'

'I didn't mean to offend you, devi,' Aman said.

'You have a keen eye for Chaturanga,' the old woman said, placing her palm on his head. 'I see an astute mind indeed . . . Oh, I remember you. I was there during your Adwaita. You're the eleventh . . . Not as daft as you look; you would have done well as the Blue Rose.'

'Blue Rose?' Aman asked.

'As in, the Eka.'

'I . . . thank you? I am no player. I just listen to my gut.'

The old woman looked at him curiously.

Aman had no idea he was talking to the revered Tritiya, third, Sadhu, Mata Kritika, who would be their next teacher in Gurukul. Upon a closer look—she had charcoal-black eyes and an old scar running down her cheek—Aman noticed he'd seen her before beside the Mother of the Valley. 'You're Aranyani's disciple, aren't you?'

'I'm many things, Aman, just like you,' Mata Kritika said. 'Like you, I too have had a life that precedes Vanyasa.'

'Where are you from?' Aman asked.

'I'm from a village deep in Rajasthan called Dakri. But I was forced to flee—or rather I was saved—in the 1600s.'

'Over three hundred years ago?!'

Mata Kritika told him of her life back in Dakri. Even back then, she had never conformed to the traditional roles ascribed to rural women. 'One night, the villagers came bearing sticks and fire to my hut. You see, they were convinced that I was a witch who had cursed the rains. And, like all tyrants, they wanted someone to blame. So, as I slept in my hut, they barged in. A man hit me with a wooden stick, which gave me this scar. And within moments, they had set my home ablaze. I still remember it: sitting there, I was sure I was going to die. But then—and we didn't have any in Dakri—a horse jumped inside my hut. I had no idea about Atmayog or Vanyasa or any of this then. Sanaka saved me.'

It shocked Aman to hear of Sanaka being spoken about in such glowing terms.

Over the next few weeks, Mata Kritika and Aman played over a hundred games of Chaturanga. One night, sitting by Pandayam Tal in the blue light of an oil lamp, Aman said, 'Did you say you were born over three centuries ago? Vanyasis truly are "immortals".'

'Not really,' she said. 'Vanyasis age and die as the people in the plains. But when in Atmayog, especially when one's atman connects to a banyan, peepal, or any long-living tree, your breathing significantly slows down. In the safety of a secluded cave, your meditating mortal body ages only a few days instead of a decade. You can then choose to resume the rest of your life in a different century. Or divide the years as you wish. Even today, over a thousand Vanyasis hibernate for a time in the future. I, too, am planning on going back up there in a few years.'

20

Pankh

Bacche,

I am terrified of knowing what stops you from replying to my letters. I know our bond has had its trials, but pray know that I cannot turn back the time—all I can do is try to make amends.

I've just got word that *you* are the Eka. Please come and pay me a visit. Two days later, on the auspicious night of the Ceremony of the Founding; it is vital. I have already lost Shakuntala to the valley; so even if it is to be my last job, I must reveal to you the trouble that awaits your path—for who will, I wonder, care for you, if not me? I am at Hathi-Paun.

Former Scribe of the Dwitiya Tier,
Your father,
Rishi Ajan

The moonlit alleys were a tone lighter than black, and in that silence punctuated only by barking dogs, Idhika did not sleep.

Although the letter was one of many she'd received over the years, this one played on her mind.

Idhika's mother, Shakuntala, had been the Eka of the valley two decades ago. She'd given birth to Idhika only a few days before the Mahayatra. Leaving her daughter behind, she had led the perilous journey with her husband, Rishi Ajan—one of the other Souls of Samsara that decade—but had eventually perished due to its unforgiving terrains. Grieving, Rishi Ajan had returned to Vanyasa to raise his daughter. But six years later, he was exiled for an unspeakable sin against the valley: the theft of Madhu.

To this day, Idhika despised him for it, for ruining their lives and leaving her without a parent. Like all the others, this letter too would have gone up in blue flames had it not been for the mention of Shakuntala. It offered Idhika an answer to the question that had always plagued her: how exactly had her mother died on the Mahayatra?

Rishi Ajan had always dodged the question, and Idhika had only one clear memory remaining of when she'd asked him—on the fateful day of his exile. Idhika shut her eyes tightly as if she could shut out the memory—it pained her greatly to recall it.

She was a wisp of a six-year-old running through the thin warrens of Vanyasa, her long uncombed hair sticking to her face. She reached a fork in the path where a gathering of women spun khadi. She realized she was lost and broke down in tears. The little girl wept, not for her father, who could take her home, but for her mother, whom she'd never known.

Idhika knew she would get no more sleep. She stood up and looked at the empty spaces in her hut, which had once held two beings. Now there was one charpai instead of two, and her father's palm-leaf shelves were empty, his writing stool and utensils broken and piled into a corner.

She approached the few palm leaves that still lay tucked to the side and dusted them off. A pankh emerged from between them. Smudges of ink faintly coloured her fingers as she walked towards the threshold with the pankh in her hand.

She was awash in the shaft of moonlight that snuck into her hut. It fell at an angle through the gateway that allowed Idhika to roughly calculate the number of hours until sunrise. Mulling over unanswered questions, she was lost in memories again.

That day, a lost Idhika did *finally find her way back home to her father. Ajan had made a successful return from the Mahayatra and was now a well-versed scribe of the Dwitiya Tier, who spent most of his life doing research, but to Idhika, he was her father, her world. She spent a lot of time in the hut surrounded by him and his work—thick bundles of palm leaves dedicated both to the history and lore of the valley.*

Idhika saw that her father was reading, and she didn't want to bother him, but his watchful eyes spotted her. He called her to sit with him.

Her face lit up, but she quickly wiped her tears before going over to him. 'Father . . . I really miss Mother today.'

He continued reading. The villagers called him the 'crazy' one because he rarely took his eyes off the palm leaves, and if he was ever drawn into conversation, he would only speak of his conspiracy theories about the valley. An oft-narrated one was that the gods were at war with Vanyasa, fighting the valley so that the gods could kill themselves. Of course, it never made sense to anyone. But then, most things Rishi Ajan said didn't.

'Tell me about her, Father!' Idhika persisted. 'Of Mother's bravery and her beauty—'

'I'm very close to the truth, bacche!' her father said. 'You won't believe it. I went to the Clearing of the Chiefs yesterday and met Chief Brighu, who welcomed me with a cup of sura paniyam. We may finally have an answer to our doubts. You see, the clans are the oldest here. They know of the valley's landscape and wield great influence over the Sabha and Samiti. And the chief did everything but confirm my doubts about where the Madhu is hidden. I was right all along.'

'So this explains how she died?'

'Not how,' her father said, 'but why, *why she had to be sacrificed . . . finally, a lot of things will change in Vanyasa.'*

'Will she ever come back? Like the sadhus that meditate in the caves for years?'

Rishi Ajan could only muster up a conciliatory smile.

'Please, Father,' Idhika said, 'I simply do not understand. You always said she was the best of the yoginis. Her beauty and strength were unmatched. She aimed the arrow best among all ten Souls. Then tell me. Why did she leave us? What happened exactly? And I don't want to hear the Song of the Valley, but the actual story!'

Rishi Ajan looked uneasily at the path, pausing as if he could hear his late wife's voice. His eyes misted as he started whispering through his congested chest, his lip trembling. 'Tucked within brambles that may, shielding boughs and keeping at bay; every . . .' At times, the words were soundless. '. . . But in the valley fortified by the one that slithers, for the sake of home—'

Before he could finish, two women entered the hut and pulled Idhika away, dragging her to the back wall. They held on to her protectively.

Before Idhika could comprehend anything, Chief Brighu, Acharya Ashwini and Sanaka entered, followed by a few other men.

Ajan had only just stood up, fumbling, when Acharya Ashwini grabbed his arms and shoved him on to the floor. The acharya stepped on his back, pushing down with all his weight, and said, 'Poor senile man. Lying to everyone, even his daughter.'

The pankh that Rishi Ajan held fell out of his palm. He managed to turn around and grab Acharya Ashwini's leg, elbowing it with all his strength until he heard the bone break. While the acharya writhed in agony, Rishi Ajan pulled out dried flowers from his dhoti, crushed them in his hands and blew them into Chief Brighu's face. The chief's eyes started to burn.

Sanaka tossed his kamandalu to the chief, who emptied it on to his face to relieve himself. Sanaka then grabbed Rishi Ajan by his hair and pinned him back to the floor.

Idhika broke free from the women and ran towards him, but one of the villagers stopped her in her tracks. However, fate afforded her a final glimpse of her father's body being dragged away, with Sanaka leading the procession. Villagers joined, chanting, 'Sinners of Madhu; they need to be banished; from the lands, they need to vanish! Sinners of Madhu; they need to be banished; from the lands, they need to vanish!'

The women had held her tight, just as Idhika now held her father's pankh—thirteen years later. Idhika retreated to her hut. She knew that the time had come to visit him.

21

Hathi-Paun

The next morning, after getting permission from Aranyani to visit her father, Idhika invited Aman, Fayza and Ujal to tag along.

'Prithvi?' Ujal asked. 'What about *her*?'

'I'm not too sure,' Idhika said. They stood by the tulsi shrubs just east of Pandayam Tal. A kamandalu was strapped to her waist. 'Can't we go without her?'

'I know she still spends an awful amount of time with Aarti, but it is you she respects as the true leader. We must take her.' Ujal hadn't ever denied Idhika anything; he never wanted to stand in her way. But lately, he had craved a sense of belonging—not just for himself, but also for his sister. He insisted on her accompanying them.

Soon, they were on the way, Idhika leading them—with Aman, Fayza, Ujal *and* Prithvi following. From the gate in the wall near Kalanag, they charged towards the Dronagiri woods. It was a hot day and the sun beat down on their heads.

As Idhika walked with Ujal, she told him about her father's exile and the letter she'd recently received. Ujal's admiration of her went up a notch as the full force of her bravery was driven home to him. She dealt with the tragedy of her past in a mature manner. Despite the fact that the Souls weren't allowed to be in romantic relationships, the Eka was an exception to the laws. He knew their developing closeness was not futile as Idhika would be allowed a partner if ever she sought one.

The further the Souls moved from Vanyasa, the thinner the trees around them became. The verdant bushes were replaced by brittle shrubs with drooping brown leaves, burnt to a crisp. The path bent and fell, and in no time, the Seven Hills looked like a place far away.

Rishi Ajan's letter had revealed to Idhika his exact location, so she led them deep within the Dronagiri. 'Hathi-Paun is where Airavata, the elephant, used to live before it began its service to Lord Indra.' For the final stretch of their journey, they hugged the mountainside and moved cautiously on a narrow path that overlooked a thousand-foot drop. The Varunasmati cut through a thick forest below.

Once they turned the mountain's shoulder, the trail opened into a clearing—a large shallow crater in the shape of an elephant's foot. In the middle of it was a small cottage. Through a grassy expanse scattered with water bowls off which glinted the sun's afternoon rays, they walked towards the hut. Idhika allowed the others to overtake her, hesitation creeping into her mind.

The hut's entrance was flung open, and a man clad in jute came hopping out, his long, forked beard swaying. 'Who . . .? How many of you are there?' His expression changed when he saw Fayza. He sniffed her, squinting fiercely, and then moved from one person to another, trying to find a familiar face. 'I apologize,' he explained. 'Reading faded words on palm leaves has left me with weak eyes.'

Idhika's heart sank when she noticed her father's dark circles and the creases near his eyes. He had aged. Her emotions were torn between love and rage. Looking into his deep, grey eyes, she saw glimpses of the father she had known in childhood—but the feelings of betrayal came rushing back with the memory of burning palm leaves and all the nights she'd spent in the hut alone.

'Bacche?' Rishi Ajan looked at her. He recognized his daughter instantly. She was now much taller, and her nose resembled that of Shakuntala.

Idhika heaved a deep sigh and whispered, 'Why? You abandoned me . . .'

Her father scoffed. 'Is that what they told you? That I *abandoned* you? Hah! Believe me, if the lal bicchu could somehow erase the *past* instead of the present, I would lie overnight in its nest.' He pretended to laugh, but a tear rolled down his cheek and his voice faltered. 'After my exile, they fed you lies. That I was a Madhu stealer.' He paused. 'They went through my notes, didn't they? Bacche, if you let me tell you the truth of my research and—'

'I. Don't. Care!' Idhika said. 'You LEFT ME!'

Rishi Ajan was taken aback by her fury. He met his daughter's eyes and gestured for them all to follow him inside.

When they entered his hut, they saw a square altar in the middle made of packed mud and filled with deadwood. Rishi

Ajan asked them to sit as he and his daughter moved to a side room to talk in private.

Aman, Ujal, Prithvi and Fayza sat there waiting patiently, sometimes in silence, sometimes making conversation about the different versions they'd heard in Vanyasa about Rishi Ajan's exile. Aman even managed time for a nap and only woke up twice in the middle when he heard raised voices between Rishi Ajan and Idhika in the other room.

Hours later, when Rishi Ajan and Idhika returned, the tension between them seemed to be no more. In front of everyone, the scribe told his daughter, 'Now you know why I haven't abandoned my research. Even now, I read under both Aditya and the moon. Either my eyes will fail me or I will find those who deserve to pay for Shakuntala's untimely sacrifice. Bacche, if I must attempt to explain to you why I had to do what I did, then I must start from the beginning . . . and simply telling you won't do. Which is why I called you here tonight, specifically on the night of the Ceremony of the Founding. It occurs once every *dashak*, every ten years.'

He left the hut and returned within moments with a lantern, which had a red, not blue, fire flickering in it. 'We have only a few minutes before the stars align themselves. I must, to all five of you, *show* on this auspicious night, how the valley was founded, the exact way the rishis learnt in the olden days. Once again, there will be a havan.' With that, he swung his arm and threw the lantern into the wood, which instantly gave fury to the *yagya*, sacred fire, and flooded the room with light and white smoke. '*Namas Swaha.*'

22

Yagya

Aman had already witnessed the Founding of Vanyasa in his Adwaita—the deity with the four arms had laid out the rules of the valley over a lavish feast. But even the Child of the Valley could not have imagined what Rishi Ajan was about to show them.

The scribe shut the lone window in the room, stuffing a cloth into its edges, and then moved to the doorway to tighten the tapestry. He stepped back towards the altar and said, 'Make yourselves comfortable, Souls. Not too close to the sacred fire. Lie down if you feel dizzy.' His hands moved at lightning speed as he pulled bowls of *parodasa*, *karu*, milk, ghee and sandalwood, among other ritual offerings, towards him and sat down on the ground.

The sun had dipped, and shadows had spread everywhere—not that it made a difference as all the light had been shut out already; only the fire emitted a glow. The rishi did not lift his head as he chanted mantras in Sanskrit from long reams of scriptures. Aman recognized none of the hymns that were recited, save for the Song of the Valley, when Idhika joined her father and sang loudly—her eyes shut and head raised.

Rishi Ajan was relentless in feeding the fire, paying no heed to the fact that the smoke couldn't escape from the closed-in room. He put in different materials, and fumes rose from the havan vessel. The smoke curled up to the ceiling and settled in, thickening in the room. Aman couldn't even see Fayza, who sat beside him, coughing.

When he put Madhu into the yagya, such a thick cloud formed that streaks of yellow started to stain the walls. They all felt a few drops on their bodies.

'Close your eyes and stick out your tongues to see the lore,' the rishi told them.

Aman obeyed. As soon as a drop landed on his tongue, a bright scene lit up the insides of his closed eyes. He saw a large, glowing human foot. He was flying in what seemed like outer space—there was a tennis ball in the colours of Earth floating in an ocean of darkness below him. He hovered up the glowing foot, crossed bulging calf muscles, up a thigh covered in white, and was soon confronted with the supple torso of this immense man.

'Don't open your eyes, only listen . . . That's Indra you see.'

Aman floated up until he reached the stars. There, Indra was not alone. Six men stood behind him in single file, each crowned in gold.

'The Devas . . . And on the other side are the seven Asuras,' the scribe announced.

The Asuras and the Devas stood opposite each other, a snake within their large palms, like a long rope. The Asuras looked equally godly, with the exception of their missing crowns.

'They hold the divine serpent to churn the Ocean of Milk. This is the only time, it is believed, that the Asuras and Devas put away their differences.'

But the deities seemed to be in the middle of a tug of war. And tug they did, just not against each other but in unison. They churned the Ocean of Milk using the serpent. Their movements were slow, but their muscles pulsated with the heartbeat of their celestial bodies. From within the ocean, with each pull, rose many offerings. When the final gift began to rise from the darkness, it lifted with itself the Milky Way like a slimy layer of glitter, which was why when the tree fully emerged, the entire galaxy shone in its branches.

'The divine Kalpavriksha.'

Indra dropped the serpent, reached out and grabbed the tree. The Asuras were too startled to react. And by the time they did, Indra was far away. He darted seamlessly through space with his arm around the trunk of the Kalpavriksha, down towards Mount Meru on Earth. The Devas followed him closely, but the Asuras lagged behind.

By the time Aman too reached Earth, well behind the Devas and Asuras, the tapestry of events in front of him had transfigured into a war involving millions, maybe more. It wasn't just men with swords, but all types of animals as well. The Asuras had led the charge towards Mount Meru, where the Kalpavriksha lay.

'This is the great unending battle between the two kinds of beings. It lasted three *Yugas* (ages). Eventually, when enough dresses were divorced from their souls, Indra found a solution—he hid the tree somewhere in the Himalayas to put an end to the war.'

The scene had transformed: everything was now calm and green. Aman saw a man plant the Kalpavriksha beside a great blue lake. The man looked around furtively to make sure he hadn't been seen.

This was Indra again. The seasons changed in front of Aman's eyes. It felt like months, maybe years, had passed. Little plants around the Kalpavriksha grew into trees and the older ones in the background rotted away. A colossal snake-demon approached the divine tree and started to plague the land around it. Indra used his lightning bolt to slay the serpent and ringed its body to form a range of mountains to protect the valley.

In the next scene, four men were sitting at the deity's feet. Indra's two hands had turned into four, and he held in them a blue fire, some grass, a rosary and the jnanamudra. He recited to the men the Rigveda, and they wrote down the verses diligently.

'The sons born of Brahma's mind: the four Kumars. You might recognize the youngest of them, sitting on the right, Sanaka—the wretched man who ruined me,' Rishi Ajan said in a tone full of hatred.

Aman saw a hut beside the divine tree where a lavish feast was going on, and although it lasted only a few seconds, it looked familiar because he had seen it in his Adwaita.

Eventually, Indra and the Kumars left the scene. A girl with dark-green eyes approached the tree and grew up into a young woman under its shadow, breathing in its air all her life. Simultaneously, the land beside the lake sprouted into a verdant forest.

'The goddess of Aranyala,' Rishi Ajan said. 'Now, slowly open your eyes.'

The yagya burnt brighter than ever, but the room was clear of smoke, and the tapestry on the doorway was drawn open.

Rishi Ajan steepled his hands. 'Now do you see? While Sanaka is alive, the other three Kumars meditate up in the caves to save their years for a time in the future. Sanaka doesn't need their support. He's got the Vanyasis exactly where he wants them—distracted and worried about danger from outside. This is what Sanaka preaches to the valley: the threat of Chayan, his potential invasion—which he overplays—and the fear of that is what he uses to bend the rules to his will. With every privilege comes a parallel suppression. *I* believe there is enough Madhu in Vanyasa.'

He continued, 'Enough Madhu and more was brought back by those who survived the snowy journey. But whatever happened to it all? Why is there always a shortage? I knew I had the pieces, and I only needed to put them together, when I started spotting men in the middle of the night under the Kalpavriksha. They weren't valley dwellers. They wore rubber on their feet and garments till their necks, which I remember from my time in the plains more than twenty years ago. And just when I was convinced that they were men of the plains, I was labelled delusional. I am sure Sanaka was behind it all; it's somehow a part of his larger scheme.'

'They're still there, Rishi-ji,' Prithvi spoke up. 'I tried telling Ujal in my first week when I was practising archery in Aranyala; I spotted a man with boots—you're right.'

'It's also what the Indian Army wears,' Fayza said, remembering what Aman had told her about his father earlier.

Rishi Ajan dug his face into his palms, his suspicions now confirmed.

Aman's head spun as he recalled his father's photographs. Idhika stared at him, horror-struck.

23

Sarp-poonch

'That's what I told you,' Aman said to Idhika after they'd returned to Vanyasa. 'If only we'd retrieved the box while it was still at the bridge.'

'You're right, Aman . . . I just . . . couldn't believe it earlier,' she said. 'But to be sure, we have to get a look at the photographs.'

'Well, my father and the others are all dressed like Vanyasis in the photographs. The Kalpavriksha is undoubtedly in the background. And he was in the army. There is no other explanation; you'll see. The box also has palm leaves with a ton of drawings, but the notes are in Sanskrit,' he said, biting his fingernails, which were longer than they'd ever been. 'And now Sanaka has the box hidden in his hut.' He implored her to assist him in retrieving it. After hearing everything that her father had said, Idhika didn't need much convincing.

The fear of what Sanaka would do to them if they got caught forced them to wait for a week. Then, on the day that the Sabha and Samiti were scheduled to meet, when it was certain that Sanaka would be at the Assembly, they stole

into his hut during Suryast and heaved a sigh of relief when
they saw the box was still there. They had decided to quickly
search the notes for information and leave the box so as not
to raise any suspicion.

'No. How could this happen? They're destroyed!' Aman
fell to his knees in front of the open box. The palm leaves
had been damaged by rainwater, probably even before Sanaka
took the box from the bridge.

Idhika tilted the palm leaves from one side to the other.
'From the little that I can see, these are very fine marks. I do
not know of any pankh that can make such thin lines.'

Aman, looking down at the photographs, said, 'Yeah.
Father probably used a pen from the plains. Can you not
make out anything? Here, look at these photographs. See the
Kalpavriksha.'

Idhika set the leaves aside and took the three photographs,
which were thankfully undamaged. She saw the men with
shaved heads standing under the zigzagging trunk of the large
tree. 'So it's true . . . Which one is he?'

Aman pointed to the man in the middle. He then turned
his face to the wall and murmured, 'We have to take the box!'

'No!' Her eyes widened. 'Sanaka will not spare us.'

'What if we just borrow it? So we can study its contents
and return it. He won't even know it's gone. We can bring it
back before he realizes.'

She shook her head.

'Idhika . . . don't you want to know?' he said. 'Don't
you want your father to return to the valley? I've already lost
mine . . . but you, your father is still alive.'

She looked at him with a torn expression. Aman knew he had convinced her.

The two made haste and left Sanaka's hut with the box. As soon as they entered her cottage, she rushed to the lantern by her rug, taking out the palm leaves so she could study the faded marks. 'Come. Look here. Although the ink has dissolved, the thin tip of the pen did leave faint cuts on the surface of the leaves. Small sections of these drawings can be recreated. For example . . . *this* one here is clearly Aranyala, and this, Pandayam Tal . . . and—these are maps!'

'And these? What are these?' Aman asked, pointing to the biggest leaf lying on Idhika's side.

'I don't know. Another part of the valley? Let's see,' she said, bringing it closer to the flame. 'I see a larger shape.'

She traced it with a pankh dipped in fresh ink until a pointy triangle had formed. It was only when Idhika said 'it looks like a tail' that Aman recalled what he'd learnt recently: that Sarp-poonch's peak was in reality the tail of the serpent Vritra.

After that, the more they looked at the remaining palm leaves, the clearer it became to them that most of the drawings were of caves in Mount Sarp-poonch.

'Was that where Father was?' Aman asked. 'In the caves up in the mountain on the other side of Aranyala?'

'No. Impossible,' Idhika said. 'The height of Sarp-poonch is never-ending. It's too steep. No Vanyasi has ever made it up there in human form. Only through Atmayog to patrol the caves—and it's not just Sarp-poonch that's insurmountable, but also upper Rohini and the less-travelled areas of Kalanag.

Guards of the Sabha and Samiti could go up there as birds, or mountain goats . . . But a human, never.'

'For people of the valley, sure,' he said. 'But you underestimate the tools available in the plains. The high caves make for a perfect hiding spot.'

Idhika thought for a bit. Later, after having further studied the palm leaves, which carried text in Sanskrit, she said, 'You'd mentioned that your father and his men called themselves "The Preservers". But that cannot be. The Preservers make up a rogue wing—one that is not necessarily attached any more to the army of your plains, from what I gather based on these notes in Sanskrit.'

Aman's head was spinning with all this information. He felt like he was at the threshold of the answer to the puzzle— but the door was firmly locked.

The next day, early in the morning, when Sanaka was at Aahaar for breakfast, they put the box back in his hut, save for one photograph. Then they went to Idhika's cottage.

Idhika sat still while Aman paced about. She was in Atmayog, her spirit up in the caves of Sarp-poonch. She had had her eyes shut for over an hour, her chest rarely moving and her Deh glowing, when she suddenly gasped for air and her breathing returned to its normal pace. 'Aman! You were right. There are people there! Two in the few caves I checked. I couldn't stay for long. A sparrow may not be the wisest animal to Atmayog into for this. One of the men even looked at me suspiciously and threw a stone, so I had to fly away.'

'Any of these men?' Aman held his breath and made her check the photograph.

'I don't know,' she said. 'But they are not Vanyasis. Are they the Preservers? They definitely belong to the plains. Because, Aman, they have *things*, objects, all colourful and well-shaped. Things I've never seen.'

'Describe the items.'

'I'll go again after a couple of days, or they'll get suspicious, but I saw a bundle of what looked like very uniform and smooth vines, like the ones that drop from the Kalpavriksha.'

'Oh! It could be rope,' Aman said. 'They must be using it to get to the caves that are high up.'

'But how did they sneak into the valley without help?' Idhika asked. 'Why are they here—no—how did they ever get past Nandana? So many questions. And we can't just ask anyone. Father . . . he was right. I'll write to him, but we need to be careful about whom we tell.'

Aman couldn't hold it in; he had to speak to Fayza. When he entered her hut the next day, she was preparing for Atmayog. Aman was unfamiliar with the asana she was practising—bent on an elaborate rug in a kneeling position, head on the floor.

'No! Wait, Fayza. Where are you going?'

Fayza ignored him.

'Atmayog later. Break out of it! I need to talk,' he said.

She kept at it.

Aman was unsure of what to do next. *Is she angry with me? What did I do?* 'Fayza? Can you hear me?'

Slowly, Fayza got up and only when she had folded her rug did she turn to say, 'I was praying, Aman.'

'Praying, in an asana?' he asked.

'Haha . . . I guess . . . I never thought about it that way. No, Aman, I was practising my faith. In Islam, we call it *salat*. In fact, I pray five times a day.'

'Oh, right,' he said. 'I guess that's why your rug is facing . . .'

'West . . .'

'Yes,' Aman said and soon told her about the Preservers' intrusion into the valley. Fayza wasn't half as surprised as Aman had expected her to be.

'The people here think absolutely no one knows about Vanyasa,' she said. 'But some do, the right circles in Rishikesh . . . Makes you wonder if many have left the valley to live in the plains, maybe even using Atmayog there. I've been thinking of all this ever since I've arrived here.'

Later in the week, Fayza joined Aman and Idhika when Idhika used Atmayog to go back to the cave. This time, she was a fly. She was right in thinking that a fly would be less conspicuous, but she miscalculated the time it took to get to the upper reaches of Sarp-poonch.

One of the people she had seen earlier was deep inside a cave, sitting in his usual spot, dressed in clothes far different from what a Vanyasi would wear. He was meditating and was unlikely to open his eyes anytime soon. This meant Idhika had enough time to observe him and the things he had around him.

Meanwhile, back in her cottage, Aman and Fayza impatiently waited for Idhika to return.

'If someone didn't know any better,' Fayza said, 'they'd think Idhika is dead. Look at her . . . sitting upright, sure, but lifeless, for her chest barely moves when in Atmayog.'

Waiting for Idhika to complete her Atmayog, Aman's thoughts turned to Fayza. He was suddenly aware of how close she sat to him. He thought of all the times he had spent with her. Fayza had been there for him in his lowest moments, and they genuinely cared for each other. He recalled charging at the kirtimukha without fear when the monster was strangling her. She was the only one who had not laughed when he had pulled the shortest twig. In fact, she was the first person in whose company he could talk about his deepest feelings. If he hadn't been brought to the valley, if he were still in school, Aman thought, he would want nothing more than to have Fayza around him. Sitting beside her, he was sure they had a future. Something inside him told him that he could do it; the voice in his head was so strong and overwhelming that all rules of the valley were forgotten—that it was okay doing what he was doing, breaking the law, interlacing his fingers with hers.

Fayza jerked her hand back. She looked away from him, towards Idhika and the front door.

Aman was so ashamed. He had been sure she liked him. *Or did she hear someone approaching and is just checking to make sure?* 'Fayza?' Aman whispered.

She didn't answer, and pulled his face towards hers. Before he could comprehend anything, he felt he was drowning. Drowning into the blurry face of Fayza. And in that half a second, Aman did a day's worth of thinking.

But finally, he did meet that watery sweetness. It was delicate, the way Fayza had come in. *I can't believe this.* Her breath smelt of jasmine. His lower lip shivered, once or twice, and his toes curled. A throaty sound escaped him, but he quelled it quickly.

Aman forgot all about his father's box and the Mahayatra that was to come. Kissing her, he felt his tension fade, clinging on to the only thing he was sure of in this uncertain world, with such vehemence that if he could Atmayog to another human, he thought, this was what the union of their souls would feel like.

It ended too soon for Aman. Still dazed from the lingering sensation on his lips that he wanted to go back to, he said, 'When I first met you, I don't know why but I felt like I knew you from before.'

Late into the evening, Idhika did finally open her eyes. Aman and Fayza were half-asleep and didn't notice at first. At that moment, Fayza wasn't aware of the fact that despite her day-long Atmayog, Idhika had aged only a few seconds—a gift that allowed many yogis to hibernate for centuries.

The first thing that Idhika told them was: 'He had notes. I saw them. He's looking for Madhu!'

'Notes?' Aman asked.

Idhika described the different objects she'd seen. Aman and Fayza managed to decipher most of them: a toothbrush, a pen, a head-covering with a peak, which was undoubtedly a cap. But the most important item was a diary. 'He's after the location of Madhu . . . and he was meditating! I am *sure* he knows Atmayog himself.'

'What?' Fayza interrupted. 'The Preserver knows Atmayog? Is there a chance he's listening to us right now—as a fly or an ant himself?'

'It's possible,' Idhika continued. 'But we have to beat him. If we can find Madhu first, we can prove my father's innocence. Show everyone that there is more than enough Madhu in the valley and the people have been lied to for long. That we need not increase the frequency of the Mahayatras . . . Then maybe we can tell Aranyani and the Sabha and Samiti. Once they learn of Sanaka's motives, he will be put under trial—and Father will be allowed to come back home.'

'So Madhu is hidden somewhere only animals can go?' Fayza asked.

'Maybe . . . likely,' Idhika said. 'And that doesn't help. There are so many places it could be. I cannot do it alone . . . Aman, Fayza, you have to learn Atmayog. And fast.'

PART III

24

Atmayog

Two months later

The Mahayatra was now a day away. The slow and subtle degeneration of Vanyasa had taken on more noticeable hues, and certainly the wisest of the residents saw the unmistakable signs.

Much had changed in the lives of the Souls. Idhika could now Atmayog into the bodies of animals outside the valley. Prithvi had vastly honed her skills and was now deserving of the title of Tritiya Archer—an honour given to few. Ujal was not too far behind. Fayza had taken up sword-fighting and was often pitched against Aarti, who was top-notch in the discipline. As for Aman, even though his arrow shots were half-decent, his swings of the sword considerably accurate and his flair for Chaturanga commendable, his attempts at Atmayog continued to disappoint.

Idhika had withdrawn further into herself, even more than Aman in his time as a plain dweller. Over the month leading up to the Mahayatra, she got into the habit of taking long walks by herself. When Aman asked what was troubling her, she told him of her worries, about the fact that she was unsure of her instincts. Was she good enough to lead the Souls to the Himalayan bee and steer clear of the Mountain Pishachus? But Aman knew there was something graver that occupied her, something she wasn't ready to tell him. She would frequently be seen spending long hours in Aranyani's hut, talking to the matriarch about things unknown to them. Yuvan was the one who ludicrously suggested, 'Since she's never had an Adwaita, isn't she vulnerable to Chayan's Atmayog?'

Their Gurukul teacher had changed in the two months that had gone by. After Mata Kritika, the students had been introduced to their Chatvari, fourth, Sadhu. A powerfully built man who carried a mace, he was teaching them the importance of physical strength and finessing their yogic exercises.

That morning, Aman was in his hut, preparing for the final lesson of Gurukul. He let smoke fill his lungs and barely flinched when a burning piece of green slipped out of his chillum and fell on his sculpted chest, creating a tiny crater in his skin.

'One just cannot go on the Mahayatra without Atmayog!' The Chatvari Sadhu's words had been bothering him. The Mahayatra was to start in a day. And time was running out for him to learn it. Failing to do so would land him neer-less in the Dronagiri woods or worse, past the Varunasmati. With that in mind, he walked up to the matka in his spartan cottage and washed his face, bracing himself for his final attempt at the ancient art.

A short while later, below the cloudless sky and the upper canopies of the divine tree that blocked out the beaming sun, Aman sat beside Fayza with the other Souls. There was much relief in the inner shade of the Kalpavriksha, the only place where Atmayog could be learnt.

The Chatvari Sadhu sat near the podium. Not too far away were Idhika and Ujal, who were now inseparable but nothing more than friends. It was clear as day that Idhika, too, reciprocated Ujal's feelings, but she refused to act on it and let him get any closer, physically or emotionally. Despite being the exception when it came to celibacy, she had chosen abstinence. The valley respected the Eka's decision.

'Any luck, Fayza?' Idhika asked her, looking distressed. Idhika, Fayza, Ujal and Prithvi had spent the last month using their newfound skill of Atmayog to keep a watch on the men hiding in the caves of Sarp-poonch, with Aman relegated to the task of keeping guard. 'The only way to prove that Sanaka is lying to the valley is to find the reserves of Madhu. The Preserver in the cave doesn't seem to have any clue about its location, but he's been trying to find it. And there's something else. Something I saw when I went there as a fly. A letter that he's written . . . but I'll reveal its contents later, away from prying ears in Maidaan.'

'How will finding Madhu help *us*?' Ujal said, playing with the head of an arrow in his quiver.

'We can bring it up when the Sabha and Samiti convene tomorrow to bid us goodbye for the journey,' said Idhika. 'If we can prove to all those who are there that there is sufficient Madhu, then we need not travel north. If we can't prove it, all eleven of us might not return like many before. Like Mother two decades ago . . .'

'. . . the teacher is calling Aman.' Fayza stopped braiding her knee-length hair and pointed towards the Chatvari Sadhu. 'Help him, guys! It's his last attempt. Any final words of advice? Ujal?'

'Umm,' Ujal said. 'Feel the energy of the tree and let the Kalpavriksha guide you.'

Aman brushed the mud off his shins and stood up. With sweaty palms and a slow stride, he reached the foot of the tree, underneath the suspended podium. *Here goes nothing, loser,* Aman thought as he relaxed his shoulders and assumed a seated meditative stance. Then, anxiously, he curled his fingers into a jnanamudra, and that was enough of a cue for the other students to quieten.

Each time he shut his eyes and let his ears take in the surroundings, different thoughts crept into his head: first, the image of Fayza's face; then, his mother's hand waving him goodbye. But this time, his determination had a different quality. Whenever he got distracted, he would push forward with greater vehemence. *What's in the letter written by the Preserver? No,* stop it! *1, 2, 3 . . . No thinking—SHHH!!!*

'Don't worry if you can't,' Yuvan teased, admiring his Deh.

Aman did not open his eyes—his ears had shut out all sound; any incident or memory that tried to sneak in was stopped in its tracks. In this trance-like state, his concentration a tangible entity, he edged towards the precipice. They say you never forget your first Atmayog, and Aman was about to find out exactly why.

Ironically, it was his straying thoughts that enabled him that day: Aman let the Kalpavriksha fill him with its oxygen. And the last thing he remembered thinking was: *Where I sit is where Lord Indra once sat.*

Suddenly, his perception changed, of himself, of who he was now and who he had been: the boy left behind in the plains. Here, Aman was one of the Souls, surrounded by his friends, and entrusted by the villagers as a potential conqueror of the Mahayatra. Here, he was visible and wanted, and here he sat at the edge of a divine tree churned from the Ocean of Milk.

His eyes were closed, and his world was already dark when everything went black. He forgot how to breathe. A pulsating pain spread to all areas of his body. He wanted to scream. Just when he could stand it no longer, the pain broke away, and it felt as though his body had finally found the first rays of sunlight after a night of freezing-cold iciness.

The next thing he knew was that all the pleasures of the world—psychological, physical, ephemeral—were his and his alone. A shiver ran down his spine; he cried and was acquainted with happiness for the first time. Such was its fervour that it seemed that this feeling of belonging would never wane or cease. Only when enough time had passed and, more importantly, when he knew the moment had arrived did he open his eyes.

He was in the middle of Maidaan, the Kalpavriksha still giving him shade. But everything was still and devoid of colour. The field looked whiter. Not a leaf moved. Neither any of his classmates nor the Chatvari Sadhu was in sight. All noise seemed to have halted, and even the sound of the wind was a distant memory.

It was another world that mirrored his own, one in which he was the only human. He recalled how Idhika had put it: *'Once in, you'll be able to perceive only the existence of the living beings that you can Atmayog to.'*

He scanned his surroundings for a companion and momentarily saw a cow approaching from afar. It looked like the animal was being ushered by someone, a human that Aman could not see. *Isn't it easier to Atmayog to bigger animals?* He figured the Chatvari Sadhu probably had the cow summoned to aid him.

Of course . . . special assistance for Aman! He knew he had fared poorly in Gurukul, but he didn't want pity. He was halfway to pulling off a successful Atmayog and he wasn't going to squander his first attempt on an easy hit. His teacher had to be proved wrong.

To hear the sounds around him, Aman shut his eyes again. After a minute, he managed to discern a faint whisper of the wind between the mountain slopes. The sound of the approaching cow reached him too. Soon, his hearing ability magnified manifold, and he could distinguish flies from mosquitoes in the buzzing that surrounded him.

Something was whirring perceptibly close to him. He centred into the noise of its flapping wings. A glint of sunlight reflected off the fly and pierced through Aman's closed eyes.

To Atmayog to an animal as small as this was no easy feat, but Aman dove in, focusing ever more intently on the fly. Slowly, he felt his mortal body vibrate, and the vibration continued every two seconds. He took a deep breath to anchor that feeling. And sure enough, his body latched on indefinitely to the vibration until he was bouncing up and down. It took Aman a while to understand that he was finally in control of the fly.

His eyes were forced open. As a fly, his perception of colour was limited, but his range of view was considerably larger than that of a human, and he was alert to the tiniest movements near him. He could see other humans now. He spotted his own body, sitting still under the podium. The Chatvari Sadhu and the rest of the Souls had their eyes fixated on the cow accompanied by a standing yogi.

'I'M HERE!' Aman shouted, well aware that he was inaudible. Aman turned himself, the fly, around and darted towards Fayza. He sat on her nose, but she swatted him away, annoyed. Aman realized he could spend his entire life staring at that face—the face that was full of concern for his well-being, that calmed him like no other could, that had lips silently moving in prayer, willing him to succeed.

'He did it!' Idhika shouted, pointing. Aman did not know how Idhika had spotted him, but he was glad she had. The entire Gurukul gathering broke into applause, and Idhika wriggled her shoulders, which Aman knew was the Child of the Valley's way of celebrating. Fayza clapped louder than Ujal, Prithvi, Jagrav and Savitri combined. They all seemed genuinely happy for him. Although Aarti and Payal tried their best to appear nonchalant, relief was clear even on their faces. There was no denying that they all feared the Mahayatra and were glad to have one more Soul on board.

Even the Chatvari Sadhu shot Aman the fly a smile.
Adrenaline rushed through Aman's miniature veins. He shot
up into the air and kept rising. Higher and higher, up the
zigzagging trunk of the tree. Eventually, through the leaves,
he emerged above the upper canopies of the Kalpavriksha and
spotted tree dwellers like flying squirrels, flying snakes and
even forest geckos. Steering clear of them, Aman flew around
the valley, taking in the sights he had come to know so well.

When he retreated to Maidaan, he could spot only two
specks beside the Kalpavriksha from far above. Fayza and
the Chatvari Sadhu were waiting for him—everyone else
had gone.

After Aman returned to his body, a great weariness came
over him.

'That happens,' the Chatvari Sadhu said, holding out a
kamandalu. 'Drink this.'

'You took your sweet time,' Fayza said, itching to give
Aman a hug but restraining herself.

'Where's everyone?' Aman croaked. He cleared his throat.

'What do you mean?' Fayza said. 'The Mahayatra starts
tomorrow, Eleven; everyone is rolling up their belongings.
What else?'

'You've done well for your first time, Aman, finding a
fly,' the Chatvari Sadhu said. 'And now that you are eligible,
make your preparations in haste. Don't forget to put in a
brief meditation session before getting plenty of rest. And
pack palm leaves for the journey, in case you need to
contact Vanyasa.'

A few minutes later, when Aman and Fayza were walking down the Chakkar towards the huts, she said, 'Not sure how much rest you'll manage, to be honest.'

'What do you mean?' Aman asked.

'Idhika is waiting for you right now. She'll only tell us what she saw up in Sarp-poonch once everyone is there.'

'The letter that the intruder wrote?' he asked.

'Yes.'

'Relax, Fayza . . . Isn't it good news that we found it?' he asked.

'Depends on what it reveals.'

25

Pandayam

Fayza and Aman found Prithvi waiting with Idhika outside her hut. Ujal was with them too, having returned from his pre-Mahayatra prayers at the Temple of Indra.

'Why must you always keep us guessing, Idhika?' said Prithvi, who was now a full-fledged member of this group. Her association with Aarti earlier had prevented her from integrating fully, but she seemed to have found her voice in Idhika's recent quietness. 'First, it was the name of the man who had ordered my kidnapping, and now this letter? What does it say? Out with it already!'

Aman shifted his weight from one leg to the other. He was apprehensive. And a little hopeful, perhaps. A part of him wished Prithvi's aggression would make Idhika react in her old way, make her resurrect her former self. But Idhika just nodded at Prithvi and went inside her hut. The rest followed in due order.

'I had gone there as a fly,' Idhika said. 'There were many letters. Some decades old and some newly written. The Preserver was going over them, and I managed to catch a few things. I don't remember every word, but the old parchment that he opened said, "Their leader is a tough negotiator, even for a village dweller. But now, his eyes have been truly opened and finally, the man has allowed us refuge up in the caves of their tallest mountain. The villagers don't come up here. While he has changed the rules of the valley in order to accommodate our nightly visits to their tree, we are struggling to understand Atmayog. *You fools think you'll learn it in a month? I'd like to see you try,* their leader told us. He refuses to share the location of Madhu, this extremely valuable hallucinogen, which, if we could get our hands on it, would greatly benefit the reach of the Preservers.'"

'So, this means . . .' Prithvi didn't need to finish. It was clear to all that they only had hours to find the Madhu. It could be in any ditch, any slope, inside any of the large trees or in a cave. Any ordinary corner of the valley could be concealing this valuable liquid.

'Aditya has almost departed for the day,' Idhika barked at them and quickly seated herself in the middle, readying for Atmayog. 'We need to divide up! Each of you, find a fly and carry yourself to a unique section of the valley. Drift into the right companion and chart your journey accordingly . . . Prithvi, identify exactly where you spotted the Preserver earlier this year in Aranyala. Go back there. Aman—accompany her—Atmayog to a squirrel and check the labyrinth of burrows around the spot. Maybe Sanaka is hiding it in an underground holding pit . . . Ujal, Atmayog into a sparrow and check the caves up in Rohini. And Fayza, why don't you take the lower canopies of Kalanag?' As for Idhika, she already knew where she was going.

Ujal unrolled the cottage's tapestry and sat down last. He closed his eyes. So did Prithvi, and then Aman. Fayza as well. Finally, Idhika also shut her eyes.

At that moment, not more than a ten-minute walk away, Sanaka too closed his eyes. Sitting in his hut, he popped a few sorrel leaves into his mouth and urged his mind to settle down. Today's Atmayog, he knew, would require even the best of him, one of the four divine Kumars. The task was one he rarely undertook, usually only a day before the Sabha and Samiti, the official gathering that inaugurated the Mahayatra. But despite its challenge, it had to be done: Madhu was vital to what he had set out to achieve.

It was known to all of Vanyasa that Sanaka and his three brothers were born four thousand years ago from the mind of Brahma. They wrote the Vedas at an early age, even before they had a chance to grow tall. To aid their pursuit of knowledge, the gods made sure that the Kumars remained children and never saw their curiosity wane. Ever since, they had been wandering the spiritual and material universes with the desire to learn and record the ways of the gods.

The four of them were tasked with assisting the goddess of Aranyala in safeguarding the tree churned from the Ocean of Milk. Sanaka was the only one who decided to stick by the Kalpavriksha. He represented his brothers at the Founding of Vanyasa as they left for the Himalayas. They would play their part in securing the knowledge that eventually birthed the oldest religion in the world: Hinduism.

So it was not surprising when, thousands of years later, Sanaka was given another task towards the same end. In the seventeenth century, at a time when many other religions had come into existence, Sanaka was urged to Atmayog into a group he was unlikely to be familiar with at all. He would be in an envoy representing Indian knowledge and texts at a European conclave organized by the Western world in what came to be known as Germany. There, the committee was to evaluate the New World's sources of knowledge in a contemporary globalized setting.

At that moment, monotheism—the idea of one god— was on the rise. When Sanaka arrived in Germany as the Indian delegate, the authorities and member countries had put up new restrictions for India to enter.

Sanaka ground his teeth whenever he remembered how they had first laughed at his explanation of the Vedic ways and then mocked the bonds between the sacred texts and religious life. They asked for 'scientific evidence', saying that the methodology used by India wasn't appropriate. Sanaka tried to show religious enlightenment as evidence of the knowledge, but the other delegates only saw enlightenment as a step backwards, not as an achievement.

The Indian delegate was laughed out of the setting, and he returned to Vanyasa humiliated. He sought counsel from his fellow yogis, but none of them wanted to take action against the non-believers.

'That's not what our faith directs us to do,' Aranyani had said upon Sanaka's return. 'Ours is the oldest religion for a reason. Its primary source of power is peace, and the ultimate aim is to understand yourself.'

'I know, but what they said is blasphemous, devi! How can you not be offended?' Sanaka said. 'They had an active agenda. How can you sit back when others besmirch the name of our Fathers?'

'Our Fathers don't need us to protect them,' Aranyani said. 'What they've done, what they stand for, cannot be undone by the mere words of a few men. True knowledge outlasts all time and hatred. Those in the West are only beginning to understand what our forefathers knew aeons ago. Forgive them, for they have much to learn.'

'So . . . we do nothing until all our gods are replaced, all our temples razed, all our yogis forgotten? Until there are no more Hindus left?' Sanaka asked.

'What do you want to do, Sanaka?' Aranyani asked.

'The fruit of the Kalpavriksha is for all agents of Indra to benefit from. We cannot be selfish. Atmayog should be weaponized by the plain dwellers to further the cause of Hinduism. India must be allowed to become once again a source of knowledge and power for both the subcontinent and the world . . . as it once used to be.'

'As noble as your plans may sound, they require the imposition of our faith upon others. They require bloodshed and manipulation. And that is what is so wrong, that is what makes it so antithetical to our belief system. Father would never approve of it. You cannot forget. All faiths must live in unison. In fact, how we treat others determines how our faith is viewed. Never forget that, brother Sanaka.'

It wasn't so much her words as the fear of Indra that had stopped Sanaka from taking any radical action back then. But as he had predicted, one by one, many foreign faiths gradually found their homes in India. A couple of centuries after he had spoken, in the 1800s, the country's colonization at the hands of the British further reduced the status of its sacred texts, until they devolved into myths and mere objects of study. According to him, the West had successfully caged the 'golden bird' by devaluing its scholarly work and focusing on the shortcomings of the subcontinent.

Even now, Sanaka's thoughts were crystal clear in his head. His loyalty to the gods was so resolute that he had had no qualms working alone over the past few decades. The only help he had was from the Alok brothers, his faithful adherents, who had only arrived in Vanyasa a few decades ago. 'The others don't deserve Madhu,' he'd told them.

Now, in his hut, a day before the Mahayatra, Sanaka adjusted his posture. His eyes remained shut. He searched for the first companion that would allow him to get to the animal he wanted to be.

All five Souls in Idhika's hut had already travelled as individual flies to their designated parts of the valley. Once within sight of their target, Prithvi and Aman made a further jump into squirrels. Ujal too jumped out of his fly self and into a sparrow, and Fayza into an eagle. Idhika, however, was still a fly, waiting to make her final jump.

She hovered above the vastness of Pandayam Tal, a buzzing black dot waiting to spot her eventual companion.

It was a while until a fish swam closer to the water's surface. Idhika caught the sun reflecting off its scales. *How different can it be?* she thought, and jumped.

Although she secured the connection instantly, Idhika should have waited to open her eyes; her first sight of the world before her was overwhelming and she instantly panicked. Breathing underwater was supposed to come naturally to her current form, but it felt like flailing around and clutching at straws. She felt weighed down in the swarm of movement around her. A snake swam past, and Idhika jerked around in shock. Rays of sunlight refracting through the water seemed to be mocking her. To steady herself, Idhika kicked her legs and tried to part the water with her arms, but her dull brown tilapia self only moved forward a few inches.

Minimal thinking was key to Idhika's survival, she realized. It took the sight of another fish—a yellow one—to distract her and allow her to breathe. This other fish uncharacteristically dove towards the lakebed, sending every creature in its path into a tizzy.

Unknown to both fishes was the knowledge of who possessed the other. As it happened, Sanaka had found himself a yellow catla. They passed each other as trains on opposite tracks, Sanaka making straight for his destination. Unlike his younger counterpart, he knew exactly where to go.

Idhika had no time to waste. The lake must have been at least a kilometre in width, but Idhika searched fast, diving just deep enough to scan the clusters of pickerelweed growing on the edges and even scouring ditches covered by dead logs or reeds.

Maybe it was her ineptitude as an underwater navigator, but she felt extremely sluggish. In fact, swarms of tiny fish and worms swam all around her at great speed. Loose strands of algae danced in the water as she passed. Even the water snails, some pink and some black, could be seen moving on the lakebed. *No, wait! Snails don't move that fast.* She had to look again. They were, it seemed, being pushed away by something.

The snails on the lakebed had alerted Idhika to the large blue hole she now saw clearly. When she tried nearing it, gushes of warm water pushed her back. The pressure varied in areas, so she had to try different angles of approach. Its western edge had a sharp cut that slowed the water, so she swam from that side and managed to close in on it, enough to grab on to the edge with her left fin. A quick second and one slender thrust into the hole, and her thin, slippery body slid into a dark marine cavern further under the lake, where the waters were calm and discernibly warmer. *Could it be?* Idhika thought, remembering what her father had told her years ago about the springs at the bottom of the lake.

Sanaka, by then, had already made his way to the lowest point of Vanyasa, the trench in Pandayam Tal. He had entered the same blue hole and slowly moved to the bottom where the springs were.

Idhika, far from being as practiced, proceeded hesitantly. She eventually reached the springs, and behind them spotted a ditch with a small opening. Since it seemed to be the only way forward, she did not wait long before entering it. A few metres in and the water started receding. *Is that the surface I see?* Before too long, as the brown tilapia, she poked her eyes out from the water to find herself in a cavernous underground chamber. It was a pocket of air at the bottom of the lake. There was a hut's worth of dry land, most of it hidden in the shadows of cave walls. But what she could not miss, deep within the darkest of the dark corners, was a faintly iridescent golden light shooting out of an open lid. Idhika gaped, struggling to breathe out of the water, as her eyes adjusted to the absence of light.

There they were. Around fifteen barrels in the shape of gigantic kamandalus—and one of them afforded her a peek at its contents. *Madhu!*

At that moment, although the fish couldn't possibly weep, somewhere inside, Idhika did break down; her nose did twitch before her cheeks swelled and eyes filled with tears. The burden Aranyani had put on her as the Eka had been lifted. *No Mahayatra!* She was relieved, ironically breathing easy for the first time as an underwater creature. She could feel remnants of her old self again, after so long. She couldn't wait to tell the matriarch.

But the relief dissipated in a few minutes and a simmering hatred began in her. Looking at the barrels of Madhu—a confirmation of Sanaka's deceit—the yogini felt anger like she never had before. One man, Sanaka, had taken it upon himself to deceive his own. He was trying to exploit the place that was home to her, and home to all her brothers and sisters. He was responsible for letting all those intruders in. Was it not enough that he was kidnapping Souls from the plains and forcing them to face the perils of the Mahayatra? *All for Madhu?* He had even separated her from her father.

But he can return home now! She imagined Rishi Ajan living close to her in the resident cottages, resuming his scribe duties. Idhika couldn't wait to go back and tell all her friends that she had actually found Madhu. *Will they even believe that it is* here?

It was indeed ingenious of Sanaka to have hidden it away from the reaches of Aranyani, far from the forest of Aranyala. And even then, if someone did manage to find it, like she had, there was no way to reach and extricate the barrels. Idhika opened and closed her eyes, trying to find another companion: an ant, spider or even a bat in the cave. She wanted to check exactly how many barrels Sanaka had stolen. But no hosts responded to her call. *How does he do it? Get to it? There's no animal to jump to. How in the three* loks *does Sanaka access, let alone move around, these large barrels? What does he plan to do with all this Madhu?*

Sanaka had entered the cave only a few seconds before Idhika's arrival, and without wasting time, after a 'Namahkrita', pushed his soul out of the yellow catla to enter the only organism in that cave: Huhu, his ultimate companion.

Vanyasa's dwellers only ever imagined the crocodile when told the story of Airavata, but having lived it, Sanaka was well aware of Huhu's existence in the flesh. The beast's powerful jaws and webbed toes vexed Sanaka and always made him uneasy as a companion. Its massive, plaited tail had a burn mark running across it where Indra's bolt had struck. Extending to an astonishing size of twenty feet, the animal was a beast of the water so primal that even a son of Brahma questioned his rank in the universe.

Sanaka lay on his belly, within the beast, hidden and unmoving in the shadow of the barrels. That was when he saw a brown tilapia uncharacteristically poking its head out of the water. Despite the fear that the Sabha and Samiti would discover his ploy, Sanaka was only momentarily fazed. That was because a plan had formed in his head. The first step was to slowly lift his tail, all hundred kilograms of it, and adjust the open lid of the barrel. And the second, of course, was to reward his companion with a much-deserved meal.

But before he could pounce on the fish, the tilapia was lost, having sunk back down into the water. Idhika was dying to tell her friends. She left behind the springs, darted through the blue hole and raced to the surface of Pandayam Tal. She flung herself out of the water with much speed— in fact, enough speed to emerge considerably and catch the sight of an eagle up in the sky. Before the fish hit the lake's water, Idhika's soul had already jumped to the eagle. That was how she made her way towards the resident huts, where she eventually found all four of her friends around her mortal body.

With her face dug into her knees, Idhika sobbed and repeatedly murmured, 'I found it . . . I found it. No Mahayatra . . . none of it!' Ujal gave her a massive hug. When she could finally speak, Idhika revealed to them all that she had seen. Prithvi, Aman, Ujal and Fayza seemed to find themselves frozen, only their eyes moving to search for assurance in one another.

Then their bodies slumped. Ujal broke into a burst of shaky laughter. '*This* was the request I'd made to Lord Indra at the temple today, and he heard my pleas.' He was filled with the pleasing thought that he would be joining the ranks of immortals in Vanyasa without going through the final test. *Mother and Father can be with us now, as part of Vanyasa,* he thought.

But unknown to him, a slow smile spread across his sister's face as she mentally charted a rough plan to find Bhavesh instead.

'Say that again, Idhika,' Fayza demanded. 'Are they really going to cancel it?' She remembered how distraught she was at being separated from her family and was glad that no new Souls of Samsara in the upcoming decades would have to go through the same pain. Her hands fell into Aman's.

Aman, eyes closed, let out a deep breath and nodded. 'If Sanaka has been helping the Preservers and he is capable of what you've just said, Idhika, I'm sure he had something to do with my father's death—or at least he knows more about it.' He urged Idhika to instantly go to Aranyani so that she could talk to the Sabha and Samiti.

But the longer they discussed it, the more they questioned the wisdom of immediately revealing what they knew. 'No!' Idhika decided eventually. 'If Sanaka finds out, he may move the Madhu and even relocate the Preservers before tomorrow's meeting of the Sabha and Samiti. We've come so far, and now we must be patient. It is in front of all the villagers that we will take him down! That way, he and all those aiding him will have nowhere to run. Once it is over, the journey north will be cancelled, and Father can return to the valley, allowing the real sinner of Madhu to get what he deserves.'

They talked about how Idhika would waylay the ceremony the next day and worked on perfecting the speech for the councils to hear. Idhika warned, 'Do not apprise any of the other Souls, no matter how scared they may be right now. It's too risky. Make sure you are not smiling when we go for the final meal of the day. And Aman, roll up your belongings for the journey, as you would, before you sleep. We don't want anyone to learn of the plan prematurely.'

All was done as the Eka had asked. After dinner, without any more discussions, the five of them retired content to their respective huts. They all slept, nervously tossing and turning, as expected of the Souls that night. Aman couldn't wait to demand answers from Sanaka about his father. He wanted nothing more.

After the tilapia had left the underwater cavern, Sanaka followed the fish as best he could. His soul had left Huhu and re-entered the catla. Eventually, he found himself at the resident cottages and then the Eka's hut. He hung about, an inconspicuous sparrow, quietly listening to the Eka and her friends plot his downfall the next day. When the five Souls left for dinner, Sanaka did not head back to his mortal body in his hut. Instead, he made straight for Aranyala.

Later that night, a lal bicchu, bright red in its tail, eyes and body, emerged from the forest and crawled to the five Souls' huts one by one for the third step of Sanaka's plan.

26

Sabha and Samiti

He initially thought he was in a dream, so he blinked a few times to be sure.

What Aman saw, through the haze in his eyes, was a bright white land before him behind a thin curtain of mist. He was walking, but he couldn't feel much—neither his toes nor fingers—other than an unusual weight on his back.

'Who has the neer?' It was Aarti's voice somewhere near him, but he couldn't make out more than a silhouette.

The weight lifted from his back.

'Oh, Indra! Already finished half of it?' Aarti said, shaking the kamandalu before taking a sip and handing it back to him.

It took a while for Aman's eyes to adjust. Fresh sleet covered his feet with each step.

Aarti seemed to be looking back at him pitifully. 'Yes, yes,' she said, 'my feet are feeling it too, or rather not feeling much of anything. And the wind is picking up, which can't be good.'

From a bird's-eye view, he was no more than a speck on a wide canvas.

'What sort of meditation is she in?' Aarti asked, pointing ahead. 'I understand that only she can find the Himalayan bee and stop us from going astray . . . But she hasn't responded to one question properly the entire day. I mean, don't we need to find neer and fruits before anything? Aditya is almost gone for the day, and the Eka has no plan for a fire. I'm telling you, boy, we will not last the night.'

No . . . it cannot be! The hairs on his body stood on end. His eyes widened, searching frantically. Around him, right above the crests of the mountains in all directions, was a green light. Further up, the sky turned an ominous blue. The trees were scarce and their leaves scarcer. It was a barren sight.

The Souls walked in a long, single file in the snow-laden land, the Eka right in front. Yuvan followed Idhika, and behind him was Dhara, with Payal. Aman and Aarti appeared to be lagging at least a hundred metres behind, but they were by no means the slowest. Jagrav and Savitri trudged along after them, and at the tail end of the contingent was Fayza, with Ujal and Prithvi.

Other than the kamandalu, Aman found a small sword hanging from his waist. A loincloth wrapped as a dhoti was the only garment on his body. His wavy hair, which had been unbrushed for a year, looked heavily sprinkled with snowflakes.

The Mahayatra has begun, Aman thought as Aarti continued complaining, something about how the Eka was leading them east, towards the Mountain Pishachus.

'Enough, Aarti! Wait!' Aman snapped at her. If his suspicions were accurate, all their hard work had been undone. *But how?*

He had to talk to Idhika. The last thing he remembered was going to bed the night before the Sabha and Samiti. *The Madhu at the bottom of the lake? The Mahayatra was supposed to be cancelled!* Nothing else after that could be prodded into his memory. He quickened his pace and kept going until he passed an irritable Payal and Dhara. Overtaking them, he soon fell in stride with Yuvan and the Eka.

'Idhika!'

'Yes, Aman?' she said and kept marching.

'What happened?' he barked.

'We'll find Madhu in the east,' she said.

'STOP!'

She didn't. 'We cannot, no matter how much your legs hurt. Remember what Acharya Ashwini said: we must always be on the move.'

'But you already found the Madhu!' Aman jumped in front of her.

She froze. 'Madhu . . .' Her face drained of colour as if she'd seen a ghost. 'I did, didn't I?' Her hands hid her face, and she fell where she had stood. After what felt like an eternity but was in reality no more than a couple of seconds, she writhed about in the shin-deep snow, looking at the tall peaks all around her and the Souls trailing in her wake.

'What are you talking . . .' Yuvan said.

'What happened . . .?' Aman asked. 'What happened to the plan, Idhika?'

'Sanaka . . . how?' Idhika was stumped. A heavy burden seemed to overshadow her once again as she panicked and examined her ankle.

Aman cursed himself for thinking things would actually work out. But before the extent of the situation dawned on him, Idhika had broken into tears. It was very unlike her. In fact, it was not expected at all of the Eka, who was tasked with leading the Mahayatra. But as Idhika sat in the snow, holding her ankle, she pointed sombrely at a sting mark. 'Lal bicchu,' she whispered to Aman, not caring for the presence of Yuvan, but well before Aarti, Payal and Dhara reached them. 'Check your ankle,' she asked him.

'Your legs couldn't have given up so early, Eka. On your feet!' Aarti ordered.

'Idhika!' Prithvi arrived only a second later from behind, having also recovered from the effects of the lal bicchu. 'We've been cheated. I don't know how but the wretched Sanaka has deceived us all! Let's just return and tell everyone of his mutiny. None of us needs to take on this impossible task!'

'What is going on?' Aarti grabbed the hilt of her sword. Yuvan and Savitri too stepped up. Jagrav didn't. He sat down and looked like he was done with walking for life.

'Put that back, Aarti, and listen for once,' Aman said. He looked at Fayza and started to tell the six who were unaware of Sanaka's machinations—Yuvan, Jagrav, Savitri, Aarti, Payal and Dhara—about how he and Idhika had first found out about the Preservers, which had led them to the discovery of Sanaka's stores of Madhu at the bottom of Pandayam Tal.

Despite her mental collapse, Idhika had to wipe her tears and get up. Hopping about to keep the soles of her feet from getting frostbite, she urged the others to continue walking while Aman filled them in on the details. Would they actually believe him? Fayza, Ujal and Prithvi piped in now and then with a point or two that Aman had missed, but the six others looked highly sceptical of whatever they had heard. The five Souls had never really made an effort to include the others, and it was a bit late to expect their trust at once. However, the sight of the identical lal bicchu marks on their ankles did a lot to convince them.

'And when I was at the bottom of the lake,' Idhika, still sniffling, cut in, 'it must have been then. There's no other way . . . Sanaka must have learnt that I found the Madhu. But how . . .? I searched for a companion, any sign of a living being down there in the underwater cave, and there was nothing.' A shiver ran down her spine, and she continued with her train of thought. 'The lal bicchu must have stung us, all five of us, in our sleep the day before the Sabha . . . When did we leave the valley?'

'Around noon, after the Sabha and Samiti this morning,' Yuvan said. Savitri looked at her watch.

'This morning? Oh, so it was only yesterday . . .' Idhika asked.

'And the five of you chose to keep it from us?' Aarti said. '. . . take the matter of our lives into your hands. Thought it best to decide for all?'

'This makes so much sense!' Dhara said. 'A month ago, I was looking for an isolated location to practise my Atmayog, but Sanaka's lackeys, Ghanisht and Ekram, wouldn't let me anywhere near Pandayam Tal.'

'Oh, of course,' Savitri added. 'I too had requested the Assembly for old palm leaves detailing the previous Mahayatras but was denied.'

'What is he doing with so much Madhu? Getting high on it?' Yuvan asked. 'Why is he stealing it? Why not come up here to collect *all* the Madhu that he needs?'

'I don't know why he's taken such blasphemous steps,' Idhika said. 'But finding Madhu is only possible through the boon of Indra. The lord passes on knowledge of the bees' location to the Eka and the Eka alone. This is why Sanaka needs us to get it.'

'All's not lost yet!' Prithvi pointed out again. 'We can simply return and expose the truth.'

A few heads nodded at this. Fayza said, 'But we need evidence. One of us should Atmayog back home and check before we turn around—'

'We cannot act in such haste,' Idhika said, looking at them with renewed confidence. 'In such cold temperatures, it is easy to forget to think. So we must proceed with care this time around. I will Atmayog to the valley and check, but it will be a time-consuming process. Firstly, will someone explain the events that transpired this morning to the five of us who have no memories since last night? What exactly did Sanaka say at the Sabha and Samiti?'

'Jagrav rarely forgets a thing,' Savitri said. 'He should tell it as best he can.'

These were crucial details so the Souls stopped walking and looked at Jagrav.

'Umm . . . okay,' he said, blowing at his blue fingers. 'I shall start as I remember, upon first light this morning, from the threshold of my hut—'

'Yogis!' the Eka said. 'On second thought, this is no place for revelations, in the middle of an open field, with nothing but mountains looking down on us as watchtowers.'

With the effects of the lal bicchu now dissipated, Idhika realized that she had led the eleven this far east, to the middle of the country, from where Chayan and his Pishachus were not far. She instantly changed course and asked them to power on, reminding them that the swifter they trudged, the warmer the soles of their feet would get.

After ten minutes of swiftly moving westwards, Idhika called for a break. She put her arm on Aman's shoulders and began to deliver instructions to all: 'Aditya's taken almost all light with him. In the remaining hour, there's much to be accomplished. Or truly our dresses will be brittle by night. Phoo!' She caught her breath for a moment. 'Gather around, all, I need your eyes, all twenty of them. As we continue west, look out for three things. First, a hollow land, hidden if possible, or a grove—any place that will shield us from the winds at night. Second, tinder, pine sticks, firewood. Anything dry. Wet things won't burn well and will make unwanted smoke. And third, large rocks, which we can heat by the fire and use to keep warm later.'

They set out again, faster, for now they had a purpose. Occasionally they would spread out a little too wide, and Idhika had to stop the journey to let everyone regroup. The fruits and neer they had would hopefully last them the night.

An hour after the sun had left, while searching for firewood, Aarti, Payal and Dhara found a thicket of branches. Behind it, the land dipped slightly into a trench. In that hollow space, only the westerlies were felt, and any other wind went past above them, off the jutted land.

'This is the place we must nurture,' Idhika announced, the numbness now seeping into her veins. 'I feel calmer here in this ditch. Let's begin by clearing the snow to make a bed for a fire. But to do so, use your feet alone because you will require the dexterity of your hands to break the firewood later.'

'I need a minute. My feet are burning!' Aman sat down, like Mata Kritika had taught him, and tucked his feet into the insides of his thighs, the warmest area of his body. This allowed him to meditate briefly and internally heat himself. He soon felt the blood coursing through his legs. Aman realized how much Vanyasa had changed him. A little over a year ago, he had been layering himself in sweaters and shawls to battle the January cold in Delhi.

Once the snow was cleared from their chosen spot, Idhika placed all the twigs and pine sticks to make a bed for the fire. Then, she collected a few bark shavings and dry grass—tinder—and shaped these materials like a huge green cotton ball. With a large branch, using her hard nails, she cut a V-shaped notch into it, and tucked the branch under her feet. The tinder was placed beside it. Picking up another stick, she placed it into the V-shaped notch and started spinning it, rolling the stick between her palms. After almost a minute, the friction brought on a thin glow from the notch. Sparks!

Aarti rushed to pick up the tinder and place it over the embers. Idhika gently blew on it and laid it on the bed of twigs.

In the valley, fire had always been blue. But the rocks embraced the odd redness of this fire, which brought to Idhika's mind the lal bicchu. 'Now tell us, Jagrav,' she said with a deep sigh.

The wind had started to pick up. The rest of the Souls gathered around Jagrav, gradually finding comfort in their island of heat. In fact, it was also an island of light, for, in the moonless night, the surroundings far from the fire were pitch black.

Jagrav pinched the scar on his temple, from when Payal had punched him. 'It was at dawn today that the Sabha and Samiti convened. All the chiefs and over a hundred Vanyasis had gathered by the Assembly to see off this decade's batch of recruits.'

He paused and stood up, away from the fire. Then he crouched to the ground, appearing shorter than he was, and started recounting Sanaka's address to the crowd: 'There, on a pedestal, he stood, probably because that was the only way he could have been seen.' He tapped his foot in frustration, imitating Sanaka, who always did that as a signal indicating everyone should settle down. 'As all in Vanyasa know,' Jagrav said in a low voice, mimicking Sanaka, 'our reserves of Madhu are running low.'

Idhika gritted her teeth while Savitri started handing out pears and apples. Jagrav continued in the same voice, 'And this has put the divine tree and Atmayog both in jeopardy.

Over the years, Madhu has served the purpose of some of our most revered rituals, and without it, Vanyasa will wither. The valley's continued existence is a testament to the fact that the Mahayatra, the most ancient of our rituals, has never failed before.'

'For *this* honour, the honour of coming to the valley as a Soul, cannot be purchased. The role of the Eka, the torchbearer, is not a position afforded to those who covet it. Instead, the lord offers it to the Soul that has it in their destiny. And every decade, the Eka has led the trek up to the ancient mountains as a mandatory service to him. It's the Eka's duty.' Jagrav paused to face Idhika. 'As it was once your mother's, Child of the Valley.'

The wind was starting to draw heat out of their resting area. Idhika picked up a rock by the fire and tucked it under her feet for warmth. Jagrav said, 'Now that I think about it, Aranyani did look exceedingly worried. And the five of you, Idhika, Fayza, Aman, Prithvi and Ujal, were standing together, not saying anything. Aman, you looked like you were sleepwalking. Sanaka went on, "Many brave yogis fulfil their purpose by taking on this treacherous journey laden with difficulties. Some are taken by the cold, some fall and feed the ridges, while the weary terrain makes a few perish. But the Eka's guidance and instincts will not only help you find Madhu but also keep the Mountain Pishachus at bay."'

As fresh flakes of snow started to rain down on them, Aarti, who already knew the events of the morning, stifled a yawn.

'"Excess weight will not be taken and only the necessities will be laden upon you. Minimum weapons for you so you can move fast and keep yourself secret from Chayan. If you return empty-handed—as per tradition—you will find the gates of Vanyasa locked. Madhu alone will grant you entry." Then Sanaka mentioned how the duration of the journey could vary between a couple of days to almost a month, depending on the sharpness of the leader. When he finished, and no questions were put forth, he said, "Don't forget, the journey lies within," and left, with Aranyani following him. We stowed our luggage into these cloth bags, the villagers accompanied us till the gates in the Seven Hills, singing the Song of the Valley and its many variations, and bid us farewell. We followed Idhika as she ventured forward.'

When Jagrav was done, all the Souls looked at Idhika for a response. She stood up, lost in thought, and began walking away from the fire, into the dark by herself. Aman thought to accompany her but knew she couldn't possibly stray far from the heat it was radiating.

And sure enough, she was back within minutes. 'I've been thinking,' she said, 'it is not a good sign that Sanaka delivered his speech this morning with so much confidence. Now, listen, do not let your eyes wander from the surroundings. Guard me. It will take me a while to go home and come back.' She sat down.

When Idhika fell into Atmayog, something told Aman to keep an eye on Aarti. He sat beside the meditative Eka, in front of the fire, alert to anything Aarti might pull. Savitri and Ujal quietly munched on dried fruits and raw vegetables next to him, each wondering privately where Idhika could be, which companion she had assumed the form of and, most importantly, what she would find when she reached home.

After a while, Aman nudged Savitri, who instantly pulled out a cloth with rolling materials from her bag. He pulled the sheet of paper and spread the green substance on it evenly. Then, pinching its two ends, and with a slick lick of the gum, he twisted his wrist while running his fingers along the vertical hem of the paper. It bonded to become the only thing that could let him digest his meal.

Aman used the bonfire before him to light the joint. As he took a puff, he looked at the smoke streaming out of the cannabis stick, almost bidding it to solve all his problems. 'Hah!' he laughed at Savitri, his voice nearly as buoyant as the smoke, 'Maybe all this is a rite of passage for us. To see what we are capable of, to take us to the edge of our skills, both mentally and physically.'

'Yeah, maybe,' Savitri said, taking the joint from Aman's shaking fingers. But, unlike her friend, she siphoned off the smoke elegantly, as if the joint was part of her hand.

Fayza eyed them as Savitri and Aman talked.

'So, did you go down into the lake yesterday with the Eka?' Savitri asked Aman. 'How did Sanaka find out? Was he in the underwater cave with Idhika?'

Before Aman could answer, he heard faint sobbing beside him. Idhika was back. She hadn't even announced herself. '. . . he moved it all . . .'

Everyone crowded around her.

'He moved it . . . and he must have asked the Preservers to leave.'

'Good going, Idhika,' Yuvan said sarcastically, throwing his half-eaten apple into the fire.

Ujal hugged her. 'It's not your fault.'

It dawned on Aman that they had missed the only chance to set right a bunch of wrongs. To save themselves from this journey. To force answers out of Sanaka that would explain his father's disappearance. To get a chance to see his mother anytime soon.

They all knew they needed concrete proof to convince the Sabha and Samiti of Sanaka's wrongdoing—as things stood, it was just their word against his. If they were to return without Madhu, theirs would be the first batch to have failed without even trying. They would not be allowed entry to Vanyasa and instead face consequences none of them wanted to ponder at the moment. They would have to continue with the Mahayatra.

WOOOOOOSH! Prithvi recognized the sound. Maybe that's why she registered it first. A thin, sharp whistle. THUD!

A spear emerged from somewhere above and pierced the top of Yuvan's head, felling him. The others watched in horror as the spearhead emerged from under his chin, having pierced his skull all the way through. His eyes remained open, and his gaze was hooked on to Aman, who was the closest and leapt towards Yuvan. But the boy was beyond anyone's help.

Prithvi dipped her arrow in the fire. Jagrav lifted his gada. Aarti's sheath was now barren. Dhara's spear was poised, and Payal heaved her mace. They all closed in to form a circle around Yuvan's corpse, looking out into the dark, ready for what was to come.

27

Chayan

Prithvi was terrified. How could she not be? As for everyone else, the visuals in front of her were too awful to comprehend immediately. But while her friends yearned for safety alone, she had far more on her mind. Her journey extended beyond the Mahayatra—to the plains, to Bhavesh.

Did that make her selfish, to not worry about her family instead? Maybe. But she didn't care. It was Bhavesh she missed. He who had introduced her to this powerful, arresting feeling called love. And it was he who was uppermost in her mind in this time of need.

Lub-dub . . . Lub-dub . . .

Without a right thumb, Prithvi tucked between her index and middle fingers the trembling arrow as she stood, part of the tight circle around Yuvan's body and the small fire beside it. Jagrav's gada was awfully close to her face while she looked out into the dark from where the spear had arrived. The thick curtain of blackness all around them overpowered the little illumination from the fire.

This is it . . . the test of all my training, the Tritiya Archer told herself.

They waited, ready to strike at any noise. But there was only stillness. It was quiet. Too quiet.

In fact, the stony silence was so prevalent, so loud, that an imaginary drumming—or maybe it was the Souls' collective hearts—started to take over. *Lub-dub.* Prithvi's heart may have been a war drum. *Is it just in my head?*

But it got louder and louder. *Lub-dub . . . Lub-dub . . . Lub-dub.*

'AAAARRRRGGHHHHHH!' Jagrav burst out of their little pocket of light into the unknown, swinging his gada frenetically.

Someone should have gone after him, but they all stayed rooted to their spots.

Almost a minute later, Jagrav reappeared, his gada lazily dragging behind him. 'No enemies here, that's for sure.'

What? How can that be? Prithvi had only just turned to the Eka when she saw Idhika's jaw drop. 'Keep me guarded!' She sat down and closed her eyes.

It didn't take long. After a few seconds, Idhika's Deh stopped glowing and she opened her eyes. 'Look up. Towards that mountain in the north above our heads. Do you see them?'

A snowy peak towered ahead of them in the distance. Prithvi could see tiny figures of what looked like a bunch of men, but in the darkness she couldn't discern much more. *How many are there?* Her grip was firm on the drawn bow. She finished her prayer and whispered to her arrow the final word, 'Ekalavya', before firing towards the mountain.

The arrow shot up towards the men on top and burnt a bright red. However, before it could reach the men and fully illuminate their area, it was met with an opposing spear that derailed its trajectory. In that split second, however, the Souls caught sight of twenty, maybe even thirty faces. And the faces did not belong to any ordinary humans. It was a pack of kirtimukhas.

Prithvi almost dropped her teer-kaman. 'No!' She reached into her cloth bag and shoved more arrows into her quiver.

Only half the Souls assembled there had ever faced a kirtimukha before. Aarti, Payal, Dhara, Jagrav and Savitri were not part of the group that had ventured to the Dronagiri woods to rescue Prithvi. Idhika recalled how that kirtimukha had easily overpowered five Souls and an acharya. *Can our months of training give us a chance this time?*

Idhika started shouting instructions. They had little time.

'How many do you think they are?' Prithvi asked her.

Idhika could see the pack of kirtimukhas stampeding down the snowy mountain, heading towards the trench, towards them. 'Not enough time,' she told them. 'Remember what Acharya Ashwini told us. We cannot reason with these barbaric beasts.'

Prithvi began chanting a mantra and fired an arrow that shot up into the air towards the kirtimukhas. It eventually descended between the running herd of monsters—blowing up like a bomb and pushing two bodies off the ridges of the mountain. However, the other kirtimukhas barely noticed what seemed like a minor loss to them.

'What do we do?' Savitri asked.

'Run? Hide?' Aarti questioned.

'We cannot possibly take on so many of them. Quickly!' Idhika looked at them all. 'We have to invoke Agni. That is our only hope.'

'What?' Aarti asked.

'Aranyani taught me. Just listen!' Idhika snapped. 'First, we have to draw a Swastika on the earth around the fire.' She rushed to grab a loose stick from the tinder and started to mark out lines in the snow. 'And to complete the invocation, four of us will have to Atmayog around the fire to attack them, in the form of any companions we can find. The remaining six of us will face the beasts with our weapons. We need to decide who the four Atmayogis are *now* so they can search for companions as soon as possible. Hurry!'

The marauding contingent of kirtimukhas was getting closer and closer, only moments away from besieging the trench. No one, not even Aarti, questioned the Eka's instructions.

'Who are the four Atmayogis, then?' Aarti asked and instantly stepped away from the fire. Payal and Dhara, on the other hand, sat down right beside it, ready to Atmayog.

'We need two more,' Idhika said. Everyone knew that sitting in Atmayog was the graver of the two options. 'The archers need to decide quickly among themselves!'

Prithvi looked at her brother. 'Ujal, why don't you fight? I'll sit.'

Ujal wouldn't ever let that happen. He would always feel responsible for her. 'No! Let me sit. Don't worry. I'll find myself a strong companion. Plus, between the two of us, you're the better archer. We need you to protect those of us in Atmayog.'

Everyone looked at Prithvi. Her brother was choosing to put himself in danger. He would be sitting in a deep state of meditation, unable to react to whatever went on around him. Prithvi knew she couldn't take the time to argue and convince him; she had to act fast. 'Okay,' she said reluctantly, taking out the Nagsutra from her finger. 'Put this on. It's the only way I'm letting you do this.'

Ujal took the amulet willingly and sat down beside the fire, with Payal and Dhara.

Then everyone's eyes turned to Aman. He knew he was no warrior, unlike Fayza. And Idhika, Aarti, Prithvi, Savitri and Jagrav—the best fighters among them. But before he could volunteer to be one of the Atmayogis, Idhika asked, 'Aman, why don't you sit down?'

Here goes nothing, loser, Aman told himself as he took a seat beside the fire. Payal and Dhara were already lost in their yog. Ujal's forearm was yet to start glowing. Aman, too, closed his eyes to search for a companion. The six who had chosen to stay in the conscious world surrounded the Atmayogis, standing in a circle.

With the Swastika drawn and the Souls in formation, Idhika initiated the final step in invoking Agni. She turned to watch the fire between the Souls and started humming, softly at first, but when it became audible to the others, they realized that Idhika was in fact reciting an intricate chant. The Eka's voice appeared to vibrate and made the flames go wild. The fire reached higher, until parts of it started to linger in the air. Soon, a yellow aura started to materialize above them. It first grew in patches, all around the Souls, and then the gaps began to be filled. When it finished, they found themselves inside a translucent solid dome; it had a light-yellow tinge.

Time was up. It was the roar of the kirtimukhas that they heard first. Then came a flurry of spears shooting out from the darkness. The spears struck the dome but left hardly a scratch.

Idhika looked at Fayza. Fayza looked at Prithvi.

Prithvi took a deep breath and looked up to the sky through the dome. She noticed a bright star, the name of which she did not know. She only hoped that Bhavesh, wherever he was, would look at the same star sometime that night.

Finally, the beasts emerged, in all their fury, from the blackness of the land. Fire glowed in the large metal rings around their necks. Prithvi could take on one, maybe two if luck was on her side. But there were at least thirty of them, elbowing one another, repeatedly pounding against the dome or trying to rip it open using their spears. Agni's protection held strong.

The kirtimukhas were of many sizes, but all of them had white skin. Only when one of them, no bigger than a well-built human, climbed over the dome, right above Prithvi, did she realize that the white skin was in fact a garment fashioned out of goatskin. The kirtimukha's eyeballs popped out and two small horns jutted out through his hair.

The siege continued. Only once did the kirtimukhas pause their efforts to penetrate the dome, when they reverentially bowed their heads as another of their kind showed up. Sporting a long forked beard, long nails that looked like a set of daggers and a smile that put his decayed teeth on full display—this was surely Chayan. He stood by himself as the kirtimukhas resumed their attempts.

A group of five kirtimukhas who were working on a particular section of the dome managed to make a thin crack in it. Overjoyed, they stepped up the force and attacked the area repeatedly until just enough of the glass-like film broke off.

One eager kirtimukha tried to squeeze in. However, as soon as he stuck his head inside, Prithvi fired her loaded bow and the beast fell away, outside the dome. The rest of the kirtimukhas swooped into the gap he left and banded together to keep chipping away at it.

Their patient work was rewarded—a large fragment dissolved into nothing, allowing the beasts to begin squeezing in, one at a time. The first to enter was a particularly bulky specimen. Idhika and Fayza took charge to make sure the kirtimukha wouldn't reach the four meditating Atmayogis.

Fayza slashed at the behemoth and tore a cut into his left leg.

'ARGHHH!' He bellowed and kicked Fayza in the jaw with the same leg. She flew backwards and fell beside Aman. Meanwhile, Prithvi had launched an arrow that grazed the kirtimukha's leg. He resorted to swiping at Jagrav with a gada—the beast had grabbed it from Jagrav. Frustrated, he brought the gada down on his massive knee and broke it into two. He lifted Jagrav into the air, but just then, Prithvi's second arrow found its mark. It caught the kirtimukha in his heart, and he fell a few steps away from Dhara in Atmayog.

Aarti, Idhika and Savitri now had to turn their attention to another, bigger kirtimukha that was trying to steal into the dome from the same gap. When he grabbed Savitri by the hair, dragging her closer, she took a moment to absorb the pain, and then spun around and jammed her spear into the kirtimukha's eye.

But as soon as these two beasts were killed, another pair broke in. The Souls fought them valiantly, their only aim to protect the four Atmayogis sitting in their midst.

And it paid off. A few minutes later, Ujal, in the form of a brown Himalayan wolf, appeared outside. The wolf moved with great speed and bit the ankle of a kirtimukha, who tried to chase it away. Both wolf and kirtimukha disappeared into the darkness surrounding the hemisphere.

He never returned. Only the wolf did, and it started searching for yet another ankle to bite.

Not long after that, a huge black bear charged into the scrum of kirtimukhas still outside the dome and, together with the wolf, took on three of them. Dhara and Ujal, bear and wolf, fought side by side.

Back in the dome, without his gada, Jagrav came up with a plan. 'I'll keep trying to distract them while you take a shot. Just aim away from my head,' Jagrav told Prithvi. He ran to the kirtimukha and swept at his leg. The beast fumbled, extending his arms and exposing his chest momentarily, and before he could stabilize himself one of Prithvi's arrows caught him in the belly.

The plan seemed to be working. As the kirtimukhas flowed in, they found their numbers had dwindled. The Souls had killed almost ten out of the thirty.

Outside the hemisphere, however, the tide had turned. Chayan's men had begun tormenting the animals the Souls had taken the shape of. When Payal arrived as a wild yak, she joined the bear and the wolf, but it hardly made a difference. 'Where is Aman?' Fayza asked, ducking, as a kirtimukha flung his spear towards her. 'Where is his companion?'

Elated that kirtimukhas had died by her sword, Aarti walked up to the edge of the dome and looked out through the translucent glass. In a fit of idiocy, she waved at Chayan, and grunted and jumped to provoke the kirtimukhas.

That was when Chayan raised his hand. All the kirtimukhas stopped in their tracks. Chayan whispered something into the ear of a slender member of his army. That kirtimukha nodded at his leader's words, marched up to the gap in the dome, and forced his way in with a strength that belied his frame.

Prithvi watched on, horrified, as the kirtimukha moved with intent. He pulled out his spear and held it horizontally, using it as a shield to block Fayza's sword. The lean opponent seemed least interested in fighting back.

'He's going for the Atmayogis!' Idhika shouted, advancing towards him, ready to deliver a blow, but the beast's spear deflected her force. She slashed her sword in a circle, swung left and then right, but the kirtimukha continued to advance. He seemed to see Prithvi's arrow coming towards him and easily side-stepped her. Jagrav tried to jump on him, but the beast threw the boy to the ground. Aarti had already backed off, but the kirtimukha dove at her. His spear somehow managed to catch her legs, making her lose her footing.

After having dealt with her, the kirtimukha continued to walk until he was within the circle of Atmayogis. He went to the fire, and kicked and stomped on the burning wood with little care for his feet. The flames withered and sparks rose. Black smoke filled the dome. Using his heel, the kirtimukha stamped out the last of the fire, and the yellow tint around them started to crack.

In a matter of moments, the dome had shattered. No more protection. They were sitting ducks. The kirtimukhas beat their chests in exhilaration and slowly drew near the Souls.

Fayza ran to shield the vulnerable Atmayogis. Just then, the wolf, bear and yak stopped fighting, and the Deh on the arms of Aman, Dhara, Payal and Ujal stopped glowing. They had severed their connections to the animals and now opened their eyes, readying their weapons.

It was now ten Souls against twenty kirtimukhas. But as the hideous beasts drew near them, Aman, who had fear written all over his face, prepared to flee the scene. 'Where are you going?!' Prithvi shouted as Aman ran into the dark before any of the kirtimukhas could catch him. Fayza couldn't believe it. But she had no time to give it another thought.

Things came to a boil. Without human companions, the three animals were scrambling around wildly. Prithvi spotted the yak running amok, slamming into both kirtimukhas and her friends.

All at once, Prithvi felt a gust of wind near her, and a sharp pain shot up her arm. Her bow fell. She turned around to see a deep gash in her shoulder and a kirtimukha standing next to her with a long, curving sword.

It was the kirtimukha who had had trouble squeezing into the dome because he was one of the biggest in the pack. He looked like an enormous ape standing upright, salivating from his lips. Prithvi looked into his glaring red eyes and saw only hatred. He waited, taunting Prithvi, before delivering his second strike. To further insult her, he let go of his sword and charged at her. He grabbed her neck with his massive arm, and his fingers latched on to her windpipe. Prithvi tried screaming, but his arm continued to squeeze the life out of her. She couldn't breathe.

The kirtimukha threw Prithvi to the ground. Just then, out of the blue, Jagrav jumped at him, allowing Prithvi to gather her bow. As he choked the kirtimukha from behind, Prithvi launched an arrow into the beast's face. It caught the beast by surprise, and before he could react, Prithvi buried a second arrow in him.

Prithvi's windpipe was burning. She paused to catch her breath and look around for her friends. She saw Ujal alongside Savitri and Fayza struggling against four kirtimukhas. Aarti seemed to be at the receiving end of a rock-hard punch. Dhara lay on the snow, gasping for breath. Payal was dodging life-ending spear thrusts. All the cloth bags and fruits were on fire, the kamandalus had spilt their contents and the smell of burnt hair lingered in the air.

'We're not going to survive this!' Idhika's voice came out of nowhere, huffing and puffing. 'Our only hope is to somehow get him.' She pointed at Chayan, who stood on the other side of the ditch, looking at the scene with a smirk full of confidence.

Idhika left to help Ujal. Prithvi realized she was no longer restricted by a dome. She decided to take an all-or-nothing approach. Dropping to one knee, she drew her bow and held it. Then she shut her eyes and started mumbling.

When she released the arrow, Chayan heard it before he saw it. He could do nothing but watch as the next few seconds passed in a blur. The dart landed right next to him and detonated upon impact. He was thrown into the air, a few strands of his beard burning and shrivelling up. He landed awkwardly on his shoulder.

Prithvi drew her bow again and closed her eyes to concentrate. But when she opened them, Chayan seemed to have made a run for it, into the darkness. Prithvi recalled the day she was kidnapped, the fear and helplessness she had felt in the Dronagiri woods. All because of Chayan—the kirtimukha had acted on his orders. *Perhaps isolated, I stand a chance against him.*

Prithvi decided to follow Chayan, leaving the battle site. He sped on ahead, and Prithvi followed the sound of his footsteps. She could hardly see anything.

Chayan and Prithvi strayed further from the others. A few minutes later, next to a rare winterberry tree in the snow-laden land, Prithvi heard the footsteps slow down.

The next thing she knew, a flash of red was dancing close to her face. She fired her arrow into the void, which seemed to have found no target, and then quickly drew her bow again. Her quiver was running low on arrows.

Chayan, in a swift motion, lunged at Prithvi's legs. She fell on him. He crawled out from under her and pinned her down, his hand clamping down on her mouth. Prithvi struggled and fired her arrow in desperation, ripping out Chayan's ear as it shot up towards the stars.

'Arghh!' Chayan bawled. He grabbed Prithvi's wrist, and she writhed in pain.

Chayan dragged her to the winterberry tree. He pulled out a small rope from somewhere on his body and tied her hands to the tree.

'Why are you tying me up?' Prithvi struggled to get free.

Chayan circled the tree, laughing. The noise of grunting kirtimukhas and screaming Souls had become faint in the background. 'To return the favour. I'll make sure you bleed to death, like so many of my men did in the past,' he said.

Prithvi felt helpless without her bow. When Chayan brushed his long beard aside, she saw an assortment of deadly weapons tied to his waist. Gasping for breath, she said, 'Barbarians indeed. Stopping at nothing to butcher all that step into these lands.' She summoned the little energy she could and spat towards him.

'Hah,' Chayan guffawed. 'Curse him! Sanaka's lies see no bounds—teaching his people that the kirtimukhas, the ancient Mountain Pishachus, are barbaric? It's a pity, child, that the truth can no longer spare your life.'

'Oh, shut it!' Prithvi shouted at the top of her lungs. She tried to rub her wrists against each other in the hope of chafing the rope and breaking free, but her hands were firmly tied. 'It was upon *your* orders that a kirtimukha abducted me from Pataan only a few months ago.'

Chayan stomped forward and slapped her. He shook his head. 'Vanyasis are fools. You're all Sanaka's puppets. Last decade's Souls believed that their Adwaita was a way to protect them from me, the man who was waiting outside Vanyasa with his army. But I've never known Atmayog. And the kirtimukhas have always remained up in these mountains. No order or kirtimukha of mine led to your abduction, of that I'm certain.'

'Quit your act! You're not alone. We know! We already know that Sanaka's been lying to the valley about Madhu and hiding it.'

'Mindless girl! I am not talking about that. What Sanaka has done in the past to the divine kirtimukhas—*that* is the greatest sacrilege. Kirtimukhas are called glorious faces because they're guardians, temple guardians in the southern plains, and guardians of something far more valuable here in the mountains. They're messengers of the gods, trying to keep alive the Himalayan bees and Madhu. And they fight with such passion because they fight for god.'

'What?' Prithvi said, trying to recall all that she'd learnt about the Mountain Pishachus in Gurukul.

Chayan lowered his weapon. 'You call us barbarians. But we have never been savages . . . We're just angry.' He turned to look at her with wicked fury in his eyes. Then, sitting right by her, he drew his beard aside and pulled out a small blade. Holding her arm with his other hand, he pushed the blade into Prithvi's triceps.

'GET AWAYYAARRGGHHH!' she screamed.

'I'll tell you why we are angry,' Chayan said as he twisted the blade. He smiled. 'Imagine this. You wake up one night to find your entire village under attack. An army of snow leopards, bears and wolves are tearing up everyone in your tribe. This is what Sanaka and his followers did to my family a century ago. Assailed and butchered over five hundred kirtimukhas with the help of Atmayog. Why? Because we wouldn't allow him the misuse of Madhu? Because he was trying to move the bees, which would have eventually killed them all?'

'So everyone in Vanyasa lied to us?!' Prithvi said. She looked down at the faint line on her finger, the place where she had once worn the fortune teller's Nagsutra.

'We are only protectors of Madhu! And when you fight for nature, nature fights for you.' With that, Chayan's dagger-like nails grew, getting sharper and blacker. He smiled viciously, and in one lightning motion he pushed his nails into Prithvi's chest and pierced her lungs. Her upper cloth instantly stained red. Chayan pulled out his nails and kissed Prithvi's forehead. He whispered, 'This is how my people felt with a thousand sets of leopard teeth in their flesh.'

Chayan tightened the noose around her wrists and then started walking back towards the screams.

This is no way to die for a Bhil. Prithvi steeled herself. *Not without my teer-kaman.* Prithvi tried to sit up but only slumped further. Her body felt like it burned at a thousand degrees.

She shut her eyes and Bhavesh appeared before her, as he had the last time she'd seen him. She looked at his arms and his nose as they both lay in the grass across the river.

'This is what I mean, love. It is becoming increasingly difficult for me. You know what?' Prithvi joked. 'I will do it. I meant it earlier. In the morning tomorrow, I will go to the southern pond . . . and wait for an hour at sunrise . . . and if you don't decide to tag along, maybe I'll find myself a boy among the city folk.'

'I guess I have no option but to join you,' Bhavesh said, laughing.

Prithvi was supposed to go back to the plains and find him. But now, she would never be able to see him. She wanted to scream, but her lungs only spurted out more blood. Her vision had gone blurry, and there was a loud ringing in her ears.

She could make out the silhouette of someone running towards her. 'Bhavesh?' she croaked.

'Oh, no! Oh, no. Prithviii!' Ujal sat by his sister.

Prithvi couldn't hear him. Or even see him clearly. She fought the tears in her eyes. 'We're finally together, Bhavesh,' she said. 'You found me.'

Ujal was furious. He thought Bhavesh had left his sister alone when he had asked him to do so. *So all this while, she wanted to return to the plains not to get Amma and Baba, but to go to that boy?!* So bitter was the hate within him that he barely mourned for his sister. 'It's me!' he said again loudly. 'Ujal!'

Prithvi heard him this time. 'Can you do me a favour, sweet brother?' she said. 'Bhavesh is not going to stop. He'll waste his entire life searching for me in the cities in the plains. Find him and tell him that I died here on this day, young and very much in love, and with only thoughts of him. Will you do that, brother?' Tears rolled down her cheeks as she felt the scent of the Bhil land, the twang of her bowstring, her hidden love, the spring of her young life— for the last time.

Then her eyes went wide, and her dreams and memories left her body forever.

Ujal went numb. 'I'll . . . I didn't . . . mean to . . .' He hadn't even mustered up the courage to agree to his dying sister's request. His heart rate increased. Balling up his fists, he stood up and ran towards the battle, where he hoped to find Chayan.

Bow drawn, wiping his tears against his shoulders, Ujal reached the trench. Fire and blood were all around. The battered and bruised Souls were cornered and surrounded by the kirtimukhas. But all of the monsters had their weapons down. In fact, it seemed like a discussion was going on.

Ujal walked around and snuck up between the Souls from behind.

'Where's Chayan? And Idhika, Dhara?' Ujal whispered, noticing that some individuals were missing.

'Dhara is no longer with us,' Savitri said. 'In fact, we should all be dead. The kirtimukhas and Chayan had us.'

'What happened? Where's Idhika?' Ujal asked, searching for her frantically.

'Chayan asked Idhika to speak to him and told the kirtimukhas to stop their attacks.'

'What?!' As much as Ujal was relieved to hear Idhika was alive, he couldn't believe she was indulging Chayan with a conversation. But apparently, before retiring to the side to discuss with Idhika, Chayan had delivered a speech that revealed to all the Souls the history of the lands—Sanaka's mass killing of the kirtimukhas to control Madhu and the Himalayan bee.

Idhika did not need much convincing that such were Sanaka's motives. Upon learning of the past atrocities at the hands of Sanaka, the Eka had agreed to engage in a dialogue with Chayan, and the two had left to talk.

He suddenly saw Chayan and Idhika step into the light from the fires.

'The Eka and I have discussed matters, and for once it seems Vanyasa has chosen to act rationally,' Chayan spoke. 'The valley dwellers, whatever is left of them, will be spared and given a kamandalu of Madhu. In exchange, they will abandon all attempts to gather more and instantly leave these lands.'

It was a difficult choice. The Souls could never have won against Chayan. But not continuing with the Mahayatra and returning with only a small kamandalu of Madhu was equally unthinkable. They would be punished and denied a place with the immortals of the valley.

At that moment, Ujal had only one purpose: killing Chayan. He considered shooting an arrow towards him, but just before he could put this plan into action, he saw Chayan display an emotion he did not think possible: fear. He was looking out towards the west, from where a large queen wasp—almost as big as a sparrow—had burst in.

The queen wasp was yellow and had a pointy red sting. It darted across and landed on one of the kirtimukhas, who recoiled, trying to swat it away.

Instantly, a large colony of wasps followed their queen and landed on the kirtimukha. After tolerating a quick burst of stings, like a high-voltage shock, the kirtimukha fainted and fell on the ground.

All the remaining kirtimukhas and Souls ran to take cover. But the wasp queen stayed away from the Souls. 'It's Aman, isn't it, as the queen?' Jagrav asked Fayza.

It happened all too fast—the queen jumped, with the swarm following, from one kirtimukha to another, until they started to fall like flies. Ujal spotted Chayan, now one of the few standing in his army, making a run for it before the wasps reached him. Ujal's sore eyes followed the fleeing leader of the kirtimukhas. That was when he realized he would rather die than let Chayan get away. The image of his sister's lifeless body was forever burnt into his brain. She had been his responsibility.

'UJAALLL!' Idhika shouted as Ujal ran after Chayan into the dark. She didn't want him to go. But the chaos and confusion around her meant she couldn't lose her focus. Eventually, when all the kirtimukhas lay fallen, the colony of wasps left the trench. The Souls examined each of the unconscious kirtimukhas, and despite the fact that killing them would make the rest of the Mahayatra easier, they could never harm them after what Vanyasa had already done to their kind. *Perhaps these are the last of the kirtimukhas alive,* Idhika thought. She knew they had maybe a couple of hours until the kirtimukhas regained consciousness. That was how long they had to get as far away as possible.

Savitri shrieked when the wound on her leg was cleansed. Others' injuries were tended to as well. The Souls gathered the little water and fruits that remained. Aman returned with his head held high by the time the remaining firewood was put together to cremate Yuvan, Prithvi and Dhara.

Ujal did not return. No one knew if and when they would see him again. But they had to get going. Of the eleven, only seven remained. The Eka was failing. Idhika led them into the depths of the mountains with a burden in her heart that she could no longer hide.

28

Eka

Aman's lips trembled. His chest felt heavy. He fainted and fell to the ground, his face touching a sharp pebble as it did so. A deep gash appeared in his cheek.

Fayza grabbed him before his body rolled down the steep slope. 'Quick. Give me the water!' she said. 'His nausea has resurfaced.'

She poured some water between his lips. After a few seconds, Aman opened his eyes.

Two days had passed since the battle. Despite the deaths of Prithvi, Yuvan and Dhara—and the departure of Ujal—the remaining seven had journeyed on into the Himalayas. They had walked tirelessly, trudging up endless mountains, surviving on a few fruits and sips of neer. When the wind became strong, especially at the ridges, they ducked and walked contiguous to the mountainside. The landscape looked the same everywhere, white and desolate, and the cold continued to ruffle the life out of them.

Their spirits were low but the seven found some comfort—thanks to Aman—in their recent victory against the kirtimukhas, allowing them to continue their search for Madhu.

Aman asked for another sip of water and allowed Fayza to help him to his feet. Still queasy, he looked at their spent faces and then turned to the Eka. 'Idhika, I feel we need to turn around,' he said. 'Instead of climbing further up this mountain shoulder, we should head back down.'

'Why?' Idhika asked, taken aback.

'I just feel that we are more likely to find the beehives in lower altitudes.'

Idhika thought for a moment but shook her head. 'No, we must continue on our path.'

'How dare you question the Eka, Aman?' Aarti said sarcastically. 'Doubt her brilliant judgement?'

Idhika's muscles tensed.

'It seems the doubt is in everyone's mind. Eka, if I may ask.' Aarti turned around, a subtle smile on her lips. 'Weren't your instincts supposed to keep us safe from Chayan?' A few nodded lightly.

'*You* are to blame for that, Aarti.' Idhika's voice rose. 'Angering the kirtimukhas with your foolish teasing. Perhaps Prithvi would have been alive had it not been for you. Maybe Ujal would have been with us—'

Aarti laughed sarcastically but her eyes turned misty. She spoke softly, 'I am truly devastated at the loss of the twins. I really am. But what about Dhara? Did you even get a chance to know her? Ever talk to her? I lost a dear friend in the battle too, Idhika. I'm not the enemy here. Your leadership is.' Then, Aarti changed her tone, addressing all the Souls.

'Jagrav, Savitri . . . even you, Fayza and Aman . . . surely you all see it too. We've been in these mountains for days and haven't spotted a bee, let alone their hives and—'

'For goodness' sake!' Baring her teeth, Idhika pushed Aarti to the edge of the trail, the steep slope just a few feet away.

Aarti only smiled.

'Quit acting so high and mighty, Aarti!' Idhika screamed in her face. 'You've pushed everyone around all year. You really think we'll forget that Prithvi was kidnapped because of you? That you then tattled on us to Sanaka?'

'What?' Payal said.

'Or when you stepped on my hand in Gurukul?' Fayza asked.

Aarti's eyes widened. 'No, no,' she said softly, putting a hand on Fayza's arm. 'Truly, that was a mistake. I was just walking towards Prithvi. Never meant to . . . I really am sorry, Fayza.' Aarti now turned to Idhika. 'And regarding Prithvi. Sure, maybe it was wrong of us to go to Pataan but we never forced her. In fact, *she* showed us the way past the wall. When the eagle took her, we were equally surprised. And we never "tattled"—'

'It's true!' Payal said.

'Payal and I were only concerned about Prithvi's abduction,' Aarti said. 'Despite the fact that Idhika had slapped me in front of everyone outside Pataan, I swallowed my pride and begged Sanaka to help Prithvi. It was only months later that I found out that Sanaka had ignored us and instead punished you all upon your return.' Fire returned to Aarti's eyes. 'Because soon after, you five banded against us.

Set up opposite camps. Weren't you supposed to be a leader to us all, Idhika? And not just the people you preferred?' Savitri hummed in agreement.

Idhika knit her brow. 'If you felt this way, why didn't you bring it up? You never even talked—'

'How could I?' Aarti looked down. 'Not after what happened on my first day in the valley. I was the first Soul from the plains to arrive and Sanaka told me to go to your hut. So we could meet and you could help me settle in. But moments before I entered, I heard you talking to someone, saying you weren't interested in meeting me at all. You had made your decision without ever meeting me. I was alone in a foreign land. Surely you know what it means to be separated from your parents . . .'

Idhika felt a twinge of guilt. She recalled the moment now—she had been plagued with her own self-doubt, her fear of being inferior to the plain dwellers, and hadn't wanted anything to do with them then.

'You see,' Aarti said. 'I learnt early on that I was alone in the fight for my survival. Especially when the Child of the Valley was going to shun me. I had to find a way out of the valley. That's when Payal entered Vanyasa, and we confided in each other. And we had no intention to harm Prithvi. Just wanted her to be our friend instead of yours . . .'

No one spoke for a while, but Idhika wasn't buying Aarti's story. It was as if deep down everyone knew, even the Eka, that something wasn't right. Looking to the sky, she noticed the dark clouds that had rolled in. Idhika led them further up the mountain, all of them walking in silence. They had to conserve their energy to forage for berries, nuts and seeds, and collect sticks and fallen branches. The one problem for which no solution was in sight was finding a place that could shelter them from the wind at night.

Until sundown, they walked steadily till they reached a group of pointy deodar trees that blocked the wind and made for a safe resting point. The sky was a mix of red and black. Idhika cleared the inch-deep snow and quickly prepared the fire. Jagrav gathered more dry branches from under the trees. For drinking water, Payal used the kamandalus meant for carrying back the Madhu to collect clean snow and heat it over the fire.

With tension in the air, everyone waited for something to happen. They rested in the snow—Fayza and Aman lay on top of their cloth bags looking up at the Milky Way. They all warmed their blue-and-black toes on the fire, Savitri throwing twigs into it to keep it going. It was starting to get late. Idhika saw Jagrav and Savitri walk up to Payal, whisper something and then help her with the drinking water.

Fearing that the Souls were losing confidence in her, Idhika decided to act. She put on a smile and walked over to Aarti, who sat on the side. 'I apologize, Aarti. Perhaps I did overlook some of you before. Tell me your story.'

The others noticed when Idhika and Aarti started talking. Aman was sure Idhika was only pretending to like Aarti. But a small part of him was happy after a long time. *Perhaps it'll all be okay,* he thought. Both Fayza and he had made it out alive. They just had to find Madhu and return to the valley. Make sure Sanaka was punished for his sins. And then perhaps, he could meet his mother, and even resolve the mystery of his father's death.

'And then?' Idhika asked Aarti.

'My parents were from Muzaffarnagar in Uttar Pradesh. They met, and I was born shortly after,' Aarti said. 'Dad was killed in the communal riots. Mom didn't have much money. But we are Brahmins, and that afforded us some standing in the community. So, we kept our chins up, and things soon started to work out for me and Mother. That was, of course, before Sanaka coerced her into giving me up.'

'Are we doing pre-Vanyasa lives?!' Jagrav said. 'Can I go next?'

'Sure.' Idhika nodded, intrigued at what she was learning about the plains.

'I'm from Mumbai,' Jagrav said. 'One of the most populous cities in the plains. My dad's an industrialist, and his job ensured our lives were very comfortable. So much delicious food to eat all the time. And we used to go on so many vacations also. But all that's in the past. I just wish Sanaka had let me bring a suitcase of my chocolates to the valley.'

'Oh, god.' Savitri sat beside Idhika. 'There he goes again with his chocolates. Back home, we didn't expect or have such luxuries. Mine is a farming family, and we lived on fruits and vegetables grown in our backyard. One day, when I was out in the fields practising my boxing, I felt a blow to my head. I fainted. Next thing I knew, I was tied and blindfolded. Sanaka kept me that way for an entire day in a jeep until we arrived in the valley.'

'He uses whatever means he can to recruit,' Idhika said. 'But not for too long. There's been much talk within the Sabha and Samiti about his methods. Once we return—which we shall,' she said, putting on a brave face, 'we will expose him, and the Samiti will deliver justice.'

'Aman,' Savitri said, 'how about you?'

'My mum tricked me,' he said, sitting up. Fayza continued looking heavenwards, not listening intently like the others, lost in her thoughts. She already knew the story. Aman explained how Sanaka had visited them; how his mother had handed him the cardboard box and promised to take him to Agra the next day; how he'd had an odd dream that night, and then the next day, when he woke up, he had been abandoned in a bus that brought him to the hills. He remembered how unwell and numb he'd felt the entire bus ride, and even later, when he passed out on the bridge in the jungle. That was until Sanaka had picked him up and carried him to Nandana. 'I was certain I was hallucinating when the tree started moving, trying to kill me, or so I thought. But he was only trying to mend my knee.'

'Wait, what?' Lines formed between Idhika's eyebrows. 'Back up for me a bit—what did you say before?'

'Well,' Aman started, 'I wasn't myself the entire day. Very dizzy. Even before we made it to the bus, I had slipped in the bathroom and broken my left knee. It was almost as if I was intoxicated.'

'No, I meant what you said before that.' Idhika's eyes narrowed. 'About the dream. And why were you dizzy? What did you eat? Anything the day before?'

Fayza sat up. Aman was gazing into the fire. 'I don't recall . . .'

'Think, Aman,' Idhika said. There was a glint in her eye. 'Did you eat anything that tasted funny?'

'What are you getting at, Idhika?' Fayza said.

'Wait . . . There was this . . . I had a glass of milk at night, as usual. But it did taste different, now that I think about it.'

'One final question, Aman.' Idhika took a deep breath. She looked into the depth of his eyes, and her next question was full of meaning. 'What exactly did you see in the dream that night?'

Aman froze. His heartbeat skyrocketed. 'But, but . . . I was . . .' He was so close. Why did it all seem so familiar? 'I was flying between the clouds over a valley . . . I think— yeah—there was a lake below. The moon in its reflection. Wait . . . in the middle was . . . the Kalpavriksha, and . . . the man beside the tree.'

'That's Sparrow over Vanyasa,' Idhika said. 'Pray tell me! Did he look at you? Lord Indra, standing beside the tree. Did he look at you?!'

Aman remembered when he had opened his father's box for the first time. How his mother had snatched it from him to 'clean' it. But there had been a jar in there—*that she never returned . . . Madhu!* A chill ran through him, his skin tingled, and then, like a blast of cold wind, it hit him. Aman's face transformed into a mask of disbelief.

'That was no ordinary dream, Aman,' Idhika said. 'Your mother wanted to put you on the bus, sure. But it seems you had your true Adwaita that night, the first time your lips touched Madhu. It was not when you came to the valley. Do you remember? They only declared me the Eka when everyone else failed, and having grown up in the valley, I was immune to Madhu. There was no way to tell for sure, so they declared me the leader, but you—'

'You're the true leader,' Aarti said with unblinking eyes. Everyone was looking at Aman.

'But the gift of the instinct?' Savitri asked.

'He . . . has that,' Fayza said with her head in her hands.

Aman told the others how, after returning from the Dronagiri woods, he had developed a certain sharpness as well as chronic nausea. And, in retrospect, that sharpness had enabled Aman to excel at Chaturanga and even save them all from the kirtimukhas twice.

'Nausea is a well-known symptom of being the Eka,' Idhika said, shaking her head. 'You should have said something . . .'

'But . . . so Vaidya Chitra lied to me when she said it was because of the kirtimukha's cut?' Aman said, pointing to the scar below his lip.

'Wait, so *you* are supposed to lead this journey?' Jagrav asked. 'Is that why the Mahayatra has been so trying for us, Eka?'

At the sound of 'Eka', Aman turned to Idhika. But it was him they were addressing.

The Blue Rose having revealed himself, far down south, the valley's leaves were a touch greener, the animals faintly quicker and the days somewhat warmer.

'Doesn't that mean *Aman* is supposed to be the exception to the laws of the valley?' Savitri asked, elbowing Fayza, paying no heed to the gravity of the situation. She was clearly referring to the rule of celibacy they all had to follow.

Aman looked across to Fayza's firelit face, her red cheeks, the mole on her temple and her bright smile. As the Eka, the valley would have to accept them as a couple, and nothing excited him more. A thick mist rolled in from between the trees. Aman and Fayza broke eye contact only moments later, when they heard Idhika sobbing.

'What's wrong, Idhika?' Aman asked her.

Idhika couldn't stop crying. Each time she looked at Aman, she wept harder, almost as though she cried for him. A minute later, she somehow managed to talk: 'Aman . . . this is a boon . . . and a burden.' She sniffled. 'I don't know if you have noticed, but for some time . . . I've been racked with pain. Holding on to a secret.' Her face was red and her eyes puffy. 'About a month ago, Aranyani had revealed to me a piece of information that completely broke me.'

The hairs on the back of Aman's neck stood on end. Before he could say anything, Idhika's lips trembled. And softly, she began to sing a familiar song: *'Tucked within brambles that may . . . Shielding boughs and keeping at bay . . . Every dashak centres a blue rose . . . Scent of which dale invariably knows.'* Idhika paused, to wipe her nose. *'Watered, it riots by the nights . . . Sheeny, eliciting awe from sights . . . But in the valley fortified by the one that slithers . . . For the sake of home, that flower must wither.'*

Idhika refused to meet Aman's eyes. 'There's a reason why everyone knows this song, why Father and I have both loved and hated it . . . Because it reminds us of Mother. And why she had to leave us forever . . . The Song of the Valley talks about the "blue rose" of the valley. The Eka.'

Fayza's stomach was in knots. Payal put a hand on Aman's shoulder.

'There's a reason, Aman,' Idhika said, 'why very early on the Eka is exempted from the laws of the valley; why they are allowed to build a conjugal bond with a partner and even allowed an offspring. Like my mother was. Because the Eka deserves to leave behind a piece of themselves in the world. Because the Eka is a flower . . . a blue rose . . . who must eventually "wither". It is the only way to gather Madhu, to execute that last step . . . The lord chose you for this duty.'

Idhika stood up and walked over to Aman. Her face was red, and she bit her lip. She fell on her knees in front of him, took both his hands in her palms and broke down. Her voice croaked. 'That's why I was trying to call a truce with Chayan earlier . . . I was scared witless. I didn't want to die!'

Aman's face turned pale. It dawned upon him that there were no surviving Ekas in Vanyasa. He looked at Fayza with the eyes of a frightened child, unable to understand how his life had suddenly careened out of control.

The others looked on protectively at Aman, who stayed silent. The night was long and unforgiving.

29

Indra

'I'll be fine!' Aman's hand waved dismissively. He stood up and started towards the deodar trees. 'Need to be by myself . . .'

He didn't know where he was going or what he was going to do. But he walked fast. There was barely a thing in his head, only the tune of the Song.

He strode into the trees and stumbled past fallen pinecones. The further he distanced himself from the others, the louder the wheezing in his throat became. His legs were growing weaker. Unable to hold himself up any longer, he stumbled to the forest floor beside a large boulder. He sat there, shaking like a leaf. Suddenly, Fayza emerged, still carrying the cloth bag.

'Aman, listen to me,' she said. 'None of this is right. It's just—it doesn't make sense. I mean, the valley's system is flawed. There is no "duty" here . . . You don't have to do this—*no one* should have to do this . . . I know it seems like you can't get out of this, that the stakes are too high, but you *can*!'

He looked down, refusing to let her see his tear-streaked face. She was always good at saying the right things, but nothing could help him.

An uncomfortable silence stretched between them. Moments later, he lifted his head. 'I don't want to die.'

Although she was devastated, she knew she had to be brave for him, try and see through the fog. As if collecting herself, she sniffed loudly. 'Listen! Snap out of it. We already found the barrels that Sanaka is hiding in the valley. Why not just return—all of us—to the valley and expose that tyrant? We'll tell Aranyani and the Sabha and Samiti.'

'Oh, Fayza. This seems to be harder on you than it is on me,' he said.

'No!' she said. 'I'm serious. Why can't we—'

'*Because* we cannot even enter the gates of Vanyasa without Madhu. And let's say we jump over the wall and somehow summon the Samiti? Then what? Don't you remember? Idhika went back to Pandayam Tal and checked. Sanaka has already moved the barrels. We were lucky the first time to stumble upon them. But without them no one will believe us.'

'We could try, Aman,' she said. 'All of us could Atmayog and search the valley before we return.'

'It's not that simple,' he said. 'Not everyone has the same goal as us. Aarti, Payal, and I think even Jagrav, they don't want to take down Sanaka; they *want* to peacefully succeed in the Mahayatra and return without complications. Maybe go back to their families one day. And for that, we have to find the bees—*I* have to find the bees.'

'Don't worry about the others! *You* are the only one paying with your life.' She paused. 'Think about your family. Abandon this madness, and run to the plains. Your mother hopes for your return . . . Yes.' She exhaled. 'Why don't you go to New Delhi? Find your mother!'

'You think I haven't thought of that, Fayza?' He shot her a miserable smile. 'It would only put her in more danger. He *will* eventually find us. For the sake of his scheme, Sanaka will never risk sparing us.' That was when it sunk in that no matter what he did, what decision he took, he was never going to win. Because winning meant a sunny day in Vanyasa, a new lease of life. Because winning meant Fayza and the friends he had found. All of which now seemed beyond his reach.

'I hear you,' she said, 'but your death cannot be the solution. What if . . . what if your mother doesn't know our whereabouts? In fact, if no one knows our whereabouts?' Her eyes dilated.

'What?' Aman said.

'The Souls could all genuinely deny culpability. That's the only way they will be spared. It's our only hope, for their lives as well as ours. Think about it, Aman. If we ran away right here, right now. If Idhika and the rest weren't able to find us, they would have no option but to return and say that the true Eka abandoned the journey. Coming back empty-handed to the valley could be justified.'

'And . . . what about us? Where will we be?' Aman asked.

'In another time,' she said, lifting his chin with her forefinger. 'We know too much about Sanaka's plan. Since only you can find the bees, you're not safe until there's

another Eka. A decade. That's how long we'll have to hide
away for . . . Find a cave, Atmayog to a banyan tree for
ten years. With our breathing slowed down, we will barely
age. And then, years later, when it is all past us, you and I
can come back to our bodies, find a remote village in the
plains and spend the rest of our days together. Far from this
crazy world.'

As enticing as that sounded, Aman also knew it wouldn't
work. Whether or not his mother knew of his whereabouts,
he couldn't bank on Sanaka showing mercy.

It suddenly started raining heavily. A wave of sadness
washed over him as he prepared himself to shoot down
Fayza's proposition. But no sound escaped his throat. 'No,
Fayza,' he said with more force, but it was as if he had
been muted.

'WHY DOES IT NOT WORK ON YOU?' It was
a deep, perceptible voice, as if someone spoke loudly in
his ear. A turbulence rose in Aman's heart. He knew that
voice; he had heard it before, moments prior to setting
on fire the kirtimukha that had kidnapped Prithvi in the
Dronagiri woods.

But there was no one beside him. Fayza seemed to have
vanished into thin air. Scared, Aman sat in the snow, all alone
among the thin trees. *Where has she gone?* Rain fell from the
black clouds above him.

Aman saw his own shadow grow in front of him, and
then felt a tap on his shoulders. Stunned, he saw from the
corner of his eye a thin fluorescent glow behind him. Burly
arms lifted Aman and turned him around. He was facing a

man draped in a lustrous white cloak. The man was barefoot, and his long hair fell behind his shoulders. His prominent nose and chin were positioned perfectly in the middle of his face. On top of his head sat a black-and-gold crown with a hole in the middle.

But only when Aman noticed a lightning blue spark in the man's crown did he realize where he'd seen him before. The feast in his dream: the Founding of Vanyasa. And although he had had four arms and was covered in jewellery, Aman was sure that the deity before him was the same being. *Indra!*

The man nodded.

Aman's rain-drenched skin flickered white in a violent crack of lightning. He got down on one knee in respect and bowed awkwardly towards the man he'd only seen in dreams or heard of in stories. He couldn't believe that the king of the gods stood before him. Only a few months ago had Aman heard the story of Indra's elephant, Airavata, and his encounter with the crocodile in Pandayam Tal. Lord Indra was not one who lived in the past, but shared and actively lived in the same time as him. Aman wondered if his own encounter with Airavata was an instruction by the lord himself.

The man nodded again. 'That's right. I tried to stop you. And when Airavata's efforts failed, I, not Chayan, let loose the kirtimukha that kidnapped one of the valley's Souls. In the hope to draw you out. I have always known you're the key to a successful Mahayatra, not the Child of the Valley, ever since I saw you in your Adwaita in the plains. But the reasons behind my actions to stop you are noble. To mend the future, once and for all. Know this, Aman: You *must* give in to the girl. Do as she says. Abandon this Mahayatra and go far from the valley,' Indra said. With that, the lord started to back away, ready to depart.

'No . . . bu-but what about Idhika? The rest?' Aman said. 'Wait, you don't want the Mahayatra to succeed?'

Indra wasn't pleased. He stopped. The sky thundered. 'Would you prefer I strike you right here and rid myself of this impediment? Do as you're told!'

'I ca-can't,' Aman said. 'For Mother's safety, I can't . . .'

Indra shook his head and exhaled. For a second, the dark clouds above parted. His facial muscles loosened, and there was a newfound kindness in his eyes. Looking above, he said, 'It seems we cannot stay here for much longer. There are hostile spirits about.'

Aman felt himself being lifted into the air. He and the lord were flying. They were heading south, towards the plains, tearing through the wind so fast that little could be seen of the mountains below.

Indra's lips did not move but Aman could hear him talk: 'Do you know how I was created? The genesis of the gods? It's as you would expect. Collective belief. Through prayer. The early man imagined us around four thousand years ago in the Vedic era and spread the idea through oral tales. Those stories painted our features, our world, and their belief slowly enabled us. But it wasn't until a thousand years later, when we found written mention in the scriptures, that our existence solidified. Our purpose, as prescribed by the mortals, was to create, forgive, shelter and provide for mankind and all living beings.'

The mountains below turned to hills and hills turned to farmland as they journeyed on. At some point, Indra abruptly stopped. The two sailed in the air, somewhere in west India, above a train station. But something seemed to be wrong: thick smoke rose from the land below. Children cried and men screamed. Aman peered down to see a passenger train ablaze. Burning passengers jumped out of it in all directions.

Before Aman could ask, Indra took wing once again, and the two departed. They soared over many clusters of light, heading towards central India. Aman struggled to keep his eyes open in the strong wind.

It was over a village that they halted. They hovered above a tree that had a man tied to its trunk. Stick after stick came down on the man as people continued to surround and shout at him, well after his last breath.

'Mankind is devolving, constantly killing in the name of god,' Indra said.

The two took off again, now going back north, towards the Himalayas. 'But over the four thousand years of our existence, no matter how much the gods tried—and we have—we were unable to rid the plains of evil and suffering. And so it festered. We sat helpless as sin spread to vast corners of the plains. Mortals, instead of being self-reliant, held us accountable for their actions. The belief became superficial. Faith that was once pure and unsullied started being misused— and we were the tools. People were whipped into submission using religion. The rhetoric of discipline and servitude was deceitfully switched with insecurity and division. And the tables fully turned when gods were no longer defending mortals. Instead, mortals defended us and fought among each other for us. Despite this, we didn't stop trying. We persisted for centuries and rewarded the few altruistic ones.'

The plains below had given way to hills. The two continued to travel deeper into the Himalayas while an endless forest carpeted the hills beneath them.

Indra continued, '. . . but over a decade ago, the plains reached a tipping point. The idea of us, of religion, started to enable more killing than salvation. Civil laws were no longer free from religious bias. And this faith was always meant to be accommodating of other beliefs, but that too stopped. So, as king of the gods, father of the mortals, I had to act. Get closer to our cornerstone objective and rid the world of evil. I did what had to be done. Passed a judgement to work on erasing the idea of god, of religion, from the plains, so all killing stops in our name. For those reasons, Aman, for the sake of humanity, the gods have to be forgotten. All religions need to be dissolved. We are trying to change the plains, transition to a world in which we do not exist. A new Yuga built on the concept of no divine power but collective consciousness powering and dictating society. However, there are many forces set on stopping us. Whether for the greater good or not, there are those who want to instead strengthen religion. And they know what it will take to stop us from wiping out the idea of god, of ourselves. They know that as long as the sole lying relic of Hinduism lives on, the gods can never truly fade away. So they protect it at all costs.'

Tall mountains had replaced the hills as they continued their flight. Over a pointy peak, and through thinning clouds,

Aman caught sight of a towering tree vast in size and width, a thousand stars glittering in its branches.

Indra pointed to it. 'There it is, the last remaining shard of divinity on earth. That which was once uprooted from Mount Meru. The Kalpavriksha.'

Aman had always known the tree was special, but never had he imagined that it was the last existing relic of a faith. But to be fair, he had never believed in god either, and here he was, surfing the length and breadth of his country with one.

'That's why, child, the Eka must not succeed. Without fresh Madhu, the Kalpavriksha *will* fade away, allowing the gods to dissipate from the memories of the mortals. What you do now will create ripples, irrespective of your decision.'

'But why me? Why now after all these years of the Mahayatra?' Aman asked.

'Because of late, the protectors of the tree have been gathering strength. They've formed an alliance with outsiders who are coming into the valley to champion its magic.'

Aman knew it was the Preservers that the deity talked of. 'Father was one of them—'

Indra was no longer there. Instead, a cloud floated away into the distance.

'Are you with me, Aman?' It was Fayza. He was back near the boulder, not too far from the rest of the Souls.

Dumbfounded, Aman looked around, but he couldn't tell if Indra had actually been there or if it was all a dream. Trying to digest all that had happened, he pressed down on his temple; the images of the burning train and the man being beaten to death flashed across his mind. *'That's why, child, the Eka must not succeed.'*

'What do you say?' Fayza asked again.

'Yes . . . yes!' Aman said, reaching out to her for comfort. 'I'll-I'll live!' His shaky laughter turned into a cry. Fayza simply hugged him, and thanked the gods.

The two discussed the plan. 'And then, when we wake up years later,' Fayza said, 'I know just the village to go to. We'll spend the rest of our lives there, by that small waterfall and pond!'

They didn't linger too long. Aman knew better than to ask if they could bid goodbye to Idhika and the rest. Time was scarce, and it was vital that they find a safe resting point for their decade-long Atmayog. What they needed was a cave so isolated in the mountains that no animal or human could chance upon it.

As Idhika, Aarti, Payal, Jagrav and Savitri awaited their return, Aman and Fayza climbed further up the mountain. With a rush in their chests and a bounce in their steps, they only stopped to collect fuel for fire. With caves usually abundant at higher altitudes, it was little surprise that once on top, they found a labyrinth of deep tunnels with big shafts.

Aman and Fayza roved about, assessing the different caverns. 'This one doesn't smell bad, which probably means animals can't get in,' Fayza said.

While she checked the inside of the cave, Aman looked out at the vast empty land overlooking the mountain. He remembered a large, bright city that he'd seen—undoubtedly New Delhi—when flying with Indra. 'Are we sure about this, Fayza?'

Fayza was exploring the cave. It wasn't too deep, around twenty metres in; the air was damp and cold. She was warming her hands over the fire she'd prepared on the stony floor. 'I'm scared too, Aman, wondering about how much the world will have changed by the time we wake up.'

Time slipped away as Aman and Fayza lay together by the fire, not talking much, each thinking of their own concerns. They wept and simply looked at each other—it would be many years until they could do so again.

Then Fayza picked herself up, and, still holding Aman's hand, led him to a ledge on the inner wall. There she sat, with her knees folded and her hands in jnanamudra. 'Our lives are only just beginning,' she said and closed her eyes, initiating her vulnerable meditation. Aman followed her cue.

The better Atmayogi of the two, Fayza's soul left her body first. As soon as she entered the banyan tree a few metres outside their cave, her mortal breathing slowed down.

With his eyes shut, Aman struggled to concentrate. He knew he was doing the right thing. It was what he wanted. What Fayza wanted. What the gods had asked him to do as well. But something didn't feel right. Their plan depended on many hopes. Hope that Idhika and the rest of the Souls would be allowed in upon the Eka's disappearance. Hope that they would believe that Aman and not Idhika was the Eka. Hope that Sanaka would leave his mother alone.

Aman's eyes forced themselves open. Beside him, Fayza breathed so sparingly it felt as if she were frozen. He stood up and made straight for Fayza's cloth bag. He had remembered that all the Souls had packed palm leaves in case they needed to send a message to Vanyasa.

He fished out a palm leaf, a pankh and some ink. In the light of the fire, he wrote a letter and tucked it inside Fayza's bag.

He stood up and looked at Fayza, who was deep in Atmayog. She had been his first true friend. But after her, Aman had met many others to whom he had grown close. Prithvi, who was no longer with them. Ujal, whose whereabouts none could venture. And more who had lost their souls in the Mahayatra.

Were all those sacrifices for nothing? Could he really gamble with the lives of his mother, Idhika and the rest of the Souls to save his own and Fayza's?

'Oh,' the word escaped Aman's lips. A cloud of doubt cleared before his eyes. For the first time, it was crystal clear where the Himalayan bees were. As he'd predicted earlier, they were in much lower altitudes than the ones traversed by the Souls. Aman could feel his instincts taking over, his body channelling the boon of Indra, dedicated above all odds to drive him to the destiny of an Eka.

Aman knew exposing Sanaka's scheme was vital. But for that, the Souls had to return to the valley, which was unlikely without him. Moreover, as long as he was with Fayza, her life too was in danger. A general feeling of panic and dread washed over him. He knew what he had to do. Something Fayza would never let him do, the same way he wouldn't let her if she were the Eka.

For Fayza's survival, for his mother's survival, Aman had to fulfil his destined role. He had to defy Indra and continue with the Mahayatra.

His shoulders hunched, Aman struggled to look at Fayza's face. It would have been impossible had she been awake. It was she who was Aman's true saviour, his new lease of life. The one who saw him for who he really was.

There was much he had never said to her, and he now wished he could. He wanted to tell her that in another life and different circumstances, he would have followed her to the edge of their days, to their very last tomorrows. Reveal to her that he'd been in love with her, or at least with the idea of her, his entire life—he only hadn't met her until Vanyasa.

Tears shone in his eyes as he recalled the warm memories of the first time he'd met her, in the first class of Gurukul under the Kalpavriksha when Acharya Ashwini had told all the new recruits that they were in their seventh and last life cycles. How Aman had instantly fallen for her and would repeatedly recall from then onwards her radiant face with the mole on her temple, the cut beside the eye that he could see now as he stood in the cave.

Suddenly, the image of an older woman with the same mole and cut on her face flashed across his mind. A woman he'd never seen before but felt like he had known forever. His head was flooded with the memories and emotions of a previous life. Of Fayza and him, of trust and habit, years ago. Fayza had been his partner for at least one previous life, maybe more. It was destiny. He was meant to find her in the valley, like he had long, long ago.

Although he was looking at her, Aman's vision took him far away, to another lifetime. He stood still as a statue. But he could no longer hold himself together. Although there was no one to see him, when his knees collapsed, he hid his face in his lap and sobbed inaudibly, jolt after jolt agonizing his bones.

With a heavy heart, and without a final goodbye, Aman exited the cave. His steps pounded along the tracks, down the mountain, his strides longer than usual. His heart full of bitter pain, he looked around constantly, checking, only to remind himself that she was no longer beside him.

Upon reaching the deodar trees where Fayza and he had left the Souls earlier that night, Aman found the fire long dead and scattered. The Souls were nowhere to be seen.

He was lost. Without Fayza, without anyone. All alone in the vast, snowy Himalayas, waiting for his imminent death.

30

Atman

There are many ways in which the human body deals with pain. Foremost among them is sleep—the mind's way to allow instant detachment from the real world. This is precisely why people often faint upon hearing bad news or being wounded.

Aman had no idea when he had fallen unconscious in the snow, near the deodar trees. But when he eventually opened his eyes, he stayed still for a very long time, questioning his decision. There was still no sight of the others.

Despite his feet going numb and the threat of frostbite—more likely to occur due to a lack of food—Aman steeled himself, stood up and began searching for any sign of his friends. He braved a walk to the boulder where he had met Indra, hoping someone might be there. But there was no one. Every now and then, dark specks ran before his eyes, so he swayed and held his arms out for balance, trying his best not to trip over a rock or stumble into a tree. Suddenly, he saw a girl approaching him.

'Oh lord!' Idhika ran up to him. 'Where were you . . .? You guys disappeared . . . we were worried sick!'

Aman saw that she was alone.

'I can't see Fayza,' Idhika said.

Aman lowered his gaze. With a knife twisting into his heart, he explained to Idhika where he and Fayza had gone and why she was no longer with him. 'That's why—promise me, Idhika—when Sanaka is served justice and the danger has subsided, you will come back and find her in that labyrinth of caves on top of this mountain. You will tell her why I had to do this. Why it was for her safety. My only option . . . And don't forget to take Madhu when you go; you'll need it to snap her out of her long meditation and—'

'Is this all a joke to you, Eka?' Aarti had emerged with the rest of the Souls.

'It was p-probably Aman's idea,' Payal said. 'More foolish of the two. Wandering by themselves in the dark—where's Fayza?!'

That was the first time Aman realized the gravity of his actions. Despite trying to safeguard everyone, his decisions seemed to only complicate the situation. He didn't know what to say. It felt as if his spine had snapped in two. He slumped. Tears started to roll down his weary, blackened cheeks like rain on a dusty pane. 'I've lost her,' he whispered.

'What happened? Are the kirtimukhas back?' Jagrav said, drawing closer to the pack. Everyone assumed the worst.

Savitri put her arm on Aman's shoulder. 'What happened to her?'

Instead of responding, Aman fell on all fours. He let out a high-pitched wail, accompanied by the whirring of the mucus in his nose and throat. 'I've lost her forever . . .'

Everyone knew better than to press him for answers at that moment. They let him be, occasionally comforting him and trying to calm him down.

'Despite tired legs, we cannot afford even a brief halt,' Aarti said after some time. 'I know we have lost many brothers and sisters in the past few days, but the problems that beset us can only be solved if we succeed in the Mahayatra. We can rest *after* we have the Madhu . . . Will you lead us there, Aman? To the Himalayan bees?'

Aman scooped up some fresh snow and wiped the taste of salt and mud from his lips. Only then did he pick himself up.

Following the Eka's instructions, they walked down the mountain at a quick pace. Within an hour of their departure, the sun peeked over the fence of hills around them. The air was crisp and cold. They crossed a thin bridge of ice, holding hands and walking shore to shore in a single file. Aman should have been leading the entourage, but instead he brought up the rear.

When Idhika slowed down and fell into stride with Aman, he told her about his flight with Indra. It was difficult for her to digest that the gods wanted the Mahayatra to fail and that they were at war with Sanaka and the Preservers, but she took his word for it.

'Aman,' Idhika said, 'you know that you won't be able to survive the final Atmayog, right? There's no way around this one. The flower *will* wither. Think twice, for now the king of the gods has given you a way out.'

As much as he was relieved to hear her say that, Aman had already weighed the options and knew that his decision was one that had to be taken.

When he refused to budge, Idhika reluctantly told him, as Aranyani had told her, the sequence of tasks he needed to execute to gather Madhu and the exact reason why his end was unavoidable.

'I never found out what happened to him,' Aman said, thinking about his father. 'And like him, I'm going to leave this world . . . You know something, Idhika. I didn't have *any* friends in the plains. Kept to myself. And back then, the idea that my future could somehow be defined by my past actions, the idea of karma, was one I would never subscribe to. I didn't believe in any of it. But then, defying all odds, I was brought to the valley, a place where Vedicism is alive. Obviously, I questioned everything I believed in . . . But all for what? Only to learn that the valley is also a cruel place? To learn that karma is a farce, a lie to whip us into submission, into collective mediocrity? Or as Indra said, "to control us"? Mine will be no "honourable" death, Idhika. Think about it: Exactly what sins am I paying for? Truly, the worst things in life are reserved for those who are good. In reality, there are no consequences for your actions. We are animals. Trivial in the eternity of time. With survival of the fittest the only law.'

Aman stopped his rant, but he knew he was right. The valley's magic, love and loss, all of it had done nothing. He was still the same person, reserved as he had always been, carefully weighing each word before he uttered it. He was unable to simply tell Idhika that this loser didn't want to die.

The Souls walked all day. Their feet found slow relief when small patches of grass started to sprout in their snow-laden path. Aman knew the general direction in which to

head, but seldom did he know the exact road, which often
meant they were blocked by boulders, or sometimes forced to
turn around from dead ends.

'Where to now?' Payal snapped. 'Eka?' The group waited
for Aman to catch up.

Aman pointed south, his arm slanted up.

'So after walking downhill all day, we have to start
climbing again?' Payal asked.

It was Aarti who spotted it. Tracing Aman's finger,
she looked far away, between the layers of blue hills, where
between them towered an odd peak. It was shaped like a
thumb, topped with a dash of snow. And below, the Souls
could see the ravine path circling up that mountain. That was
the route they had to take.

Aman, Idhika, Aarti, Payal, Savitri and Jagrav trudged
on for a few more hours under the last rays of westering
Aditya, the sun god, until they arrived at the foot of the final
mountain, the top of which was shaped like a thumb. As they
mounted, the path thinned, until there was no possible way
forward. So they took to the steep hillside and ascended as
fast as they could to the summit.

After covering the final stretch, Idhika eventually lent her
hand and helped Aman crest the very top of the thumb.

The wind whistled in his ears. It seemed like he was on
top of the world. He walked to the edge and looked down
at the deep canyon spread out before him, split by a rushing
river. And there it was. A few hundred metres below his feet,
jutting out of the stone in the vertical fall of the mountain, a
thick branch with a wide crown and many leaves. Scared of

getting swept away by the wind, Aman stepped back but could still make out what looked like large golden fruits hanging off the branch. 'They're huge,' he said, 'the honeycombs.'

The Souls set down their bags and joined Aman to look on in amazement. The bees danced in an intricate pattern around the four hives stuck to the sturdy branch. Quickly, but with care, the Souls carefully cleaned the kamandalus in preparation for storing the Madhu.

The sky had changed colour to the dark of an early night. It was time and Aman knew it. He only hoped for some strength. The leader of the Mahayatra wasn't supposed to feel this way, but again, he didn't know the first thing about it. He had been an odd backbencher in school; and then the odd eleventh recruit in the valley; and finally, the odd inexperienced leader to the Souls—without training or any time to process the responsibility. He was just a glorified Eka with an ill-fated destiny. And when he died, no one would remember his sacrifice—not even the people of the valley, let alone the world outside.

But it was almost poetic. *Dying for the same valley that sank my father. Perhaps, they will remember me. As the foolish one. Daft enough to believe in himself. Only to pay the price for the choices of others. Perhaps they will tell stories. Make an example of me. To teach kids to make the best of each day, make the most of little moments, because the bitter truth is that oftentimes, entire lives can amount to absolutely nothing. Not everyone finds happiness or attains something great. Most lives are insignificant and thus blown away into the sands of time.*

'Promise me you'll live,' Aman told Idhika. 'On my behalf, you'll return to the valley and expose Sanaka. You'll live to be the proof that I existed. My legacy and my goals. Tell Ma and Fayza my story. Don't let them all forget me, Idhika.'

His chin trembling, Aman walked up to Jagrav. 'Don't cry, brother, or I won't be able to go.' One by one, he hugged each of the Souls.

He wanted to run back down the mountain. But as if guided by an invisible force, he stepped up one last time and wiped the tears streaming down his burning cheeks. At the edge of the cliff, he cleared the pebbles and sat down. Despite his blurry vision, he could see how at times the clouds hid and at times revealed the stars above.

Aman took a deep breath. And then, for the last time in seven life cycles, he closed his eyes. Remembering Idhika's instructions, his soul searched for an appropriate companion, and in no time latched on to a fully grown Himalayan vulture with aged feathers and droopy eyelids flying a little way above him. Through his sharp vision, half covered by his white beak, Aman spotted the Souls, and at the edge of the cliff, his own body in meditation. And below that was his target, the branch with the bees. His broad wings straightened until they lay flat against the wind currents, allowing him to glide towards the honeycombs.

Idhika had told him that the Himalayan bee's hives were often on inaccessible terrain, which made it difficult to collect the Madhu, even with a bird as a companion. There was no way to separate the hives from the branch. And if the bird managed somehow, its claws would tear into the cells and waste precious Madhu. And because of these reasons, Vanyasa had perfected a unique system.

Aman raced past the Souls, and in one hard flap of his wings, gained momentum towards the wide branch. Through his razor-sharp eyes, he could see how the branch grew horizontally from within a lone patch of grass surfacing the stony face of the cliffside. Truly, Aman realized, nature is tenacious and finds a way to survive in the harshest of terrains. Within seconds, the head of the vulture met with full force the middle of the branch. Although this shook the beehives up and down violently, Aman had failed to break off the branch.

Aman then flapped his wings and distanced himself from the bees as fast as he could.

The Himalayan vulture now hovered a long way directly above the branch. As soon as he was ready, Aman folded and tucked his wings close to his body until he was one large ball of mass suspended in the air. The vulture fell with increasing speed and eventually crashed upon the branch. The branch wobbled oddly, and then, like a brittle piece of chalk, snapped. But the top half, with all the hives, did not separate. Instead, it hung limply by a few fibres.

All of a sudden, the bees scattered; some made straight for the bird that was Aman. The vulture desperately warded them off mid-air, moving up and down, trying to dodge as many, but the deadly insects stung it repeatedly. They injected their venom through the creature's neck, abdomen and even tail. Aman screamed and writhed in agony, and the bird let out a screech that reached the Souls who were watching from far above.

For the first time, Aman's Atmayog connection felt a little too tightly secured. He remembered what Idhika had told him about the bee stings but tried not to think about it.

Somewhere in this mayhem, the last fibres of the branch undid themselves and the top half with all the beehives fell. It sank for a long time towards the canyon below and eventually descended into the cushion of a leafy foliage around the river that flowed through the forest.

The venom of the bees spread through the vulture's veins, and Aman felt his strength wane. He dove, beak first, towards the branch and found it perched comfortably between tree leaves near the river. Bees around the hives were now few in number.

Using the last of his power, he pulled the branch with his talons and just about managed to carry it to the top, where the Souls stood. A few metres away from his meditating body, Aman let go of the branch, moments before the vulture hit the ground awkwardly.

Aman drew his final breath. Although Idhika had told him it wasn't possible, he put in a last-ditch effort to jump back into his mortal body. But the bee stings he had endured blocked all attempts. He was stuck in the dying frame of the vulture. *But in the valley fortified by the one that slithers, for the sake of home, that flower must wither.*

Sure, nature was tenacious, but it also knew how to surrender. The warmth in his body grew. Aman wanted to smile, to feel fully the happiness within him. He saw his mother's laughter from a time much before his father had left, a memory of a time far, far away. He saw his first sight of the Kalpavriksha. Fayza's smile and her eyes. And he and Fayza speaking at the Temple of Indra.

From the corner of the vulture's eye, Aman spotted the Bhuts' white bodies and heads full of hair circling the sky around him. Before he could avert his gaze, his droopy, pallid face lost colour.

The clouds above broke, revealing a starry band across a completely black canvas—the graceful arc of a billion celestial bodies making up the heavens from horizon to horizon.

Idhika saw the exact moment Aman's soul left the vulture. Slowly, but with energy, it rose, and she felt a profound emotion as the soul made its way up to Brahman, the ocean of souls from whence Aman had come many lives ago, at the beginning of his cycle of Samsara.

'Whether you've considered yourself a servant of god or considered yourself god, you're still an atman,' Idhika said softly.

'He was truly the best among us,' Savitri said.

The Souls did not go near Aman's mortal body, for it was the vulture in which he truly resided in the end. They surrounded the bird and wept. And eventually, it was the vulture they cremated.

They waited for the last of the bees to clear from the hives, and only then did they drain the Madhu into their kamandalus.

With the ticket to the valley in her hands, Idhika said, 'And now, we must let the world know the truth about Sanaka.' She led them down the mountain, and they began the journey back towards Vanyasa.

Epilogue

The clouds above were dark, and the sky behind it was purple. Idhika, Aarti, Payal, Jagrav and Savitri descended the mountain with their Madhu-laden kamandalus. No one said anything. They simply walked down the slopes of the thumb-shaped summit.

There was much distance between them and Vanyasa. The path ahead was curved like a river. And in the cold, hazy wind, little could be made of each other except for the scrape of the heavy steps on the loose pebbles. But Aarti could tell when Idhika, who walked ahead, halted every now and then, and assuming no one was looking, knelt and bent down, weeping.

Making sure to stay near Idhika, Aarti walked faster. She had to turn the tide in her favour, and with Payal at her side, her confidence grew. So, it was her plan more than her empathy that made her reach out to Idhika. 'Let us rest here,' she pronounced to those still a few steps behind.

'Why here?' Idhika's nose whirred from the mucus in her throat.

Aarti paused and waited for Payal, Jagrav and Savitri to catch up, letting them register Idhika's condition, and then spoke, 'It is as good a place as any. We're all tired. And we finally have Madhu.'

'A chance to find something to eat,' Jagrav said and sat down, letting his sprained ankle unbend.

'No, we are to head back instantly,' Idhika said, hiding her swollen eyes. 'Already our gait has slowed due to these kamandalus, and in the little time that is left before we are greeted by Lord Aditya, we should cover much ground. In the day, against these white mountains, the kirtimukhas will spot us from miles away.'

'Listen to me, Souls!' Aarti barked. 'You've all fought valiantly. This is nothing more than much-needed rest. We are at least a day ahead of any of those beasts. There's no worry or rush. And our heavy kamandalus are our tickets to a hero's welcome, not our burden. Our licence to the air around the Kalpavriksha, to the different gifts of the valley . . . including immortality. We must embrace this victory.'

'Don't let your mind wander,' Idhika said. 'We shall not forget the wrong done to us; we have to bring justice. Before Sanaka finds out that we have Madhu and a way inside the valley'—she said looking up at the sky—'we must reach there and expose him. Reveal to all that he has hidden barrels of Madhu, lied for decades and allowed the Preservers to weaponize the divine tree. Therefore, we must haste, reach before sunrise and enter the valley with warm faces, not revealing anything of our plan until we are in front of the Sabha and Samiti. On your feet, Jagrav.'

Jagrav held his ankle in pain and did not get up.

'Don't worry, brother.' Aarti bent beside Jagrav. 'I'll help you up. Not to walk further but to assist me to gather wood. I'm building a small fire here. We can heat all the clean snow by that tree and allow ourselves some water—and Payal will see if she can find some berries for you. We must take care of our own. Cannot lose another soul like brother Aman.'

How dare she?! Idhika thought. 'Aman went of his own choice. Let me reveal something to you all. He had an option to abandon us. And that would have meant that the rest of us roam these terrains with no Madhu or a way back. But he chose his way so that our return could be guaranteed. So that we could go back and foil Sanaka's plan, once and for all. He went for no fault of his.' Her voice dropped. 'He suffered an untimely and tragic end, without any moment to comprehend what was asked of him. And he did it for us, for Vanyasa.'

Jagrav begrudgingly stood up and put his hand on Idhika's shoulder. 'We shall walk until our legs allow.' With that, he started slowly limping forward. Idhika followed and Savitri joined her. Payal too pulled Aarti along with her before the others went out of sight.

Little time was wasted after that brief pause in their journey. Aarti was lost in a deep conversation with Payal for most of the way. Savitri walked Jagrav, holding up his weight by her arm across his back. Idhika carried Jagrav's kamandalu for him. And after hours of walking downhill, while simultaneously staying alert to any danger, the five remaining Souls reached the threshold of the clearing of Hathi-Paun, home to Rishi Ajan.

Idhika bolted towards her father's hut, eager to meet him after their recently rekindled relationship. She reached a couple of moments earlier than the rest and rushed straight in. She saw him busy in his palm leaves, oblivious to her charge inside his hut, and said, 'Namahkrita.'

In a fit of surprise, Rishi Ajan dropped his pankh and shot up. 'Bacche! What—how . . .? But you're the Eka.' His eyes misted and he gave her a tight hug. 'I've never known happiness until now . . . Thank you, Indra, for sparing my daughter.'

The four other Souls joined her in the hut. Idhika recounted the events that had transpired since her last visit to her father. She told her father how they'd found Madhu at the bottom of Pandayam Tal, only to still find themselves in the Mahayatra because of the lal bicchu's sting; how Chayan and the kirtimukhas were victims of Sanaka's past actions. She took him through the evening when they learnt of the true Eka of the valley, and the events that transpired after that, which was why none of the other four souls he'd met earlier were with them. But the biggest revelation to Rishi Ajan as well as the other Souls was when Idhika recounted Lord Indra's wish for Aman, right before his sacrifice.

Upon hearing that the lord himself wanted the Mahayatra to fail because of what Sanaka was trying to achieve with the Preservers, Savitri and Jagrav fully embraced Idhika's plan to go back and expose Sanaka. However, all this while, Aarti and Payal stood silently to the side. It was clear to them that they could no longer prolong their suffering in this land of the gods where, ironically, the only rule that persisted was the survival of the fittest. And that they had to foil Idhika's plan when the time was right.

Just then, another man entered the hut from the back door. Even from a distance, Idhika could see that there was a thick layer of dandruff in the man's long, unmatted hair that wantonly fell to his waist. His skin was parched and looked like crumpled paper. Each time he coughed, dust rained down from his head. 'Won't you introduce me to your daughter, brother Ajan?'

'Come forward, bacche,' Rishi Ajan said.

That's when Idhika saw it. The same slouch to his stance. The same nose. And a familiar set of dark-brown eyes below light eyebrows. 'Namahkrita, Idhika,' the man said in a voice that was soothing, and for a moment it evaporated all of Idhika's guilt, for it sounded friendly.

'Aman?!' Savitri blurted.

The man's eyes widened.

The colour drained from Idhika's face. She said, 'Father . . . who is this?'

'Avi . . . Avi Chandra,' Rishi Ajan said.

Idhika fell to her knees.

'Ajan. Was my son here? Was Aman *here*?!' Avi said. 'Where is he?'

'Aman was the last Eka,' Aarti said from a little ways away. 'Aman Chandra.'

Rishi Ajan's jaw dropped.

Silence befell.

Idhika registered little of what followed. She looked down at the mud floor for over an hour. By the time she looked up, she found the other Souls lounging on the floor, surrounded by empty banana-leaf plates and kamandalus that Rishi Ajan had provided. Avi Chandra and Rishi Ajan had left the hut. The two could, however, be heard from the backyard outside.

'How could you not tell me there was a Chandra among the Souls?' Avi said loudly. 'You should have woken me up!'

'I didn't know, Avi. I didn't know Aman was your son,' Rishi Ajan said. 'Let alone that his last name was Chandra. If only he'd mentioned once that his father was in the army . . .'

BOOM! A thunderous sound reverberated around them, instantly followed by a strong gush of wind that rattled the hut.

Rishi Ajan and Avi rushed in.

'What was that?' Jagrav asked.

'Something divine,' Rishi Ajan was quick to point out. And then he lowered his volume significantly. 'The sound emerged from the south . . . Vanyasa,' Rishi Ajan said.

Before long, Avi, Ajan and the five remaining Souls were on their way to the valley. Their pace was quick, and Ajan led the way despite his reservations about returning to the land from where he was banished. He hoped that accompanying victorious Souls coming back from the Mahayatra would grant him a warm welcome.

As they walked, the trunks of the trees around them grew thicker. Aarti mentally rehearsed her plan to iron out the specifics. Idhika looked forward to correcting the wrongs that had plagued her home. When Avi tied his long hair into a ponytail behind him, revealing previously hidden parts of his face, Rishi Ajan tried to lighten his spirits. 'You haven't aged a day, my friend, since you went into Atmayog thirteen years ago.'

'You look just like Aman,' Jagrav said, oblivious to the painful reminder he'd sent Avi's way. 'Only a couple of years older.'

'Sanaka did this, didn't he?' Avi said to Rishi Ajan in a fit of rage. 'Aman was brought to Vanyasa to draw me out of hiding.'

'I've been thinking, Avi . . . One cannot just recruit a boy to bring to Vanyasa,' Rishi Ajan said. 'Is it possible you became an inadvertent Tapasvi? You did spend long hours every night under the Kalpavriksha. Sanaka must have realized this—and that your child would automatically make a Soul of Samsara.'

'Aman mentioned that Sanaka had visited him and his mother, and only after that did she let go of her son,' Idhika said. 'But how could you be a Tapasvi, Avi? Only residents of Vanyasa can be.'

'Avi has spent a great deal of time under the Kalpavriksha,' Rishi Ajan said. 'It was Sanaka himself who allowed Avi and his men to practise Atmayog under the divine tree at night. You see . . . thirteen years ago, a few years after I'd returned from the Mahayatra as a Soul of Samsara without Shakuntala, I started having my suspicions about Sanaka, and in desperate search for Madhu, I ventured into Aranyala at night. I found an intruder; Avi was alone foraging for fruits to take back to his hiding place up in Sarp-poonch. With the help of a fallen log'—Avi rolled his eyes—'I knocked him unconscious. I tied him up and brought him to my hut.'

Ajan took a sip of neer from his kamandalu. Miles ahead, the dark green ring of the mountains of Vanyasa could now be seen, and with thick clouds surrounding the peaks, the Seven Hills looked like an enormous palace in the heavens. Ajan continued speaking as the group veered east and headed towards the gate above Mount Kalanag. 'Avi stayed tied for days and I wanted to confide in the Sabha and Samiti, but couldn't trust anyone. So I questioned him relentlessly. When I learnt of his identity as a Preserver, and that Sanaka had granted him and a few others entry into the valley, I went to the plains as a sparrow in search of their headquarters, as Avi had described it. After a week of searching, I finally found it. And then every day I went to New Delhi. It was during one of those visits that I heard a conversation between Avi's superiors. "Avi is no longer of any use to us. After leading the men into the valley, he had successfully negotiated terms with their leader for time under their tree. But for some reason, he has gone missing recently." To which his manager replied, "Get the others to find him, and kill him. He knows too much about the larger plan. And once we have confirmation on that, kill his wife and son, so no questions are raised."'

Ajan continued, 'The sinister plans of the Preservers had already opened Avi's eyes, but the tipping point perhaps was learning of their intentions for him and his family. I continued to listen in on both the headquarters and the other Preservers up in Sarp-poonch, kept a close track of Sanaka's actions while simultaneously searching for Madhu, and in the evenings, Avi and I discussed our next steps. We realized that we had to wait until the time was right and the valley could start to see Sanaka for what he was. And for the sake of his and his family's safety, Avi would have to disappear, far from the reach of the Preservers. He wanted to go back to his family, but one sitting of Atmayog revealed to me that the neighbours in their apartment were Preservers, keeping a close eye. The Preservers could not risk touching his family in case Avi returned for vengeance. They had to kill him first. So I sent him to a place where he could disappear, Hathi-Paun, for a long session of Atmayog. And, upon my exile, I too joined him there, and guarded him for the sake of our plan.'

'. . . son, I will never forgive myself for bringing this upon you . . .' Avi surmounted the side crest of Kalanag, but instead of looking at the emerging gate in the Seven Hills before him, he looked up at the sky with tears streaming down his face.

'Stop!' Idhika said as soon as she saw it. The gate was covered by a large black cloth. Something was wrong.

'What now?' Ajan asked.

'I know another way,' Idhika said, and led them further east until the loose brick in the wall was in front of them. One by one, each of them climbed the wall and started the brief journey to the Temple of Indra, the crest of Kalanag. A spot-bellied owl, a dark omen, circled their heads, but Idhika kept mum.

Upon reaching the temple, as the valley came into sight, they found it teeming with intruders. Sunrays reflected off a jet-black chopper that hovered above Pandayam Tal, a steel rope dipping into its waters. On the other side of the valley, men with guns stood guard by the entrance to Shreyan's tunnel. Smoke rose from the village below them, and they all watched in horror as a group of women ran across the Chakkar. Aranyani led the running women towards the Kalpavriksha, but it became clear that it was towards Aranyala that she ran when she raised her hands towards the sky and screamed, and the forest beyond Pandayam Tal came to life—the trees started moving, birds of all colours rose in a frenzy and the earth started vibrating—but it lasted only momentarily, until another chopper dropped an electrified net on her. The only area that seemed unaffected was the north, where lay the Clearing of the Chiefs.

There was no time for discussion. It was clear to them all that the Preservers had taken over the valley and were pulling out Madhu from Pandayam Tal. 'We have to alert them, and bring out all the fighters from the Clearing.' There was a fire in Idhika's eyes. 'I don't know exactly what weapons they're using, but whatever it is, we have something better. Atmayog. We cannot give up.'

'Avi, you're the best Atmayogi. Reach out to Chief Brighu as soon as you can,' Ajan said.

Avi immediately sat down and closed his eyes. *Here goes nothing, loser.*

BOOK II

To help build the second book in the Samsara series, see
a detailed map of Vanyasa and join us on our quest to locate
the valley of the gods, visit **www.sakshamvgarg.com** or

You can also share your thoughts about Samsara with the
author on social media @sakshamgarg94 and join the discussion
through our Discord: **https://bit.ly/SamsaraVerse** (case-sensitive)